THAT PROSSER KID

That PROSSER Kid

by Lloyd Pye

ARBOR HOUSE
NEW YORK

Without these people, my task would have been immeasurably more difficult:

Jacquie Borda
Dan and Benjamin Sharp
Bob and Susan Dawson
Linda Kay Lee
Alexander R. (Sandy) Smith
and L. M., who gave a stranger a break

To My Mother
Nina
For the love, support and
encouragement she gives to
everyone in her life.

THAT PROSSER KID

SEPTEMBER 14

Friday

MY POSITION as senior manager of the Cajun State football team requires adherence to a few basic commandments, one of which is: "Thou shalt never interrupt or try to influence the natural flow of events around here." Consequently, even though I like Wheeler and consider him a friend, I had to leave the note tacked to his door when I went in to wake him and his roommate.

The dormitory's fluorescent hall lights flushed the dawn from the left side of the narrow, twin-halved room. As usual, Wheeler's immaculate, military-style bedding tucks had barely loosened during the night. From the clothes in his closet to the books above his desk, everything in Wheeler's half of the room was tidy. Even his hair seemed to stay combed when he slept.

I glanced right to check Quink Thompson, his roommate. Sound asleep. I stepped down the middle aisle between the two beds and began gently shaking Wheeler by the shoulder.

"Jimbo," I said quietly, "Jimbo, it's time."

His eyes creaked open and began to focus on me.

"Are you awake, Jimbo? Do you understand me?"

After a couple of confused blinks, he spoke in a voice barely audible and cracking with sleep.

1

"Yeah. . . . I'm awake. . . . I understand you."

As always, no problem with him. He accepted what had to be done and got on with it. I turned to face the Quink.

A Quink is defined as someone short enough to fart in a bathtub and break the bubbles with his nose. This Quink was only a shade under five feet nine, but dense, knotty muscles widened his frame enough to create the image of a much shorter man. Those overly taut muscles projected a bristling physical intensity that stayed with him even at rest.

Waking the Quink during two-a-days was not my favorite task. At his best he was surly and difficult to rouse in the morning, but these two weeks of double practice sessions put him at his worst. Without my extreme size advantage over him, I'd have been hesitant to make him get up. I reached for his shoulder and heard Wheeler's sleep-slurred voice behind me.

"Wait . . . is another note stuck on the door?"

I turned and stepped back into his side of the room.

"Yes," I whispered, "there is."

"That fucking Everett," he muttered angrily. "What does it say?"

"It says: 'Stoner has muscles in his freckles.'"

Wheeler suppressed his response and smiled ruefully in the dim light. "That's probably true."

Three days ago it had become obvious that Wheeler had first team sacked and, barring injury, in nine days he would start the first game of his Varsity career at center against the defending National Champion Texas Longhorns. He would be head-up against the man considered by many to be the toughest middle linebacker in all of college football, a heavily freckled mass of speed and power named Keven Stoner.

As a junior last year, Stoner had been elected to nearly every all-American team in the country. At about six feet four and two hundred and forty pounds, he was certain to be a high first-round pick in the pro draft, but much of his future worth depended on how well he performed this year. He'd be at his very best for the first game of the season, especially against a weak team like ours.

Wheeler was five-eleven, weighed about one ninety, and had

slow feet. He didn't have a hope in hell against a monster like Stoner, and everyone connected with the team accepted that fact; everyone, that is, except Wheeler. He grimly refused to confront his probable fate, which was one of the principal reasons he was starting. Successful self-delusion is a skill without equal among football players.

The first note appeared on his door two mornings ago, a good-natured attempt at establishing reality that said: "Stoner is God." Yesterday morning's said: "Stoner eats nails and shits bullets." Wheeler would endure those reminders of doom until game day, and by then he'd be strung out tighter than a highwire over Niagara Falls.

"Just do your best against him, Jimbo," I said. "That's all anyone can expect."

I turned away and stepped back across the thin strip of white tape that ran down the length of the floor. That strip divided the room into halves as a boundary beyond which even Quink's cigarette smoke was not supposed to pass. As ridiculous as that seems, the reason for it was sound.

Shortly after Quink and Wheeler became roommates, they discovered that although they got along fine in everyday activities, they were completely unable to live together comfortably. On our team, roommates were assigned instead of chosen, so they had to make the best of their situation. Since a wall was out of the question, their only recourse had been the strip of tape. It did little more than isolate them symbolically from each other, but they found its presence comforting.

Quink lay in a twisted heap of sheets, dirty clothes, cigarette butts, crumpled skin magazines, and one lone shower sandal. His whole side of the room looked as if a tiny cyclone had passed through in the night, and he looked, as they say, like death warmed over.

I try to wake all the players gently because they sleep so poorly during two-a-days. They toss and turn all night in an effort to find comfort for their aching bodies. Fear keeps them checking the clock whenever they wake up enough to remember who and where they are. Most discover the inevitability of time watching phosphorescent hands sweep darkness toward

3

these particular dawns. Some have difficulty accepting it.

"Quink," I said, shaking him easily by the shoulder, "Quink, it's time."

He jerked his arm away, turned his back to me, and crammed the bare pillow over his head.

"Quink, you've got to get up. It's nearly six-fifteen."

He lay unmoving. I reached out and shook him again, a little harder than before. Without warning he swung a vicious backhand that barely missed my left knee. I was on him in an instant, pinning his shoulders with my hands.

"Listen, you little asshole, I'm not going to take that kind of crap from you! I'll put the fucking horn against your head tomorrow morning and blow your damn eardrum out!"

It never failed. He went limp in my hands. No matter how rotten and angry he must have felt, not even Quink would risk revival of my predecessor's wake-up technique, a harsh but effective process that involved walking from one end of a dorm hall to the other blasting everybody out of bed with a hand-held, high-compression air horn.

I prefer my slower, quieter method of getting them going, but I'm not above bullying when I have to. For the two weeks of two-a-days my first responsibility is to get everyone checked in for breakfast by 6:45 A.M., and this was the next-to-last day of that early-morning obligation. Nobody had been late during my two years of seniority, and I was determined to prove decency as effective as that goddamned horn.

I glared hard at Quink and shook him again. "Well . . .?"

Quink was reckless and it wouldn't have been beyond him to fight back in some way, but it's hard to be reckless with two hundred and thirty pounds kneeling on your chest.

"All right . . . all right . . . I'll get up."

Before I released my grip on his shoulders I shook him one last time and said, "You'd better." I eased off him and headed for the still-open door to complete my wake-up rounds.

As I reached for the knob on my way out, Quink spoke from behind me. "Hey, Sage?"

I stopped and turned to face him. "Yeah?"

4

"I'm sorry, man. I didn't mean anything. This shit just fucks me up sometimes."

I looked at him for another second and then said, "You almost found out what fucked-up is." I stepped outside and closed their door.

Then I heard Quink's voice from inside. "What the hell's the matter with *him?*"

Wheeler replied, "You almost hit his bad knee."

And then the Quink. "Ho-lee shit, no wonder."

ALL PLAYERS shuffle toward breakfast wearing variations of the same basic costume: sandals, cut-off jeans, and a T-shirt of some kind—rarely anything different. An enormous density bears down on each of them, a pressure they can't escape, and their outfits are a visible attempt to lighten the load, as if their coolness and brevity could oppose and balance the heat and weight of what would come later.

Their destination is Seward Cafeteria, known as "The Sewer," a dining hall halfway between the dormitory and the stadium. I check everyone into The Sewer by six forty-five and by seven they've all finished nibbling or sipping whatever they've chosen to eat. Then they go to the dressing rooms beneath the stadium's west side: Varsity to the south or "front" end, Freshmen and Redshirts to the north or "back" end.

In the dressing rooms they begin the agonizingly slow ritual of preparing for a hitting practice. Time begins to stand still for them, so they counter by stretching the tiniest actions into major projects: a sock has to fit exactly right; a loose screw has to be tightened; shoulder pads have to be adjusted a dozen times—anything to fight that excruciating wait.

The only thing lightening the mood today is the fact that it's the last day of double sessions. There's still an important scrimmage tomorrow that officially ends the two-a-day period, but after today's two practices the worst will be over. Each player wants nothing more than to get through the day unhurt, but they all know it's highly unlikely everyone will.

After breakfast I go to the equipment shed which is located just opposite the Varsity's "front" dressing room and my assistant, Chris Stanton, and I pull equipment for practice. We load blocking dummies, football bags, towels, and Gatorade into the bed of an ancient green pickup, then Stanton drives it out to the practice field to put everything in place and I go into the training room.

The training room is a swirl of muted voices and movements. Players, trainers, and occasionally coaches pass in eddies of sound felt more than heard in the hushed atmosphere. Whirlpool baths located in the rear produce background white noise as some injured players try for a last-minute loosening of knotted muscles and bruised joints. Others sit or stand with jockstraps beneath the towels around their waists, waiting to be wrapped or treated in whatever manner necessary to get them through another practice.

Senior managers have enough experience to participate in caring for minor injuries, so I usually spend this time taping ankles and covering abrasions. I work at a rear-corner table away from the front-wall tables of the team trainer, Trainer Hanson, and his two assistants, Bud and Raymond. They care for most Varsity players and all serious injuries, while Redshirts, Freshmen, and routine tape jobs usually come to me. We can talk safely at my table if we keep our voices low, and that provides some relief to the grimness of what's going down all around us.

"Heard anything about Prosser this morning?" Quink asked.

I shook my head. "Not a thing."

Quink was getting his left ankle taped and referring to a favorite topic of his. Pete Prosser was a player of singular ability and indifferent attitude who was also the Redshirt tailback.

Redshirts are players suspended between the Varsity's three offensive and defensive units. They're no longer Freshmen, but they've been unable to achieve Varsity status, which makes them expendable. They're forced to imitate each week's upcoming opponent in practice, which renders them into little more than cannon fodder for the varsity, and as a result, their life expectancies as players are easily the shortest of any sub-group on the team.

"I heard Teekay, Junior, said the coaches might move him up if he has a good day today." Quink's thick black eyebrows pinched in toward his nose. "You think they might?"

Quink was running at third-team tailback and considered himself fortunate to be there. As with all third-teamers who live on the bubble like that, his greatest dread was of getting rolled down to the Redshirts. Which would happen if Prosser got moved up.

"Who can tell? They could go back to the single wing and not surprise me. You've been here long enough to know how they are."

Quink's hair-trigger temper flared.

"Goddammit!" he said, "I want to know what you think!"

I felt sorry for him, but I knew a specific answer was too much for him to handle. Irrefutable generalities are what bubble riders need to hear when they're anxious.

"I think any fucking thing can and will happen. Things don't make sense around here, they just happen, so why worry about it?"

He seemed to accept that—it was true, after all—and changed the subject.

"What about him?" he asked, nodding toward where Don Slade stood on Trainer Hanson's table. "How's his knee holding up?"

I glanced over at the heavy, crisscrossed tape job being applied to Don's right leg from mid-thigh to mid-calf. He got wrapped that way before every practice to prevent licks like the one he took yesterday from buckling his knee. It had been torn up nearly as bad as mine, and I'd never been able to understand how he could play so well on it.

"They say it's just bruised," I said. "It ought to be as good as new in a few days."

Quink smiled slightly. "Then that's the end of his shot at the Bull, isn't it? He can't afford to lose even one step."

The Bull—straight name Ken Rowley—was Quink's best

7

friend and the team's starting fullback. Slade had been challenging him for supremacy since last year's spring training. Ken went at football and life in general "like a bull in a china shop" and his superior size and speed made him our best all-round back. Don's bruised knee would slow him just enough to permanently remove what little hope he had of rolling the Bull off first team.

"That's true," I agreed, "but second team behind the Bull is a damn sight better than where he was last year at this time."

I was just finishing Quink's ankle when he spoke up again. "What about Prosser, though? Do you think he'll move up?" He looked worried.

"Let me put it to you this way. He deserves to move up, doesn't he?"

"Well . . . ahhh . . ."

"Then he probably won't, so relax," I said, slapping the sole of his foot to indicate I was through. After all, merit never figured in coaching decisions about someone like Prosser.

Brrrraaaaaaakkkkkkkk!!!!!!

I signaled taking the field for calisthenics at precisely eight-fifteen. The Cajun State practice field lies just outside the stadium's north end and is surrounded by an eight-lane quarter-mile cinder track bounded by a field house, tennis and racquetball courts, a baseball field, and, to the west, a chain-link fence that separates the track and football area from a long row of residential homes. The air horn woke everybody in the neighborhood who might still have been asleep.

The sun was up and sweat already pouring down when the players broke into position groups at eight-thirty. Each specialized group went off with its respective coach to its particular area, while Freshmen and Redshirts avoided cluttering the practice field by running through plays over on the adjacent baseball outfield. Surveying all from atop his portable coaching tower was Head Coach T. K. Anderson, Senior.

Anderson was an enigma. He was starting his second season as our head coach after spending many years as the top assistant at Auburn, and he brought a big-time attitude to this job. I'd never understood why a man like that would come to a school like Cajun State, because he had nowhere to go but down.

I walked over to my usual position near the south end of the west sideline. From there I could survey each drill at a glance and be ready to sprint to anyone who might need, say, a quick fix on his equipment. I was so absorbed with what was going on in front of me I didn't notice Randall Webber come up from behind.

"How's it going this morning, Larry?" He clapped a hand on my shoulder.

I looked down into his round face and smiled. We'd met at a couple of preseason press functions for the team and had hit it off reasonably well. He was my age and just getting started as a junior sportswriter on one of the city newspapers. Built like a troll, short and squatty, he hung his gut right out front and always kept a ramrod-straight back. He had the carriage of a guy who wouldn't hesitate to knife you in a brawl, but his black horn-rims spoiled the effect.

"Pretty good," I said, "it's the last morning workout and they're really cranked up about it. How've you been?"

After the opening day of practice, Randall had written an article about our status as a "breather" on the schedules of powerful teams. Our value, he said was that we were good enough to be a spirited opponent but bad enough to always lose against superior teams. Randall hadn't been around since then, and he didn't have to tell me why.

"Ahh, my chickenshit boss got a call from your asshole boss suggesting I make myself scarce for awhile. I've been covering a bowling tournament and a ladies' golf match."

"Sounds about right."

"Bullshit."

We both looked out over the field for a few seconds, then I asked him what he'd come by for.

"Nothing special. . . . I just wanted to get a look at that Prosser kid. He's what I've been hearing about down at the office during my 'suspension.' Prosser this and Prosser that—hell, they make it sound like he could run through a rainstorm and not get wet."

9

I grinned at the cliche, which in Prosser's case was damn near the truth. "Almost, but not quite."

"Is he really that good?"

I nodded. "He's the best pure runner I've seen here . . . or anywhere else, for that matter."

"Then why is he a Redshirt?"

I looked sideways at him. "Because of his *attitude,* man. He won't play their game . . ."

"Such as?"

"Such as he won't swallow the coaches' shit with a smile on his face."

"Just what does he do that's so bad?"

"Mostly he lets the coaches know exactly what he thinks of them. He never actually *says* anything to them, but he makes it clear he thinks they're a bunch of pricks—"

"Which most of them are, right?"

"Sure, that's what being a coach is all about, but you're not supposed to make a big deal out of it."

"So the best runner on the team is a Redshirt because he won't play kiss-ass? Is that it?"

"That's about the size of it."

"But the object's to win . . . don't they put their best people on the field no matter what?"

I was beginning to get uncomfortable. "Look, why don't we talk about something else?"

Randall bowed up like a bantam rooster. "Because I want to know whether or not they put their best people on the field to try to win football games or whether . . ."

I thought about trying to explain it to him . . . about how the difference between three or four players at any one position is often harder to find than a gnat in an elephant's asshole, and how coaching decisions about who plays ahead of whom often become capricious and arbitrary and the coaches defend against having to make sense of them by setting up themselves and their decisions as sacrosanct. The worst breach of protocol is even remotely to question a coach's absolute authority . . . I may have been only a wrecked ex-player, but I was still hesitant to open up with all this in front of a reporter I hardly knew. I decided to keep it short.

"I'll come looking for your ass if this ever comes back to me," I finally said, "but it goes something like this . . . Of course the object is to win, but only on their terms. It would cost them too much face to let a guy like Prosser play. They can't afford it."

"Shit!" he muttered. "No wonder this team stinks every year."

"C'mon, Randall, that's not the reason. It's the same for every team in the country—shape up to the mold or you don't play. It's basic to the system."

"Then the system stinks."

STANTON BLEW the drill-change signal and the specialty groups immediately broke up, the players scurrying to their new areas in order to avoid punishment laps for failure to hustle. I led Randall across the field to a spot near where the half-line drill would take place.

"You're going to get a chance to see Prosser in action now," I told him as we walked. "The Redshirt offense goes full-speed against the Varsity defense in this drill."

The left side of the Varsity defense—linebacker, nose guard, tackle, end, cornerback, and safety—was joined by the Freshman offense on the twenty yard line's far hash mark. The Redshirts joined the Varsity's right side defense on the hash mark nearest us. Only half the offensive lines would go on each snap, and the ball would always move toward the short side of the field. Since the Varsity defended the short side in both halves of the drill, things were pretty heavily stacked against the offense, but practice wasn't held for the benefit of Redshirts and Freshmen.

"Which one is Prosser?" Randall asked as we watched the drill set up.

I pointed out the slender figure who stood off to one side with his arms folded across his chest. All the other Redshirts seemed nervous about the impending contact as they fidgeted in a dozen different ways.

"He doesn't look like much, does he?" Randall observed.

"No, he doesn't. That's another of his problems."

It was true. At close range the uniform's illusion of size dissipated and you could clearly see how thin Prosser was. Worse, he was extremely blond, almost albino, and that gave him a ghostly aura of fragility.

"How big is he?" Randall wondered.

"About five-eleven, a hundred and sixty-five, but he's tough as a hickory knot and quick as anyone you'll ever see. Don't make the mistake of judging him by the way he looks."

Teekay Junior, Coach Anderson's recently graduated son, stepped in front of the Redshirt huddle and assumed his position as signal caller while Tom Everett, the quarterback, stood respectfully to one side. Part of the humiliation dumped on Redshirts was not letting them call their own plays, or even giving them credit for enough intelligence to remember plays. It was still worse that Teekay Junior had gotten his job through nepotism, which, ironically, he tried to justify by imitating T.K. Senior. Before each snap Teekay Junior would produce notebook-sized cards with basic plays diagrammed on them and say, "This one. On two. Got it? Break!" The huddle would then break and the Redshirts would shuffle up to the line and into position.

Tom Everett took his stance behind center and handed off to Prosser in a straight dive over left guard. Bill Hopper, a mammoth defensive tackle, threw his man aside and smothered Prosser at the line.

Randall winced. "Not much there."

"Not much anywhere," I added.

The next play, a power sweep, was snuffed when Andy Ferragino, the cornerback, neatly stripped away the blockers and left Prosser naked.

"Can't those guys block any better than that?" Randall asked. "Prosser's getting creamed!"

"They're just following their motto."

"What's their motto?"

12

"C'mon, Randall, give me a break."

"No, seriously, I've never heard of it. What is it?"

I could see he wasn't kidding. " 'Do it wrong the first time.' "

"What?"

"It's like this . . . if the Redshirts run a successful play, it means someone on the Varsity fucked up. When that happens, the coaches make everyone do it over until the Varsity gets it right. Getting it right means creaming the Redshirts, so it's to everyone's advantage to make sure the Redshirts blow it."

Prosser was getting smeared on a trap while I was talking, but Randall didn't seem to notice. He was muttering to himself.

"Do it wrong. . . . I bet there's a story in that . . ."

"You'd better forget it," I advised, "if you don't want Anderson to ban you from here permanently."

Randall kept silent until after Tom had handed off to Dave Duggan on a fullback dive.

"I don't understand why I should pretend Redshirts don't exist," he said.

"Look, nobody pretends they don't exist, and you'll have no trouble doing a party-line story on how much their selfless dedication helps the team. What I'm saying is that you can't get into what it means to be a Redshirt, and you certainly can't tell the truth about what happens to them."

Randall stood silent again until after Tom had run a bootleg left, then shrugged and said, "We'll see."

TWENTY MINUTES later Randall sighed with disappointment. "I guess this just isn't his day. I'm going back to the office."

The Redshirts had run about twenty plays and Prosser, carrying the ball on half of them, had shown nothing. I'd half expected him to respond to the rumors Quink had heard, but he was giving the standard Redshirt performance of into the line and onto the ground. He knew he didn't have a chance in hell of moving up, and he wasn't falling for any of Tom Everett's ploys. It was relatively easy to stir up the illusions of players like Quink and Wheeler, but Prosser was another case entirely. A hard case.

13

"Why don't you hang around a little longer?" I suggested. "Maybe you'll see something when they bring the defense together after the water break."

"Nah, I've had enough. I'll come back this afternoon to see if things pick up then."

"Can't blame you. Morning workouts are usually like this. See you later."

At that moment Randy Colter, the first-team safetyman, came tearing upfield to help stop a sweep. He speared Prosser late and much harder than necessary, which could only mean that Wade Hackler, the head defensive coach, had decided to stir things up a bit by ridiculing Colter in the defensive huddle. He'd probably told him he tackled like a "dick-licking pussy" or "mamma's worn-out douche bag." Colter was a square-jawed redneck who responded with a vengeance to Hackler's prodding. As a matter of fact, that was the primary reason he was a starter. Coaches loved the ones whose insecurities were big enough to manipulate easily.

Prosser normally didn't respond to late hits or any other outrage that got laid on him, but I'd seen him tangle with Colter before. A quick look passed between them as they got to their feet.

"Stick around," I said to Randall as he started moving away. "I think we're about to see something."

The next play was an end run, shallower than a sweep, but still leaving Prosser plenty of room to maneuver. He took Tom's short pitchout and headed left behind Dave Duggan's fullback escort. Will Jensen, the defensive end, sensed what was coming. He shed his blocker to the outside to force Prosser to cut back inside, but as soon as Jensen stepped with him to fill the hole, Prosser jumped back left with a quick hop. Jensen crashed to the ground empty-handed, and Corky Ames, the linebacker who had joined Jensen in anticipating the inside move, found himself tangled up in the two interior double-teams that had neutralized the nose guard and tackle.

Prosser's move left only two people with shots at him: Ferragino at cornerback and Colter at safety. Ferragino had outside responsibility and so had no choice but to take on Duggan's

14

block. That left Prosser and Colter one-on-one in the defensive secondary.

Prosser stuck his nose straight upfield for his first two strides beyond the line of scrimmage, but then inexplicably swerved toward the sideline. That move exposed his right side to Colter's unbeatable angle, and Colter, like a shark smelling blood, accelerated for the kill. Three yards away from contact he lowered his head toward Prosser's knees—and the instant his eyes went down Prosser reacted. He pivoted directly toward Colter and lowered his own head, stepping full force into the blow.

The helmets made a sickening crunch that drew startled glances from all parts of the field. Colter, totally unprepared for that kind of lick, dropped like a rag and lay stunned. Prosser drove on through the contact point and only had to touch his free hand to the ground to regain his balance, then jogged several more yards downfield until he crossed the goal line.

"God-Damn-Shit!" screamed Coach Hackler. "Get your pussywhipped asses back up on the line and run it again!"

He stomped over to Colter's still-prostrate form and kicked him in the butt. "He made you look like drizzle-shit, Colter! Get your lazy ass up and pay him back this time! Stick him!"

Colter staggered to his feet and weaved over to his position while Hackler grinned behind his back. Hackler was a grossly overweight ex-substitute defensive tackle with jowls like a blue-ribbon hog and the disposition of a constipated rattlesnake. It was widely agreed that the only difference between him and a tub of shit was the tub, but he was the most important coach we had after Head Coach Anderson.

Every coaching staff needs at least one blatant asshole to attract and focus the players' hatred like a lightning rod grounds electricity. They are usually men who channel their shame at having been mediocre, unaggressive players into success as ruthlessly vicious coaches. Hackler was rumored to have played without courage or talent at a small midwestern backwater.

None of the defensive personnel acknowledged Prosser as he threaded his way through them toward his own group. Even his Redshirt teammates weren't sure how to react. Their football instincts applauded the beauty of his run, but their survival instincts damned him for humiliating the defense.

"What now?" Randall asked.

"They run it over until Prosser looks worse than Colter."

"How many times?"

"Usually once, but sometimes twice when they really want to get the point across. For Prosser it will probably be twice."

The Redshirts assembled at the line. There was no need to huddle, everyone knew the play. The defense waited eagerly because they knew exactly who was coming at them and from where. There was no reason to play the usual position football, so they could afford really to tee-off on their opponents. The Redshirts nervously took their stances.

The ball was snapped. Prosser took the short flip from Tom and went left. The defense instantly reacted and went after him, but after four steps Prosser hit the brakes and cut back inside over tackle. The entire defense overpursued and Prosser blew by them all. He quit running twenty yards downfield.

"Goddammit!" Hackler screamed again. "How many fucking times do we have to tell you: *Don't overpursue!* Now get your asses over here and do it again, and this time do it right!"

The defense held their ground and waited for a hint of Prosser's same inside move. When he gave it they all froze and he had no trouble changing direction back outside. In five steps he had turned the corner and shown them his heels. He hadn't been touched in two plays.

"Jesus fucking goddamn Christ!" said Hackler. "You look like a bunch of limp-dick pussies! Can't you hit? Can't you pursue? That's a fucking Redshirt over there doing that to you, for Christ's sake? Now get up there and stop his ass! Kill him!"

The air crackled, adrenaline flowed; Randall began to breathe in short gasps.

At the snap the defense fired out and stopped every Redshirt charge at the line. After being burned every way possible, they weren't going to fall for anything else. Prosser must have seen it because he cut into the hole without a fake. As the defensive line sagged in on him, he leaned into their waiting arms.

They were heading for the ground and the play seemed over

when Prosser executed a violent spin that twisted him out of their relaxing grips. Standing clear, he found himself face-to-face with Ames, the linebacker. Ames lunged and made solid contact with Prosser's right thigh, but as he slid his arms around to lock the tackle, he found himself holding air and falling. Prosser had given him a classic limp-leg and was now pointed as before, straight at Colter in the secondary.

Colter had learned. He came up in full control and maintained a perfect hitting position—head up, feet apart, tail low. Prosser didn't even bother with a fake. He lowered his head five yards away and left Colter no choice but to do the same.

One stride away from contact Prosser suddenly straightened back up. Colter was fully extended with his head down and didn't see the move, so he dove into the contact point and continued on into the ground. Prosser, meanwhile, had jumped straight up, and now hovered for an instant with his cleats above the small of Colter's back.

It seemed certain that Prosser would stomp Colter into the ground, but at the last second his feet spread and landed on either side of Colter's kidneys. Staggering more than striding, Prosser jogged the required extra yardage. Exhaustion was beginning to show, but his mastery was intact.

Stanton blew the water-break horn as Prosser turned to head back upfield for the fourth straight time. Usually all football activity stops when that signal comes, and everyone goes directly to the break area. Not this time.

"Goddammit!" Hackler shouted as he yanked his baseball cap off and threw it on the ground. "None of you chickenshit motherfuckers move!"

Everyone stopped dead in their tracks.

"I'm gonna find someone who can tackle that son of a bitch if it takes all goddamn day! I want every last one of you pussies to get after his ass and nobody stops till he's down! Move!"

The entire defense began running full tilt toward Prosser. I don't know if he was being defiant or was simply too winded to run anymore, but for whatever reason he made no effort to get away. He calmly wrapped both arms around the ball to prevent a fumble, then lowered his head slightly. He seemed totally relaxed when Colter smashed into his chest. Three or four others piled on, and then a whistle blew from midfield. It was Coach Anderson's signal to end the work period and start the break.

As Randall stared at the spot where Prosser had been plowed under, subdued players began jogging past us toward the break area.

"My God," Randall said, "I've never seen anything like that!"

"Like what? Prosser's ability or Hackler's assholery?"

"Both . . . together . . . I mean . . . Hackler . . . shit!"

"As the saying goes, old stick, you ain't seen nothin' yet. It's even more entertaining when the coaches do their own dirty work. Come on, let's get some Gatorade."

I started toward Soupbone's handiwork. Soupbone was the team's assistant equipment manager, an old black man with off-white hair. During each two-a-day workout he set up a table between the track and the stadium, then covered it with pint cups full of Gatorade. If not for those fluid breaks, most players would dehydrate into heatstroke by the end of the day.

Randall grabbed my elbow as I moved away.

"Are you saying what just happened is routine around here? There's nothing peculiar about it?"

"It's routine for the ones like Prosser. Don't let it get to you. He'll be better off after they get rid of him."

"Get rid of him? He's amazing! Why don't they use him?"

"Look, every time he puts on a show like that it makes the coaches look stupid for having him on the Redshirts, and they can't move him up off the Redshirts because he doesn't show proper respect. The better he is the worse it is. So they've got no choice but to get rid of him. He's a bad influence on the rest of the team. All clear?"

"Are you putting me on?" Randall demanded. "It sounds like Catch-22."

"Yeah, sort of. Now, come on, let's get something to drink."

We walked over and took places at the very back of the line. After the players had been served we each took a cup and threaded our way through the sprawled, gasping bodies, careful to avoid being spit on. When a player's dehydrated, a phantom layer of cotton seems to cover the mouth and it's got to be cleared out regularly.

Prosser was squatting on his helmet near the outside edge of the track. His head was hanging down, his sides were heaving for air and all you could see of his face was sweat dripping off his nose. He hadn't been able to drink any of his Gatorade, and the full cup was extended in front where his arms rested on his upraised knees. Randall and I took a position near him, but out of everyone's hearing range.

"Look's like he's in pretty bad shape," Randall said.

"Most people wouldn't even be able to sit up."

Randall nodded and took a sip of his Gatorade. "Tell me about him. What's his background? What kind of a guy is he?"

"I can tell you about his football career, but I don't know much about him personally. He's a real quiet type. Sticks to himself and doesn't say much."

"All right, then," Randall agreed, "tell me what you know."

"Well, year before last he was signed out of a small north Louisiana school that played six-man football. As you probably know, scholarships are almost never given to six-man players because there's no way to judge their eleven-man potential, but Prosser's statistics were so incredible—something like ten thousand yards in four years as a starter—the coaches decided to take a chance on him. So, last year as a Freshman he blended into the wall during two-a-days, and nobody thought much of him until the first Freshman game. They put him on the kick-return team for that and he ran back the only two balls he touched."

"All the way?"

"All the way. Naturally, that got everyone's attention, so the coaches decided to take a close look at him. That's when they found out about his attitude, and they've been down on him ever since. They didn't play him any more as a Freshman, and they spent last spring training trying to get rid of him. The only reason he's here today is because he lucked out and survived the Shit Drills."

"Shit Drills? What are those?"

I seriously began to wonder about Randall.

19

"C'mon, man, don't you even know what Shit Drills are?"
He looked flustered for a second, then he smoothly replied.
"They must call them something else where I come from."
I couldn't imagine what else they might be called.
"They're the drills coaches use in spring training to get rid of
the players they don't want around anymore."

"Ohhh," Randall said. "Those!"

I looked at him strangely, but before I could speak I noticed
Hackler break away from the circle of coaches inside the track
near the standing dummies. Coaches can never for a minute,
especially among themselves, cease the game of trying to prove
one man's worth at the expense of another. Ridicule is the most
frequently used method, and Hackler had apparently had
enough needling about what had just happened to his defense.
He stormed toward Prosser with a scowl on his face and both
fists clenched into white-knuckled hammers.

"Uh-oh," I said to Randall. "Trouble."

Without breaking stride Hackler kicked the cup of Gatorade
from Prosser's outstretched hands. Prosser didn't look up.
Hackler reached down with his left hand and grabbed a fistful
of curly blond hair, then snapped Prosser's head up and back
with a vicious jerk and thrust his ugly red face down level with
Prosser's blue eyes.

"Listen to me, you little cocksucker!" he began to scream.
"Don't you ever pussy-out on me again! When I tell you to run,
goddammit, you run! Don't stand there like a fucking statue!
Statues belong in parks, and we play football out here! You
understand me, boy?"

Prosser, somehow, managed to look bored. No other word for
it. Anyone else would have been shitting in their pants. Prosser
just looked uninterested. After a while he turned his head left
and spit on the ground.

Hackler's face went from red to white. He swung a round-
house punch that caught Prosser on the left cheek and snapped
his whole head right from the impact. Even his hair slipped
through Hackler's grasp. Before anyone could recover from the
shock of the blow, Prosser had turned back to spit between
Hackler's feet.

Hackler roared and swung again, but this time Prosser's head was free and he was able to duck under it. Hackler was thrown off balance when his bloated body followed the violent arc of his arm and he flailed out for support with his left hand. In the abrupt silence, we all heard the familiar snapping sound of a bone breaking as his left wrist smashed into the raised concrete edge of the track.

Coaches hurried over to aid their stricken comrade, who was now rolling on the ground and squealing like a stuck hog. Even Trainer Hanson seemed to be hurrying, and Trainer Hanson normally took great pride in the stoic way he reacted to other people's injuries.

During the commotion caused by getting Hackler on his feet and into the ambulance jeep, I noticed Prosser move away and blend into the crowd of nearby players. I happened to be looking at him when a figure stepped up and surreptitiously slipped a fresh cup of Gatorade into his hand. I checked to see who had dared such a thing.

It was Quink.

WHEN HACKLER had finally gone on his way to the infirmary, Randall turned to me and said, "Serves that bastard right."

"Come on, lighten up. As bad as it is, he's just doing his job. Somebody has to get rid of Prosser. The sooner they get rid of him, the better off he'll be."

"Jesus! What a callous asshole you are. I don't understand any of this—"

"You can say that again. For someone who's supposed to be a hot-shot sports reporter, you don't know a fuck of a lot about football, do you? Where did you go to school?"

He mumbled something indistinctly.

"Where?"

"Columbia."

I smirked down at him.

"Hell, Randall, even piss-ant Ivy League schools fuck people over. You must not have gone to many practices."

He looked at me and stiffened. "All right, dammit, look at this goddamn body. I'm short and dumpy and I've got bad eyes, so I was never any kind of athlete. I'm a damn good chess player, I play tournament bridge, and I can hustle pool with the best, so don't give me any holier-than-thou shit. Now, all right, I admit I concentrated on political coverage in journalism school, but I learned the mechanics of sports coverage too. Just show me the inside stuff and I'll do the rest."

"This isn't exactly city hall."

"Fuck it! Dirty laundry is dirty laundry, I don't give a shit where you find it."

Just then Stanton blew the horn to signal the water break's end.

WHEN SOMEONE gets nailed like Prosser had been, player reaction is usually no more than, "Thank God it wasn't me." Verbal and physical assault from the coaches is an integral part of the game, and no one thinks much about it. This instance, though, was something of an exception. Prosser had been scourged for doing well, not for screwing up, and most everyone but the coaches found it hard to justify the fuck-over.

And even though Hackler had gotten his, the water break episode caused an immediate downer throughout the team. Practice turned into fumbles, dropped passes, missed assignments, poor execution. Coach Anderson could see what had happened as well as I could. He called me over to his tower twenty minutes before the scheduled end of practice.

"Blow the horn," he said.

The team members jogged from their various work areas to the middle of the field and surrounded the tower's south side. Coach Anderson looked down into a hundred-plus sweating faces and began his postpractice pep talk.

"Men, we had a good workout this morning," he lied, "but I can see we're getting a little tired. We're going in early so we can get some rest and put some zip back in our legs."

A halfhearted cheer went up on cue. Nearly everyone knew the real reason for cutting it short.

"So let's go on in and take care of those injuries. Get some rest so we can come out this afternoon and have a good one to end two-a-days on. What do you say, men?"

The standard growling cheer went up followed by "All right!" "Get it up!" "Let's have a good one!"

"All right, then!" he shouted. "Hit the showers!"

One last cheer and the players took off at a run, slowing to a walk only after clearing the practice field's end zone back-line. Football tradition allows no walking on the field itself, as if walking on it at ordinary times would produce an uncontrollable urge to walk during a game.

I was loading stray equipment into the pickup when Randall approached me. "Larry, I want to apologize for getting hot a while ago. I just—"

"That's okay, pal," I said with a shrug, "we all screw up now and then."

"Look, I have to file the Hackler story now, but I'd like to talk again this afternoon. You're right, I've got a lot to learn."

Before I could respond I saw Paul Marshall, the head offensive coach, coming our way. That meant Randall was still on the coaches' shit list, and *I'd* screwed up by talking to him so much.

"Get lost!" I muttered. "Here comes the heat."

Randall took one look at my face, glanced at Coach Marshall's. "Right, see you later," then turned and walked toward Coach Marshall with a cheery greeting while I stooped back down to the dummy I'd been lifting.

Coach Marshall was Hackler's opposite number in nearly every way imaginable. He was a lean, craggy-looking man with alert, darting eyes and a voice like number-six sandpaper. He'd fashioned that raspy marvel through years of screaming at people who couldn't possibly play football with the skill he'd displayed as an All-SEC end at Ole Miss. Unlike Hackler, his toughness was genuine and he was respected for it.

"How's it going, Larry?"

I looked up from the sand-filled dummy. "Fine, coach, just fine."

"Here, let me help you with that."

He grabbed the lighter top end while I muscled up the heavy bottom and we heaved it into the truck bed.

23

"It's a heavy sombitch, ain't it?" he said with a wink. "Lots heavier than the ones we used to hit."

"Is that a fact?"

"Are you finished now?"

"Yes, sir, that was the last one."

"Good. Let's head on in, then."

As we started walking toward the dressing room, I knew what was coming. My only concern was how deep I'd gotten myself into hot water.

"What'd that ol' boy from the paper want?" Coach Marshall asked. "You and him seemed to talk an awful lot."

"Aw, nothing much, he just wanted to know about basics. He never played football before and doesn't know much about it."

"Hah!" he rasped. "It figures. Most of them fuckers are like that. But listen, Larry, try not to be so friendly in the future. You know we like to let Coach Anderson do all our talking and explaining for us. Next time he comes around asking questions, you send him on up to the tower. Okay?"

"Sure, okay." Relief. This wasn't sounding bad at all.

"Fine. I'm glad you understand."

We walked in silence until it was time for us to part. Coach Marshall stopped and looked at me. "I sure am sorry you're not able to play any more, Larry. With an attitude like yours, I bet you'd have been a good one."

I actually felt myself flushing and heard myself saying, "Thanks, coach," as he gave me a pat on the shoulder and turned away.

Old soldiers never die, they just hang around.

THE "BACK" dressing room is really two separate rooms connected by a common shower and toilet area. There's a fairly large room for the Freshmen and another room half its size for the Redshirts. I always check there immediately after each practice session because those two groups get shorted first, especially when the schedule is disrupted.

"Did you all get oranges?" I shouted from a central spot near the showers. No answer. "How about ice?" Still no reply. Everything seemed in order. I moved on into the Redshirt room, where Tom Everett motioned me over. "How about it, Sage? What do you think?"

Though mired as a player at Redshirt quarterback, and blessed—or cursed—with a choirboy's innocent face, Tom was an authentic natural leader. People just trusted and had confidence in him. As the Redshirt's man-in-charge he did his best to sustain their physical and emotional welfare, which he was especially worried about now.

"I think they'll ease off this afternoon. They'll want to get some work done, but I can't see them exhausting everyone. They need good film of tomorrow's scrimmage."

He nodded and then raised his voice to the room. The post-practice hubbub immediately died.

"Listen-up, everyone! Sage and I talked it over, and we think it's going to be an easy one for us this afternoon. There might be some hitting somewhere along the line, but mostly they'll want to save the Varsity for tomorrow. That means we can relax and look forward to surviving two-a-days!"

A cheer went up and the conversations resumed.

"What about Hackler's 'accident'?" I asked.

Tom's thick brown hair was splayed over his forehead by a particularly unruly cowlick, and I watched him push it up for the millionth time as he answered my question.

"In a way it's a damn shame. It practically guarantees special Shit Drills for Prosser."

I glanced at Prosser sitting across the room, unlacing a shoe while holding an ice bag to his swollen left cheek. He didn't seem worried, but Tom was right. Special Shit Drills were for sure now.

BEFORE GOING into the Varsity dressing room, I stopped at the equipment shed for a quick conference with Cap'n, the team's equipment manager and also my immediate superior; an intense, orderly little man who'd been at his job for fifteen years, during which time he'd established a direct pipeline to the secretaries in the front office. The secretaries told him nearly everything and I'd gotten my nickname, the Old Sage, because of the inside scoop he often gave me.

"You hear what Prosser did this morning?" I asked.

Cap'n replied without looking up from tightening the cage on somebody's helmet. "Yeah, Soupbone saw it. I don't know what they gonna do about that boy. I hear the coaches want him gone before reporters start hangin' round ever day."

"Any word on starting special Shit Drills for him?"

Regular Shit Drills are used almost exclusively in spring training to get rid of what the coaches call "deadwood." They're savage exercises in mayhem designed to produce crippling injuries. As soon as one injury heals sufficiently, another is inflicted until an unwanted player gets tired of being hurt and quits. It's a nearly foolproof system, but occasionally someone like Prosser gets through the spring sessions on talent, guts and luck. That usually precipitates a session of *special* Shit Drills, and no one walks away from those.

"Not yet," Cap'n answered, "but I expect 'em any time now. Prosser ain't the kind to turn tail without a boot in his ass."

I WENT into the Varsity dressing room and looked around. Most players were naked by now, and several had already showered. I noticed Don Slade having trouble cutting the heavy bandage off his knee. "I'll get that," I said, reaching down for the tape cutter.

Don winced as the blade passed over the jagged pink scars on both sides of his right kneecap.

"Sorry," I said, "but it can't be helped."

"I know, I know. Just get it off."

It had been twenty-two months since his knee had been injured, but swelling was still evident. Of course, yesterday's bruise had added something to it, but stripped knees never really look the same.

When the bandage was off, Don leaned back in his cubicle and closed his eyes with relief. A deep calm came over his broad, deeply tanned face, which somehow fitted more the image of a farm boy, which he was, than of a doctor, which he wanted to be.

He opened his eyes and smiled up at me. "Thanks, Sage. You still clear for Sunday?"

Don and his wife, Annie, had invited several of us to a big Sunday dinner, and we were looking forward to it almost as much as the end of two-a-days. "Wouldn't miss it for the world."

"That's great! Annie's psyched out of her mind for it. She's gonna lay out a hell of a feed."

"She better. Tell her we'll Redshirt her if she doesn't."

I headed across the room to Quink's corner locker. He was sitting in front of it picking at the tape on his ankle.

I reached down and rumpled his dark, sweat-soaked hair. "Hey, boy, that was damn fine out there, slipping Prosser that Gatorade. I thought you were worried about him rolling you."

"I don't want to get rolled by him or anyone," he said, "but I just can't stand the crap-ass way the coaches treat him. Why the hell can't they give him a break—"

"You know why."

"Fuck it, I'll never understand."

AFTER PRACTICE a good many of the players spend time in the University Center where they perform one essential function and exhibit one basic tendency. They replace lost body fluid with various soft drinks and milk shakes while eyeballing any attractive females who happen by. During two-a-days the New Orleans humidity saps ten to twenty pounds from each per practice session, so the need to replace fluid is almost constant. Mercifully, there are few decent women around during the summer break, so temptations are scarce and easy to resist.

Now that two-a-days were ending, though, the pattern was reversing. Practice became tolerable and curfews were extended at precisely the right moment. The summer drought ended with the next day's class registration for the fall semester, and it seemed part of some grand celestial design to have girls return to campus exactly when the players could begin to take advantage of them.

"Jesus," said the Bull, "look at the freaking wheels on *that* one. Nine-fives at least, maybe nine-fours."

"No fucking way," Quink shot back, as much to be argumentative as anything else. "Nine-seven, tops."

Quink, Bull and some other players were sitting at the counter grading female calves, a criteria they all knew well and judged themselves by. Under their system women were rated by the projected speed at which their sons might run a hundred-yard dash. It was all based on a seat of power each player understood and could relate to. Muscular, well-developed calves—male *or* female—commanded immediate and deep respect.

"Speaking of fucking," the Bull said, "is anybody going to Peso's show tomorrow night?"

Most had dates of their own and all had serious intentions. Practice twice daily and team meetings nightly combined to make two-a-days a period of constant football and little else. If absence makes the heart grow fonder, abstinence surely makes it hornier.

"I'd love to see it," Wheeler said in behalf of the majority, "but I have some other things planned—"

"Well," cracked the Quink, "give one of us a call if she wants more than you've planned."

Wheeler threw a sugar packet across the counter at him while everyone broke up. Just as the laughter was dying down, Tom walked into the huge room holding a small paper bag.

"Oh, shit," Wheeler said softly, "who's he gonna stick it to this time?"

Despite Tom's choirboy looks, he was the brain and nerves behind nearly every major hoax, con or practical joke pulled off on the Cajun State campus. He was a virtuoso schemer with unlimited capacity for mischief. His notes to Wheeler were so insignificant as to almost be beneath him, but in a way that was only further testimony to his art. He saw possibilities everywhere and never hesitated to exploit them.

Tom leaned over the counter's end and pointed to the bag he carried. "Gentlemen, a little Rabbit action is about to go down. Anyone care to come along?"

"Not again!" someone moaned as we all slid off our stools. "That poor bastard . . ."

RABBIT IS as much an enigma as Prosser, but in exactly the opposite manner. He's the poorest excuse for a football player on an admittedly poor team, but he somehow manages to stay on the Varsity at third-team wingback. Doubly puzzling is the fact that the coaches never criticize even his grossest mistakes, and they've made the seemingly incredible decision to put him at safetyman on our kickoff team. His habit of dropping passes whenever he hears a defender's footsteps earned him the nickname "Rabbit ears," and most consider the space between those ears to be one of nature's few true vacuums.

Rabbit is basically harmless and totally unhindered by any notion of reality. He thinks of himself as a good player and believes everyone on the team wishes him well. He accepts the miseries put on him as a normal part of his everyday life, never seeming to question how or why such things happen. In short, he's an ideal, deserving victim for the players to take out some frustration on.

"Okay, men," Tom whispered, "silence from here on."

We were two doors away from Rabbit's room, Tom leading. The paper bag in his hand had been replaced by two thick white towels, one soaked in the lighter fluid the bag had contained.

By the time we reached Rabbit's open doorway, Tom had gently stacked the towels over Rabbit's left shoulder as he lay sleeping on his right side, his bright red hair contrasting eerily with the white towels. The match Tom struck hardly made a sound and the topmost towel ignited just as quietly. Flames danced two feet up off Rabbit's torso.

"Rabbit," Tom said, whispering directly into his ear from the head of the bed, "Rabbit, you're on fire."

No response.

"You're on fire!" Tom repeated with slightly more urgency. "Rabbit, for Christ's sake, you're on fire!"

"Uhmmmmm . . . wha . . . ?"

Tom was on his way out at Rabbit's first flicker of movement. He'd just closed the door in our faces when it began, the most bloodcurdling, unearthly howl. We took off down the hall to the Bull's room, and once inside let go . . . Even though I never *really* approve of what gets done to Rabbit, damn it, the guy does ask for it . . . come to think of it, in one way or another all of Tom's victims do . . .

"Mother crammer!" the Bull said when things finally began to quiet down. "What's gonna happen to that geek next?"

Tom looked up. "It's already in the works. Sunday. About five o'clock. Be here."

NEARLY EVERYONE takes naps between practices; Rabbit's misfortune was that he had started too early. Now we all went to our rooms for an hour or so of restless sleep. I was nervous because my responsibility increased when practice shifted from group work to unit work. I played a fairly important role in certain aspects of unit work, and I had to prepare myself mentally like everyone else. Well, not quite like everyone else; I knew I'd be walking at the end of the day.

As it turned out, by the time practice was almost over only a freshman guard named Dirk Hatfield had been wiped out. He broke his right collarbone during the first tackling drill of the day and had long since been removed to the infirmary.

Hackler had returned to the scene of battle. He'd stomped about like always, brandishing his elbow-length cast like a shiny new toy, but he'd given no indication of what he intended to do about the way he'd acquired it. Was it just possible Coach Anderson's sense of fair play might spare Prosser an immediate reprisal?

Except for Hackler's appearance and Hatfield's injury, practice had been uneventful. The Varsity had gone through the tedious routine of polishing its offensive and defensive sets, and the Redshirts had had no difficulty maintaining a low profile. Tom's easy-workout promise would hold up because the toughest drill of the day, which had been saved for last, didn't include the Redshirts.

Randall arrived just as the serious hitting was about to begin. The Varsity was going to go against itself in a goal-line defense drill, and these next twenty minutes would be an abbreviated version of tomorrow's two-hour scrimmage. Since this drill occasionally determined who got the most game time in goal-line situations, the contact was always fierce.

"Sorry I'm late," Randall said. "Did I miss anything?"

"Yeah," I told him, "you missed me getting my ass chewed out this morning for spending so much time with you."

He winced.

"It looks like you're the Prosser of sportswriters around here, so I suggest you go on up to the tower and start kissing Anderson's ass."

"I'm in that deep, huh?"

I nodded. "No shit, Randall, I really was told to steer clear of you from now on, and I guess I don't have any choice but to do it."

"Does that mean you won't talk to me somewhere away from here?"

I considered the implications of what he was asking. The coaches wouldn't like it if they found out I was fraternizing with someone I'd been told to stay away from, but on the other hand, they'd never find out unless Randall screwed me, and I couldn't picture him doing that.

"All right, I'll fill you in, but it'll be strictly off the record unless I say otherwise. If you tell anyone or I see a word of it in print, you'll be damn sorry. Understood?"

He said it was.

I PERSONALLY supervise ball placement on goal-line drills because quickness and accuracy are essential. The ball is centered on the ten yard line, and the offense has four plays to take it in for a score. The first-team offense goes against the second-team defense and the first-team defense faces the second-team offense, and the rivalry between the two top units is never more intense.

"First and goal at the ten!" I shouted, and the drill got under way.

I took my position straddling the line of scrimmage ten yards outside Loop Watson, the second-team left defensive end. From there I could control the ball and call offsides if necessary, but the coaches invariably beat me to it. "Goddammit, so-and-so!" they would shout at whoever jumped. "Get your head out of your ass and listen to the fucking count . . ."

The first-team offense snapped into position over the ball and the second-team defense dug in. The first play was a dive by the Bull over right guard, and he got three tough yards by going directly through a linebacker.

"Way to hit in there, Bull!" came a shout, and then from Coach Marshall, "Way to run, Ken!" The Bull was our best short-yardage runner and everyone liked to watch him work, but Coach Marshall always seemed especially appreciative. Talented people seemed to share a special bond.

"Second and seven!" I shouted.

Ronnie Davis, our starting quarterback, rolled left on a keeper and picked up five.

"All right, Ronnie! Way to work!" . . . and from the other side, "Come on, defense, dig in!"

"Third and two!"

The Bull slammed into the line and the defense pinched in on him . . . it had only been a fake. John Lawrence, the tailback, took Davis's pitchout and came steaming around end toward me. It was all I could do to get out of the way as Watson, who hadn't bought the fake, cut Lawrence down for no gain.

A groan went up from the offense, a cheer from the defense.

"Fourth and two!" I called out. It would be the last chance to score in this series.

The linebackers anticipated a fullback dive and disguised a stack against it. They were waiting when the Bull hit the line and caught him high and low in a vicious cross-tackle. There was no sound of ligaments or bones snapping, but everyone

32

heard him scream. Dead silence fell over the field as the pile untangled. The Bull was on the bottom, twisting in pain and holding his left ankle.

On goal-line defense the action stops for injury, but only because it's too time-consuming to reassemble at the other end of the field. In all other instances the ball is simply moved away from the injured player, a gesture that illustrates how quickly the unfit are isolated. No one looks at him and he is automatically replaced with hardly a beat missed in the continuity of practice. In football, when your function ceases, *you* cease; your existence, your value as a player are immediately and thoroughly discontinued.

"It's not broken," Trainer Hanson said after a hasty examination of the ankle, "but get him over to the infirmary anyway."

Hanson then taped an instant ice pack over it. Two Redshirt linemen familiar with the procedure were standing by, and they carried the Bull toward where Stanton was revving up the ambulance jeep. That white clinker was always parked just outside the track that circled the practice area, a four-wheeled symbol of the high-grade danger each player faced whenever he stepped onto the field.

"All right, men," Coach Anderson boomed through his megaphone, "let's get back to work."

The two sides huddled uneasily as I watched the Bull being loaded into the jeep. Then I noticed Coach Marshall glaring across the line at Hackler, who wouldn't look back.

I couldn't blame Coach Marshall for being pissed. He knew the linebackers hadn't called that stack, we hardly ever used it against ourselves. Hackler had called for it to make sure his defense didn't get scored on. He'd protected his ego at the expense of Coach Marshall's best runner. Marshall, I suspected, would find a way to pay Hackler back.

It took only one series of downs before the Bull's injury seemed forgotten. Don Slade moved up to first-team fullback while Roger Johnson took over the second-team spot. The injury was a golden opportunity for both substitutes, who ran hard and acquitted themselves surprisingly well. The Bull would be missed, but no one was irreplaceable. . . .

33

"All right, men," Coach Anderson said at the end of practice, "we had a good workout this afternoon, we had some injuries, and that's unfortunate . . . it means the rest of us have to tighten our belts, suck up our guts, and get after those other folks just that much harder.

"Now, just because this is the last day of two-a-days and you think the worst is over you shouldn't make the mistake of letting down mentally. We've got an important scrimmage tomorrow that's going to be the last chance for some of you to show us that you want to play this season. You'll all get an opportunity, so each of you should do everything possible to be at your best. Be sure to get a good night's sleep and remember . . . there'll be fans out there, and reporters, and the Big Eye will be watching every move you make. Give one hundred and ten percent effort on each play and you'll have no problems; loaf and we'll all know about it. The ones who stand up are the ones we want to put on the field against Texas next Saturday night.

"All right, tomorrow morning is class registration and I want all of you in front of the Registrar's office at nine o'clock sharp. We've arranged for you to have the first shot at every course, so I don't want any excuses for afternoon classes. If it looks absolutely essential that you cut into practice time with a lab or something, see Dr. Westrum and try to make other arrangements. We've been assured full faculty cooperation in scheduling around practice, so I don't expect any problems.

"Questions?"

That was a cue for silence.

"All right, then, take it on in!"

A cheer went up as the players broke for the showers, and as usual I stayed behind to gather up equipment. I had just started working when I noticed Richard Biggs jogging through a few postpractice laps around the track. He had a pulled hamstring, and was testing it out. Biggs was a second-team cornerback with the inevitable nickname "Big Dick," an innocuous-looking guy who wore granny glasses most of the time but was what we all respectfully termed a "heavy hitter." He was as tough a tackler as we had on the entire squad, and only frequent injuries had kept him off the first team.

As I loaded the last hand dummy into the truck he puffed up to me, looking pleased with the workout.

"How does it feel when you run on it?" I asked.

"Fine," he said between breaths. "I'll be ready Monday."

After we'd walked in silence for a few steps he turned to me and said, "Bad luck losing the Bull like that."

"Yeah, he's our big gun."

"Can Slade and Johnson take up the slack?"

I shrugged. "They have to now."

Big Dick lapsed into another silence. "In a way, you know, I'm really glad for Don," he finally said. "I'm not taking anything away from the Bull, but anybody who works as hard as Don deserves a chance to play. Of all the runners out here, Prosser included, Don is the one I really hate to come up against."

Coming from such a hard-nose, that was high praise.

"Why's that?" I asked.

"Because the fucker is so damned determined. He never stops scratching and clawing for those few extra inches. Prosser just makes you look like a fool, but Don stings you."

It was true. The Bull had the most natural ability, but Don had the fiercest heart. Maybe this would be the break he needed.

I went into the back dressing room, checked everything out, then headed for Tom's cubicle. He glanced across the room at Prosser. "Could you believe that shit about everyone playing tomorrow?"

Tom was probably Prosser's biggest booster. He didn't know him any better than the rest of us, but he worked with him every day and appreciated his pure football ability. Also, like many others, he admired Prosser's guts and vicariously enjoyed his defiance of the coaches.

"What did you expect Anderson to say? 'Everyone will play except Prosser'?"

"I know he has to pretend to be fair and impartial," Tom said sourly, "but I still say he's got a hell of a nerve trying to put something like that past us—"

35

Abruptly, he changed the subject. "What about Don? Can his knee hold up against Texas?"

"You know Don Slade. He'd play on a nub."

I LEFT Tom and went into the Freshman room to clean out Hatfield's cubicle. Hatfield was the guard who'd broken his collarbone in the early part of practice. Whenever players were injured seriously enough to go to the infirmary, I was responsible for getting their clothes and personal belongings over to them, and so usually was the first team-related person to visit them. They were almost always scared and upset over the injury and worried sick about how their team status would be affected, and I had to at least try to be calm and reassuring with them. I lied a lot.

Fortunately today's visits would be minor. Hatfield was a cocky kid who was good and knew it. He'd be down but not devastated. As for the Bull, anything short of a compound fracture wouldn't faze him. He knew where he stood if anyone did.

I was picking up the Bull's gear in the Varsity dressing room when Helmut Moedle approached me. "Helmet" was our German-born, soccer-style placekicker, and the only certified star on our team. Even though we managed few drives sustained enough to exhibit it, his kicking leg was acknowledged as the best in the South, if not the whole country.

"Sagely," he said, "Have you and Carla an engagement for tomorrow evening?"

He was referring to Carla Andrews, my steady lady. She was a second-year mathematics instructor at Cajun State.

"We're not going out, if that's what you mean."

"Good! You must excuse such brief notice, but there is a party which was arranged only today. It is to be a small affair for a Belgian industrialist at the home of a friend. I would like you and Carla to join with me as my companions for the evening. Will you come?"

Helmet was the son of a wealthy German diplomat, and his courtly manners and Teutonic good looks made him a big favorite along the local social circuit. As might be expected, he was the object of much female admiration, but too often it was the underage or married kind, and consequently he liked to have chaperones along in certain awkward situations.

"Aw, hell," I said with dramatic wince, "what a shame! Carla's math department will be meeting through most of the weekend getting ready for the start of classes Monday. There's no way she can go."

Helmet smiled with his usual good humor. "It is as I expected; arrangements of the last moment always create the difficulties. Tell me, Sagely, would you care to come alone? Surely Carla would not wish you to sacrifice in her behalf."

"No, no," I hurriedly replied, "but thanks just the same. I've already made other plans."

Carla was one of those people who fit in anywhere, but I'd never been comfortable with the people who circulated at Helmet's level of sophistication. They were into art and theater and world affairs, and they hardly knew what a football was.

"Some other time, perhaps," Helmet said with a shrug.

"Absolutely."

HATFIELD WAS even less of a problem than I'd expected. He'd grown up within a mile of the stadium, and his parents were already in his room when I got there. He was still in considerable pain, so I just delivered his clothes and offered a few words of encouragement to him and his parents.

The Bull, on the other hand, was alone and in bed when I got to his room, his ankle propped up on two pillows and packed with ice.

"How's it going, champ?" I asked when I looked in on him.

"Sage! Great to see you, man, you gotta get me some booze, these geeks are gonna keep me here overnight and you know how I hate to sleep alone . . ."

His smile was tight and he was talking too fast, kidding around to play down his need. Maybe he wasn't an alcoholic in the classic sense—yet—but I worried that he was on his way. I decided to play his game. "The last thing you need to do is sleep alone, turkey. There's four candy-stripers outside foaming at

37

the mouth. Looks to me like you can have your pick of them, buddy."

"No shit?" he said, genuinely amazed. He was exceptionally handsome and went through women like a chain saw through balsa, but he never seemed to appreciate his own attractiveness, which Tom pinpointed as the secret of his success.

"Scout's honor, old buddy, there's a redhead out there who's gonna have to be put on a leash as soon as I leave . . . booze is the last thing you'll need tonight . . . besides, you know the rules, if we got caught I'd be right in here alongside you with my ass in a sling."

He forced a grin, but I knew he wanted it more than either of us would let on. It wasn't something to risk talking about just then.

"What's the word on your ankle?" I said, changing the subject.

"No breaks," he said without emotion. "Just a bad sprain. Right now it looks like I'll miss two or three weeks."

"Lucky fucker. I heard Stoner wanted to pick his teeth with your bones after he goyaed Wheeler and the rest of the line."

We both loosened up over that. A few years ago one of the players came across a print of Goya's painting of *Saturn Devouring One of His Children.* That grisly picture of the monster holding the half-eaten man quickly gained fame as the winner's reward in the "Goya of the Week" contest. The person voted to be going up against the opposing team's toughest individual had to keep the picture above his locker the entire week preceding a game. In time the name "Goya" came to mean the actual act the painting represented, and you'd hear . . . "Goya that son of a bitch," or "That motherfucker goyaed my ass . . ." It was dying out now only because Anderson banned the picture when he took over as coach, but old hands like the Bull and myself still got a big kick out of it.

Suddenly the Bull's smile was gone as he looked at me and spoke in a dead serious tone.

"How about some beer, Sage? You know I haven't had a drink since two-a-days started. If I'm gonna be out two weeks, what can it hurt? Huh?"

"Come on, man, don't put me on that kind of spot."

"Yeah . . . okay, okay, forget I asked . . . I've made it this far, I can make one more day . . ."

The Saturday night following the end of two-a-days was traditionally a blow-it-out-the-tubes night. The Bull had waited for it as eagerly as anyone, and I knew he wouldn't be denied tomorrow night. I just didn't want to contribute to the early start he had planned.

"That's the ticket," I said, heading for the door. "Get yourself some candy-striper instead."

"I sure will," he promised.

Sure you will, I said to myself. Sure you will.

EVEN THOUGH I maintained a room in the dorm for occasional sack time, I'd lived with Carla for almost two years in a place four blocks from the stadium. Actually, I lived "off of" her more than "with" her since she worked and paid most of the bills, at the same time protecting my feelings so that I never really thought of myself as kept. Besides, I intended to make an honest woman of her after I graduated at the end of this semester.

The best part of coming home was the way Carla always greeted me. No matter how her work had gone, no matter how lousy she might be feeling she made it seem like the highlight of her day was when I walked in the door.

"Hello, darling!" she said in that beautiful husky voice, coming over to give me a hug and a kiss. Carla was an imposing lady, five-nine and built like God's little sister, but she was as warm and open as a puppy. Her voluptuous figure, long black hair and delicate facial features made her a treat I never got tired of.

"How did it go today?" she asked.

"Not so good. We lost the Bull with a sprained ankle. He'll be out for a couple of weeks."

She leaned back in my arms and looked upset for a moment, then broke into an unexpected smile.

"Well, that's a tough break for Ken," she said, "but it means Don will get to play a lot, doesn't it?"

"Honey, I like Don as much as you do, and I love Annie, but

39

this is business. The Bull is more valuable to the team than Don, no matter how you cut it."

"More valuable?" she shrugged. "They were both good enough to make the team, weren't they? Besides, Annie's been dying to seeing Don play ever since they moved him up off the Redshirts . . ."

I knew how hopeless it was to argue with Carla, she always let herself get emotionally involved. But over the supper table I made the mistake of telling her about the incident involving Prosser and Hackler.

Carla's normally cheerful features tightened. "They'll be getting rid of Prosser soon, won't they?"

I nodded. "Probably special Shit Drills early next week."

"Oh, Larry, why can't the coaches correct their mistakes without hurting people? Why are they so barbaric?"

"Well, it's a barbaric sport. And Prosser is just more than they can deal with."

Carla stared at her plate, then looked up at me with that familiar glint in her eyes. "Why do you stay in football, Larry? It's not you."

She'd asked that question many times before, and each time I tried to explain my addiction.

"Football has been the major part of my life since I was ten years old, Carla. It's the thing I know best and feel closest to. Can't you see? I know how bad it is, but I love it anyway. I get a satisfaction from it that I just can't explain."

She looked at me. "What will you do after this season when you're no longer part of it?"

"What's for dessert?"

SEPTEMBER 15

Saturday

WAKE-UP WAS at seven-thirty, so I had no difficulty getting them going. Most had taken Coach Anderson's words to heart and gone to bed early, and even Quink was awake, sitting cross-legged amidst the madcap jumble of his bedding while Wheeler slept on. Quink was smoking a cigarette, poring over a class schedule booklet; the four butts in the ashtray beside his knee meant he'd been at it for some time. It was typical of him to be planning his semester class schedule less than two hours before reporting to the Registrar's office.

"I need a crib philosophy course, Sage," he said as he looked up at me from the booklet. "Any suggestions?"

"I don't know any easy professors, if that's what you mean, but I once got an A in a history of philosophy course. It was about the earliest philosophers. Even you should be able to deal with a time when people were just beginning to think."

"Suck a hairy banana."

"How about you, Jimbo?" I said as I looked over at Wheeler. "You ready to get up-and-at-'em today?"

He nodded sleepily. "What's today's note say?"

I went back to the door to read it because it was long and I wanted to get it right. "It says 'Look! Up in the sky! It's a bird!

41

It's a plane! It's Stoner! Yes, Stoner, strange visitor from another planet who came to earth with powers and abilities far beyond those of mortal men. Stoner, who can leap tall buildings at a single bound; change the course of mighty rivers; bend steel in his bare hands; and who, disguised as an all-American middle linebacker for the University of Texas Longhorns, fights a never-ending battle for fame, women, big bucks, and the demise of Cajun's Jimbo Wheeler.' "

"How cute," Wheeler said.

I grinned sympathetically and turned to finish my wake-up rounds. Quink's voice came from behind.

"You figure Prosser will play much this afternoon?" Prosser's mercurial ability still haunted him.

"Don't worry. He won't get in at all."

"Wait a minute," Wheeler interrupted, "didn't Coach Anderson say everyone would get a chance to play today?"

Wheeler was a damn good player who had never been down on the underside for a day in his life. He also tended to be a straight arrow, giving the coaches the benefit of every doubt.

"Prosser isn't like everyone else," I said.

"But he looked good again yesterday," Quink went on. "How can you be sure he won't get in for at least a few plays?"

I thought he knew the answer to that as well as I did. "Because it's okay if he looks good at practice in front of local reporters who're under the coaches' thumbs, but it's another matter entirely if he cuts loose in front of a few thousand fans."

Wheeler persisted, "I say if Prosser doesn't play it'll be because he doesn't deserve to play, and not because the coaches are afraid of what he might do."

I looked at him for a long moment but decided to let it go. "Well, Jimbo, does it really matter?" I turned to go to the door. "After all, he's only a Redshirt."

AT BREAKFAST I ran into Peso Rodriguez, a stocky third-team guard from New Mexico. "How about tonight, Peso?" I asked, sitting down at his table. "Everything still all squared away?"

His olive skin creased into a happy smile. "Fuckin' A, man," he said with only the slightest trace of Spanish accent. "It's all set. You're comin', aren't you?"

As I looked at Peso's bristling black hair and broad, sloe-eyed face it was easy to see why he was the team's number one hustler and wheeler-dealer. His upbeat attitude and teddy-bear appearance took in suckers by the score, and tonight's scam was only another in a long, nefarious string. He had talked a local barmaid into staging a public sexual encounter with him, and splitting the profits down the middle. At two dollars a head minus a charge for the bar's back room he figured to clear fifty dollars for his night's work.

"What time does it go down?" Quink asked.

"Late. Midnight earliest. It's got to be after closing time so there's no hassle with regular customers."

"Too bad," I said. "I promised Carla I'd be home by midnight. And the rest will be drunk or shacked up."

"Aw, come on, man," Peso wailed, "it'll be worth it, I promise. Come drunk, bring your women. It'll turn them on!"

Everyone hooted him off and he sat in dejected silence for a few moments.

Suddenly his fingers snapped. "Never mind, assholes," he said. "I don't need you. I just figured out how to pack the house."

"How?" said Quink.

"Go stuff yourself with a cream cheese dildo."

EVERYONE WAS in front of the Registrar's office by eight-fifty, frantically discussing ways to clear every possible obstruction from the path of least resistance.

"Goddammit, it's a fucked course and he's a fucked instructor. I had him last year." . . . "C's, that turkey gives C's, never gives D's or B's." . . . "Look, it's like this—stick an elbow in her tits every now and then, you get a C with no sweat. Brush her ass a few times, you get a B. Go to her house to ask her a question, you get an A locked . . . and that ain't *all* you get either!" . . . "Physics? Why the shit do you want to take physics?

43

Hey! Did you guys hear that? Wisner wants to take fucking physics!" . . .

And on and on. Football cost them fifty to sixty hours per week during the season, difficult courses had to be avoided at any cost.

I sat on the grass with Tom Everett. "How's it feel to have only one last semester before you graduate?" he asked me.

"I'm scared shitless. I keep wondering if I'll be able to handle whatever comes next."

"Really? I thought you'd be stoked. Hell, the night Marty graduated he was so happy he cried."

"I'm not surprised," I said. "Not many people could have taken what he went through."

Marty was Tom's older brother. He'd been a high school all-American quarterback who went to Georgia Tech as a dropback passer, but there'd been a coaching change at the end of his freshman season and the new coaches installed a winged-T. They decided Marty wasn't quick enough to operate a rollout offense and—what else?—put him on the Redshirts to get rid of him. He stayed there until he graduated.

Being a four-year Redshirt is as rare as being a three-time all-American, except you get no credit for what you've done. It's certainly a much harder thing to accomplish, the physical and psychological battering is unbelievable. No wonder Marty cried when it was over.

"Do you ever think of getting out of it," I asked, "instead of going through what he did?"

Ironically Tom had come to Cajun as a dropback passer and a similar coaching change had happened to him. Now he was starting his second year as Redshirt quarterback and couldn't expect much more than his brother had gotten.

"Sure, I think about it, but at least I've got it in a little better perspective than most. Charlie's college career matched my high school career year for year, so by the time I was a senior in high school and he was a senior in college I had a pretty clear picture of what went down. I came here for the education. It doesn't matter whether I play a down or not—"

"Jesus, you sound like the coaches when they're out recruiting some poor schnook."

"I do, don't I?" he said, smiling. "You know, when they sat there telling us my education would always be their foremost concern, it was all my family and I could do to keep from laughing out loud. But we held on and just plain old-fashioned out-lied them. We made them think we believed all their bullshit."

"Your father's a successful dentist, isn't he? Why go through all this crap? Why not let him put you through? Even working full time would be better than this?"

"Well, I probably know this system as well as you do, Sage, and that's saying a lot . . . anyway, I've got a pretty good idea what it can do to me, but I still want to stay with it as long as I can. . . . Let's just say that at this point quitting would be tougher for me than staying on."

I thought back to the time five years ago when I made my own decision to quit. I'd been a scared eighteen-year-old kid with a shattered knee and no older brother to measure myself against. I was so ashamed I couldn't even face my own family.

"What if you get hurt or never get to play?" I asked.

"What if?" he countered. "At least I know the football part only matters to me. Most of those other poor bastards think it matters because of someone else—family, friends, hometown, you name it. Sure, I'll carry scars if I get hurt or never play, but mine won't be as deep as for those who think it really matters."

I looked at my own scarred knee and felt a pain in my gut. Five years ago and it still mattered.

THE ATHLETIC Department smooths out registration for two reasons. First, it's a nightmare of confusion and frustration for an ordinary student, especially one unfamiliar with the process or the professors. Second, it gives virtually no excuse for missing practice because of class-scheduling conflicts. When problems do come up, they're handled by Dr. Westrum, the team's academic counselor. The real coaches refer to him as our "brain

45

coach" when assuring a prospect's parents that their son will be well-looked-after mentally as well as physically. The fine print is that help is given selectively according to status on the field.

"I need a three-hour humanities elective at eleven o'clock Monday-Wednesday-Friday," a starter says at registration. "What have you got?"

Dr. Westrum looks up from his desk and smiles benevolently. He is a small, rat-faced man with the morals of a '59 Buick, but he takes good care of the hands that feed him. He checks his class files and says to the starter, "History of Western Civilization, H-203, Dr. Clarkson."

Dr. Clarkson accepted a ride on the team's charter flight to Charlottesville when we played Virginia last year. As I recall, his mother was sick and he wanted to visit her. Anyway, while Redshirts, freshmen, and the injured stay behind, empty seats on the team plane get filled with assorted jock-sniffers and people whose influence the coaches consider valuable. Those professors like Dr. Clarkson, who sell out for a favor, invariably find a clutch of athletes in their classes. But only the top athletes.

"I need a three-hour humanities elective at ten on Monday-Wednesday-Friday," a Redshirt says to Dr. Westrum. "Can you help me out?"

"Sure," Westrum says with the same benevolent smile. Again to the class files. "Got just the thing for you. Psychology of Interaction, P-300, Dr. Blandings."

When Westrum offered Dr. Blandings a ride to his hometown of Atlanta, Blandings told him to take the ride and stuff it up his ass. Unfortunately, that pungent reply only allowed the coaches to manipulate his outrage to their own advantage. They now send nothing but marked players into his classes, and he obliges by making life miserable for those unfortunates. As a result, Blandings helps the coaches get rid of their unwanted athletes while thinking he's getting back at them, and that makes him as valuable to the Athletic Department as Dr. Clarkson.

No MATTER how carefully the Athletic Department structures registration to prevent it, occasionally someone *has* to take an afternoon class. Those situations almost always involve once-a-week labs, and they present their own unique difficulties for players with brains enough to qualify for them. The first of those difficulties is keeping the decision-making process out of Westrum's hands.

"Sage, I need some help and I know Westrum will fuck me over if I ask him."

I was sitting at one of the long tables that were set up in the gymnasium to facilitate completion of class-confirming computer cards. I looked up and saw Sir Henry the Wolf, a Redshirt tackle, looking down at me.

Sir Henry was an erudite nineteen-year-old with a large head and thin face. He was deadly serious about life, and it was considered a major achievement to make him smile. Even so, the look on his face betrayed more than his usual degree of angst.

"What kind do you need, Hank?" I asked, not at all sure I could be of any help. Sir Henry was extremely bright. He aimed to be an engineer, and I knew almost nothing about the courses he would be taking.

"I have an option between a fluid mechanics lab on Tuesday afternoons and a hydraulics lab on Thursday afternoons," he explained. "The fluid mechanics professor doesn't like football, the hydraulics one does. I have to take one or the other, and there's no way Westrum can rearrange it. I also have to make a B or better in either one. What the hell should I do?"

A classic scheduling problem. Thursdays are fairly easy practice days during the season, but Tuesdays are the roughest, especially on Redshirts. Logic dictated taking the Tuesday lab to avoid that tough practice day. On the other hand, a professor with a grudge against football could make a hard class even harder and possibly put a critical dent in Sir Henry's grade-point average. He was caught between the rock and the hard place.

I considered all the implications I could think of, then offered my best shot. "I'd take the fluid mechanics on Tuesday and

47

hope for the best with the professor. They'll get rid of you a lot quicker on the field than in the classroom."

"Amen," he said as he turned away.

LUNCH FOLLOWED registration and then began "The Wait," the hour from twelve to one to be filled before reporting to the stadium to dress out.

Helmet filled his open time by doing whatever he felt like and without a care. Practice was never a problem for him. He'd mastered his skill so thoroughly that the coaches wouldn't allow him to be hit under any circumstances. It was even dangerous to jostle him in the dressing room. Helmet was magic.

Rabbit didn't worry about practice either. The coaches never said a harsh word to him, and his existence as a football player seemed every bit as charmed as Helmet's. Rabbit usually spent open time sleeping.

Everyone else sweated it out.

Peso would play cards if a money game was to be had, otherwise he'd try to dream up new get-rich hustles.

Sir Henry would close the heavy black drapes in his room and play dirges on his stereo in the darkness.

No one knew for sure what Prosser did . . . long walks off campus maybe, or stints in the library . . . nobody bugged him. Tom usually spent the time on the phone hoaxing folks, but this time he was busy on final details of Rabbit's weekend fate.

Wheeler would tidy his half of the room, sweeping, dusting, shining shoes, ironing clothes.

Quink and the Bull would man the counter in the University Center, wisecracking and checking-out women.

Big Dick would tinker at his motorcycle.

Most of them had to deal with an inner fear and tension impossible for a nonplayer to understand or a player to communicate.

Since Don Slade was married he lived in a separate dorm for couples, so open time left him with no particular place to go. He solved that problem by visiting from room to room, which had

48

built him the widest circle of friends on the team. Don was probably our best-liked and respected player.

Whenever he felt like sack time he'd come down to the fifth-floor room Stanton and I shared. Since we both lived primarily off-campus with lady friends, we nearly always had an unoccupied bed available. We'd given Don a key, and I woke up to the sound of it scratching in the lock.

"Oh, I'm sorry, Sage," Don said, "I didn't mean to wake you. I thought you'd be with Carla—"

"She's busy today," I said through a yawn. "Come on in."

"I just wanted to take the pressure off my knee for awhile," he said as he stretched out on Stanton's empty bed. "Today's a kind of big day for me, I want to give it my best."

"How does it feel to be first team?" I said, asking the all-time cliché question. I wasn't fully awake yet.

"Great!" he answered with the same enthusiasm he'd probably been asked to show a hundred times by now. "Even if it's only for a few days—"

"Only a few days? The Bull told me he'd be out for at least two games."

Don shook his head. "The official medical report came in just after lunch. Bad sprain, not much else. He'll be able to run on it by next Saturday night. He just won't be able to cut on it too well."

"I don't know whether to feel glad for him or sorry for you."

"Well, the best man ought to play."

Which was exactly what I'd expect Don to say. He was so decent it hurt.

"Yeah," I said, "but you came back from a long fucking way down, and you worked your ass off to get where you are."

"You got that right." He laughed. "Last year at this time I was lower than whale shit."

Last year at this time Don had been the Redshirt fullback, and the skids were being greased for his imminent departure. He'd gotten a severe knee injury the previous year as a freshman and the coaches lost patience when it didn't come around on schedule. He limped through the entire season and took all the punishment the Varsity had to offer. He never quit rehabilitating himself, though, and just before spring training we found out why.

He'd gone to Coach Anderson and asked permission to get married. He'd been in love with Annie, his high school sweetheart, for years, and now they wanted to start a family. Marriage is by no means an automatic option for Redshirts or borderline players. Permission is reserved for those who are a proven commodity, but it's also used to stimulate performance. Coach Anderson agreed to Don's marriage provided he had a good spring training and made the Varsity. Which was exactly the deal he'd hoped for. He knew the coaches would watch him closely, and he came out fighting for every inch. Only the Bull's sheer natural ability had kept him off first team.

Don and Annie were married as soon as the school year ended, and she'd become pregnant during this past summer. Several of us were going to be godfathers next spring, and we were all stoked by the prospect.

"How's your knee since the bruise?" I asked. "Is there much fluid buildup?" I knew all about fluid buildup in a knee.

"Yeah, some," he said. "They're going to drain it in about an hour."

My stomach flipped at the image. Draining's a grisly procedure in which a giant hypodermic needle is jammed into an injured joint and then moved around in search of fluid pockets to be sucked dry. The pain reduces even hard-bitten pros to screams, and I knew what Don must be feeling. About all I could manage was, "Hang in there, kid, you've been through it before."

"Yeah. I know."

THE DRESSING room tension before a big scrimmage is only slightly less than before a big game. The quality of Varsity scrimmage performances sometimes determines who starts in the games, so the top-level players prepare religiously for an all-out effort. The lower-echelon third-teamers and Redshirts are under even more pressure to perform; their playing time is mostly a matter of luck and nearly always much less than they'd like.

"What're you doing back here?" Tom asked as I came into the Redshirt dressing room. "You're supposed to be up front taping ankles.

I offered a weak shrug. "They're draining Don's knee."

"That shit still freaks you out, doesn't it?"

I nodded as I sat down next to him. "I guess it always will."

"So, how's it look outside?"

"It's a beautiful day for watching football, but a crappy day for playing. No clouds and ninety-plus heat."

"You figure we'll play much?"

"Hard to tell right now. If the Varsity is sharp and execution is crisp you ought to play a lot. If they drag-ass in the heat, then I imagine the coaches will work them into the ground. Remember, tomorrow is an off-day."

He nodded and glanced across the room at Prosser, who was leaning back against his cubicle with his eyes closed, looking like a twelve-year-old towhead suited up for a Pop Warner League game.

"What about him?" Tom asked. "You think he'll get in?"

I shook my head. "No chance."

"Isn't it a bitch? The only way to get off the Redshirts is to look better than the people above you, right? But everything's fixed to keep that from happening. What's a guy like Prosser supposed to do? What are *any* of us supposed to do?"

I noticed Sir Henry trying to struggle into his shoulder pads, and got up to go help him. "Hope for a miracle," I said.

ON THE second day of two-a-days Hank Wolf had bruised his sternum, one of the most painful injuries you can get but from the coaches' standpoint the perfect Redshirt injury . . . it's not crippling and the victim can be made to play in excruciating pain. The only way out is to quit.

Hank had survived by designing his own protection—a foot-square sheet of foam rubber that covered his entire chest. The fist-sized hole over his injured breastbone had reminded Tom of a jousting target, and he'd been Sir Henry the Wolf ever since.

"Let me help you, Hank," I said as I began squeezing the foam sheet under his shoulder pad breastplates. It was a tight fit and difficult to adjust properly, but once everything was in place all pressure was directed off the weak spot over his heart. It was a very ingenious design, and Trainer Hanson had already stolen it to treat a Varsity guard with the same problem. Thanks to Sir Henry the Wolf at least there'd probably never be another Cajun State Redshirt going down the toilet because of a bruised sternum.

"Thanks, Sage," he said when I'd finished.

I looked at his normally deadpan face and saw the faintest outline of a smile tugging at the corners of his mouth, a cheeser grin on anyone else.

"What're you looking so smug about?"

"Nothing, really," he said noncommittally. "I just have a feeling today might be my day."

I winked at him. "*Some*body back here ought to get a break once in a while."

"Yeah, just as long as it's not a bone."

CAP'N MOTIONED me over as I passed by the equipment shed on my way into the Varsity dressing room. "Fat boy in a white shirt and tie come by lookin' for you a while ago," he said.

"What'd he want?" I asked, knowing it had to be Randall.

Cap'n shrugged expansively. "Didn't say. He did say he'd be in the press box during practice but he'd talk to you after."

"Okay, thanks."

Everyone was ready inside. Last-minute dumps and whizzes were going down in the toilet area. The Wait had been screwed down one more turn . . . helmets spun nervously by taped and padded hands; mouthpiece ends chewed to shreds; fist-and-jaw-clenching psych-ups; endless finicky equipment adjustments . . .

"How do you feel, Quink?"

He looked up at me with a faint smile, the best he could manage.

"How about it, Jimbo? You doing okay?"

Wheeler's heels were bouncing up and down in a nervous frenzy, but his face was a mask of calm and purpose.

"I'm ready," was all he said.

Don and the Bull sat together talking, the Bull's new crutches laid parallel between them. Their rivalry was a friendly one based on mutual respect.

"Good luck, Don," I said. "Have a good one."

Don glanced up. "Yeah, you too."

Under pressure like this, even Don got distracted. He'd forgotten I wasn't a player. I wished I could do the same.

MOST CIVILIANS think scrimmages are held in the stadium at least partly for their viewing comfort. Actually it's mostly because it's easier to get good film there. Well, what fans don't know can't hurt them, or their enthusiasm, which was considerable when the team hit the field at two-thirty. I stood to one side watching calisthenics with Big Dick, the Bull and several other injured players dressed out in shorts.

"What size crowd do you figure?" Big Dick asked.

"I'd guess about a thousand," said the Bull.

"More like three," I corrected. "Maybe even five."

"Come on, you've got to be kidding!"

"No, I'm not. This place swallows them up."

The Cajun State stadium is indeed cavernous; low and wide, with a capacity of more than eighty thousand. It's easy for three or five or even ten thousand to look insignificant inside it.

The crowd was the usual mix of friends and die-hards, but this last Saturday scrimmage always brought another contingent— newly arrived students drifting over between bouts with registration's madness to sit in the sun awhile, check out the new year's team and then prepare heavy analyses for fraternity parties later the same night.

Coach Anderson stayed in the press box during scrimmages

so he could be with reporters assigned to cover it. Public relations is a crucial part of any head coach's duties, and none of them exactly shun it. Coaching itself is a questionable skill—either you've got the horses or you don't—but there's no substitute for a man who can manipulate the press. Coach Anderson was very good at it.

While he was busy upstairs, Coach Marshall became the acting head coach on the field. At two-forty-five he blew his whistle to start the scrimmage, and the field cleared of players except for the first-team offense and the second-team defense. Professional referees had been hired so I was free to join the remaining players along the sideline below the press box.

"First and ten at the twenty," an official yelled.

There were no kickoffs in scrimmages, but otherwise game conditions were in effect. That meant there was no stopping to run anything over, which was fortunate, because the first play was a perfect trap up the middle that made the defense look like stomped shit. Hackler roared with anger while brandishing his cast, then threw his cap down and disgustedly kicked it. Wheeler had blown his man into the next state, and Don had picked up fifteen yards.

"All right, big offense, way to roll" . . . "Dig in defense, hold 'em" . . . The sideline chatter would go on for the next two hours.

"First and ten on the thirty-five!"

The offense kept its drive alive for two more first downs, then finally had to punt from the defense's forty-two. The punt ended in a touchback so the second-team offense took over on its own twenty against the first-team defense.

The action was crisp and fluid. Marches went up and down the field, good runs were followed by crushing tackles, long completions led to fumbles, and all gains seemed to be balanced by equal losses. And then suddenly a man was down, rolling in pain and holding his left arm.

"Who is it?" someone on the sideline asked. "Can you tell?"

"Looks like a lineman," someone else answered.

All substitute linemen tensed and each stomach knotted.

"It's Dean," someone finally said . . . "hurt his arm."

54

Ralph Dean was the second-team offensive right tackle, and his arm looked to be broken.

"Jennings!" Coach Marshall shouted. "Where the hell is Jennings?"

Rick Jennings was the third-team right tackle and therefore automatically next in line to move up into Dean's spot. He stepped forward from the sideline and said weakly, "Right here, coach."

It's a first-rate disaster to be singled out in the eyes of God and everyone else while injured and wearing shorts. Jennings knew the unwritten rule as well as anyone: there is absolutely no acceptable excuse for not being ready when called upon. The coaches would never forgive or forget that Jennings wasn't available when he was needed.

"God*dammi*t," Coach Marshall bellowed, "Jennings doesn't want to play! Give me a tackle who wants to play!"

Sir Henry, sharper than most, immediately grasped the situation. Dean's spot was being thrown up for grabs to the first man with balls enough to take it. Sir Henry's helmet was on and his chin strap secured when he broke from the sideline. Two other reserve tackles made bareheaded moves, but Sir Henry had too much of a jump on them.

"All right, Wolf," Coach Marshall said. "Wolf wants to play. Get in there and show me what you can do."

Excitement ripped along the sideline. Coach Marshall was hard but fair, and he'd give Sir Henry a decent chance to prove himself. It wasn't often a Redshirt managed to rise out of the mire, and everyone took a special interest in the prospect.

The next few plays went away from Sir Henry, so he couldn't show much, but they finally ran his way on a cross-buck. He got under his man in perfect position and drove him cleanly out of the hole.

"All right, Sir Henry!" . . . "Way to block!" . . .

The Redshirts knew that coaches can't see everything and often listen to the sideline shouts to determine who's playing well. The noise was a way of sticking Sir Henry's name in the back of their minds.

"Old Wolf did pretty well out there today," they might say

later, not having particularly noticed his performance, but remembering all the yelling. And when they graded the films later on, they might be inclined to give him the benefit of the doubt on any questionable efforts.

As scrimmages go, this one was a B-plus. The heat drained everyone into puddles of sweat, and the coaches began to substitute liberally after the first hour. Don scored two touchdowns on short plunges and gave every indication of being able to fill a large part of the Bull's big shoes. Helmet kicked three medium-range field goals, which showed that he'd lost nothing since last year. Sir Henry was hanging tough and giving an excellent account of himself. Even the third-teamers and Redshirts were getting their promised chance to show what they could do, and except for Prosser they were all performing well. As expected, Prosser hadn't been called in by the time the scrimmage was nearing its end.

Without warning Quink now popped through the line on a simple dive and blew right past the linebacker. He shot into the secondary and tried to run over Colter, The two hitting at full speed in a violent collision. Quink's move was the kind that frequently produced injuries, but it also was one that won points with the coaches.

"All right, Thompson!" Coach Marshall called out, "that's the way to run, that's the way to stick it in there!"

Every coach—including superior ones like Marshall—in his heart prefers savage contact over long, untouched runs, and Coach Marshall was beaming as Quink wobbled back to the huddle.

"That's the way to hit in there, little stud," he said to Quink. "Take a break and sit out a play." Then, without thinking about what it meant, Coach Marshall turned to the sideline and shouted, "I need a tailback for one play."

Prosser was the next man up after Quink, and at the moment there was no way for the coaches to avoid using him after Coach Marshall had called for him. As Prosser headed onto the field, Hackler abandoned his defensive group and hurried across the line of scrimmage to have a word with Marshall. He needn't have worried. Coach Marshall immediately realized his mistake and leaned into the huddle to call the next play, and was behind the huddle, smoothing Hackler's tail feathers, by the time Prosser jogged into place. We all knew who *wouldn't* carry on the next play.

Marshall took no chances and called a simple fullback dive over left tackle. Roger Johnson took the hand-off and headed into the line while Prosser swung behind him faking a run around left end. Chip Martinson, the defensive tackle at the point of attack, shed his blocker and threw himself at Johnson. His helmet hit squarely on the ball, which squirted from Johnson's grip into the backfield. Prosser was about five feet from where it came to rest. He ran back toward it, and suddenly everyone realized what could happen next.

"Fall on it!" the coaches shouted.

"Pick it up!" the rest of us screamed.

Prosser picked it up and surveyed his situation. The defensive flow had pursued left with Johnson, so there was nothing straight ahead. He had no choice but to swing right and reverse his field. His path led him directly into the cluster of coaches who always stood behind the offense, and they scattered out of the way as they usually do. All of them, that is, except Hackler. He'd stayed with the offensive coaches for this one play, and he alone seemed to realize the consequences of what was going on. He stood his ground and waited as Prosser came streaking at him with his head turned upfield toward the defense. With exquisite timing, he faked a pathetic little stumble and then stuck his foot out to trip Prosser.

I'll never know how Prosser didn't go down. It was as clean a trip as you could ask for, and the surprise should have gotten him if nothing else. He staggered like a terminal wino for about ten steps, keeping himself off the ground with his free hand, then finally regained his balance enough to stand upright. What he saw then was worse than what he'd seen before. The defense had pursued with him to the right, while most of his own men didn't know what had happened behind their backs. As a result he was on the right side of the field facing most of the defense while his own men were to the left and facing each other. That left him no choice but to go back where he'd come from.

57

This time Prosser kept his eyes on the coaches as he nego-
tiated through them, and had no difficulty dodging a frantic
swipe of Hackler's cast. He left Hackler roaring obscenities
behind his back as he turned his attention upfield. He was
getting behind his blockers by then, and they were starting to
knock holes in the pursuing wall of defenders.

Suddenly, as he neared the left sideline, Prosser stopped for
a brief instant. All the defenders hesitated in anticipation of
what he might do next, and that slight hesitation provided all
the opening he needed. He darted through it as if someone had
jabbed a hot poker up his ass, and from there he ran like a
scalded cat, zigging and zagging through all the open spaces
among the strung-out defenders.

Thirty yards downfield Prosser was totally in the clear. He
had so far outdistanced his pursuers that he began to ease up.
They gained ground on him all the way into the end zone, but
the closest one was still five yards away when he turned and
tossed the ball back to the trailing referee. The stands were
going crazy as he wearily jogged back to the sideline. It had
been a sixty-yard run from scrimmage, but he'd traveled well
over a hundred yards to complete it.

"Judas H. Priest!" exclaimed the Bull. "Can you *believe* that
guy?"

Prosser silently accepted all the back slapping and congratulations, then I noticed him looking anxiously back upfield as he
tried to see past those around him.

"Where's Wolf?" he asked. "He took a bad hit on a block."

Everyone became silent when he spoke because it was such
a rarity. We looked for Sir Henry and sadly found out what had
happened. He was still on the ground upfield with Trainer
Hanson already bending over the familiar ugly angle of his right
arm.

"Dislocated," I muttered bitterly. "A fucking dislocated
shoulder."

THE SCRIMMAGE ended immediately after Prosser's run. Hackler called his entire defense onto the field and told them they

58

looked like hog shit, then made them run ten punishment laps around the track so they wouldn't be seen by the fans. Not to be outdone, and perhaps feeling guilty about his mistake, Coach Marshall made the offense join in the laps. Prosser returned to his goat status as quickly as he'd become a hero.

Gloom, as they say, hung heavy in the Redshirt dressing room when I went to get Sir Henry's clothes. A lot of vicarious hopes had ridden on his back, and now those hopes were as crushed as his shoulder. In a way he was also now on a level with Prosser as far as the coaches were concerned.

Once it becomes obvious that someone is doomed, the other players must react as if he's already gone. There's a very real fear of guilt by association. Today's friend is tomorrow's liability. Even a marked player's best buddies will break off the relationship rather than risk what the coaches might think about it. Which doesn't mean there's any pleasure in doing it. It's just got to be done to survive.

"Just when he had it in the goddamn bag!" Tom exploded.

"Come on, Tom," said Gene Skidmore, the other Redshirt tackle. "It happened and it's done. Accept it."

"Fuck you, Skid," Tom snapped as the anger and frustration spilled out of him.

There would be no confrontation over Tom's harsh words. Skid was a gentle giant who always made an effort to cool hot tempers. Besides, everyone felt as bad as Tom. Even Prosser showed it, sitting there with his head hanging down.

"Look, guys," I finally said, "Sir Henry looked good out there and the Big Eye saw it all. The coaches might remember the films and give him a shot later on."

"Goddammit, Sage, that's bullshit!" rasped Tom, jumping to his feet. "They're gonna get rid of him now for sure and you *know* it. A Redshirt lineman with a fucked-up shoulder is as good as gone—"

"Maybe it won't be that way," I said as I picked up his clothes and carried them toward the door. "Maybe he'll get lucky one more time."

Of course, I knew I was only pissing in the wind.

RANDALL WAS waiting in the shadows under a stadium ramp when I walked out the door. He motioned me over.

"Gee, pal, you look like hell," he said.

"Yeah . . . what are you doing here?"

"I'm protecting you," he said with a self-satisfied grin. "This way the coaches won't know we've been talking."

"I appreciate your caution," I said sarcastically, "especially the part about asking around for me before practice."

"What? The old guy up front?" Randall dismissed Cap'n with a careless shrug. "He's cool. I told him I'd do a story on him later this year."

"Listen, asshole, that 'old guy up front' is probably the sharpest son of a bitch around here. You fuck with him and he'll put your hide on a wall."

Randall blinked. "What kind of wild hair got up *your* ass today?"

"Hey, look," I said, forcing a smile, "I'm sorry. The guy who hurt his shoulder on that last play is a good friend of mine, and I have to take these clothes over to him in a few minutes. I guess I'm a little uptight about it. What did you want to talk about?"

"Well, the thing I wanted to tell you before practice was that two assistant coaches from Texas flew in this morning to scout the scrimmage. They spent the whole time up there in the press box with Anderson and us reporters."

The only thing unusual about that was the fact that there were just two of them. Our city is a "plum" scouting assignment because of its night life, and we were often scrutinized by whole flotillas of coaching staffs. It occurred to me that Texas just might be taking the upcoming game with some seriousness.

"So," Randall went on, "and this is the beautiful part, when Prosser started dancing around out there, one of the Texas coaches said, 'Where the hell you been hidin' *that* one, T.K.?' When it was over you could have heard a pin drop up there, and then the other Texas coach said, 'What's his name, T.K.? You been holdin' out on us?' They seemed pretty annoyed."

I nodded. "Coaches don't trust each other for shit."

"Okay," Randall said, "so Anderson turned around and gave

a little halfhearted laugh, then said, 'Look, fellas, that boy's just a Redshirt. He got lucky, that's all. It's late and the defense is tired. My grandmother could have made that run and she's ninety-nine.'

"Well, the first Texas coach said, 'Horseshit, T.K., that's the fastest man you've got.' Anderson said, 'They were gaining on him the whole way.' The first coach just turned away with a funny look on his face and the second one said, 'Come on, T.K., the kid let up. A blind man could see that.'

"That was all Anderson could afford to listen to in front of us. He jerked those two aside where we couldn't hear and then really gave them a jawing. When they came back it was all smiles and good humor, and Prosser wasn't mentioned again. I'm not sure I know what to make of all that . . . I wish you could have been there."

I shook my head emphatically. "I didn't need to be. What he did was tell them about Prosser's head. Coaches are the same everywhere. I already told you how it is . . . they feel threatened by anyone who isn't afraid of them. Texas gets rid of them just like we do."

"Larry, don't laugh, I want to change some of that. I'm going to do a headline story for tomorrow's edition: 'Prosser Shines in Last Cajun State Scrimmage.' What do you think?"

"I think you'll be wasting your time and putting a noose around your neck. It won't help Prosser because the coaches will stick with their lucky-break story and then get rid of him that much quicker. You'll also find yourself damn unwelcome around here. You'll be covering bowling tournaments and ladies' golf matches from now on."

"To hell with it . . . the public has a right to know about Prosser—"

"Dammit, Randall, the public doesn't give a shit! They don't *want* to know. Go stop ten fans on the street and try to tell them football is fucked. Tell them it makes zombies of their sons, they'll run from you like you just got loose from the nut house. They don't want to know about all that. People want the image because the reality is too ugly. Randall, believe me, they'll de-

6 1

stroy you if you try to fuck with that image. . . . Look, we'll have to finish this some other time, I've got to get over to the infirmary. I'm behind schedule already."

"Yeah, right. . . ." he mumbled.

"Will you hold off on the Prosser story? It can only hurt both of you."

"Yeah, I guess, but I'm still not convinced you're right."

"Just wait until we've had a chance to talk," I said as I turned away. "I'll convince you."

He thought that over as I walked off, then yelled after me, "I'll give you a call next week—Tuesday."

I could hardly wait.

I DROPPED Dean's clothes off first. He was in surprisingly good spirits and not at all displeased with his broken arm.

"If I had to get one," he kept repeating, "this is as good as any. I just don't want a knee. You know yourself, Sage, fucking knees never heal worth a shit."

But Sir Henry was anything but cheerful. He sat propped up in bed with the entire right half of his upper torso covered with tape. He'd been brought into his room only minutes before I got there, and was still in serious pain.

I asked how he was feeling and he answered through tightly clenched teeth. "Every fucking breath hurts."

"The pain-killers will take effect soon."

"I sure as hell hope so."

"I'll go now and let you rest," I said, turning to leave. "I'll come back later to see how you're doing."

"Wait! I want to ask you something."

I knew what it would be and hoped against it.

"What's going to happen to me now, Sage?" he asked hesitantly. "I mean, what are they going to do with me? I want the truth."

I stepped back alongside the bed and gave it to him. "Things are going to get pretty ugly for you, Hank, if you try to keep on playing. They won't repair your shoulder with surgery because you might tear it up again. That means you'll have to play with it taped into place, but the tape won't do much good on a solid lick. Your shoulder will start popping out of place more and more until you get gun-shy and start favoring it. You'll become an embarrassment to yourself, the aggravation will catch up with you, and eventually you'll be forced to quit. And that's the truth."

Sir Henry had been here long enough to know that scenario by heart, but it always took a while for the reality of it to sink in. The most gut-wrenching part of my job was helping terminally injured players through that initial rejection stage.

"But I can't quit—" he blurted, then winced from the pain and toned himself down. "What would my . . . friends think?"

"They'll think you're a quitter."

"But I'm not, damn it. I'm no quitter!"

Being forced to quit, becoming known as a quitter . . . there it was, the strongest, most ingrained fear a football player has to deal with, even stronger than physical injury. Good men, real men, are never weak under any circumstances. Football players are the elite, the most macho among red-blooded American males—as long as you play football, your manhood can't be questioned. Quitting forces you to take your first honest look at yourself, and the view can be pretty damn terrifying.

"You know you're not a quitter and I know you're not a quitter," I said, "but don't expect too many others to understand. They've all been brainwashed by the same bullshit that's making you feel so guilty right now, and there's not much you can do about it except learn to live with it."

He sat there staring blankly for a few moments, then slowly nodded. "Well, I'm damned if I'll give my scholarship back. They said I could keep it no matter what, and I'm going to hold them to that—"

"They won't let you keep it," I said quietly. "That scholarship deal isn't worth the paper it's printed on once you're off the team."

"But it's a fucking legal document! I can sue those bastards if they try to take it away!"

"They don't need to take it away, Hank. They have enough ways to get it back legally. Look, that scholarship gives them the power to make you scrub out toilets in the dressing rooms. If you go along with that, they'll find something you won't do. As soon as you refuse to do anything they say, it's all over—"

"They can't do that!" he shouted, and couldn't control the tears starting to fill his eys. "It's not fair, goddamn it." He began to cry, and pounded the bed with his good hand, which hurt his shoulder even more.

I'd been through this whole scene several times before, but that only made it harder to take. "Listen to me, Hank. If you keep on trying to play you'll only make your shoulder worse than it is, and the coaches will put you in Shit Drills this spring anyway. If you quit and try to hang on to your scholarship, they'll humiliate you until you give it up. One way or another they're going to get rid of you *and* get your scholarship back. It's always been that way and don't bet it always won't be.

"What about Sutherland? *He's* still on scholarship! Why can't I be like Sutherland—?"

"Sutherland is a special case and you know it."

Last year Hackler had devised a special way of making defensive linemen fire out of their stances more quickly. He'd spot someone slowing down and then sneak up behind them at the snap and kick the target hard in the ass "to help get him going." It was an effective stimulus. Then, during last spring training, he snuck up behind a third-team tackle named George Sutherland.

Somehow Hackler missed Sutherland's ass and hit his crotch instead. Sutherland's testicles were crushed and he was hospitalized for several days; then word came down that he was sterile. The Athletic Department had to fork over fifty thousand dollars cash *plus* the full scholarship before Sutherland's old man backed down from pressing charges against the entire coaching staff. Of course, not a line was ever printed about it.

"You quit way back, didn't you, Sage?" Sir Henry said. He seemed to be calming down.

"Yes, I did."

"How long does it take to get over it?"

"You never get over it."

As I WALKED across campus enveloped by the warm, sweet air of late-summer evening, I was hoping we'd at least have the same kind of weather next week at this time. Then I checked my watch and realized that in exactly one week it would probably be time for the second-half kickoff.

Carla went to bed early that night after a rough day of faculty meetings, so I decided to look around and see what was going down. Which usually meant Tom's room.

Sure enough, Tom and two henchmen were operating when I got there, so I quietly stepped inside and nodded silent greetings to Skid and Wizard Burke.

"That's right, sir," Tom was saying on the phone in his 'Joe College, Freshman Honor Student' voice, "I'm certain it was fireworks. Yes, sir, right out in the quadrangle, sir. Right in the middle of it, sir. Yes, sir. I hope you catch them, sir."

Tom hung up and turned around to face the room. He always worked turned toward a wall so the expressions of onlookers wouldn't crack him up in the middle of his routines.

"Hey, Sage," he said, "good to see you, man. You're just in time for a little Greenie Cop action."

"Green Tide" for the team, "Greenie Cops" for the campus gendarmes. A favorite and deserving target of Tom's, the Greenies were hopelessly incompetent and gullible.

Tom now got up and walked to the large window that faced out onto the large quadrangle six stories below.

"Come over here and check out the quadrangle while I tell you what we've got set up."

I walked over and joined all three of them at the window. The quadrangle was faintly illuminated by lights from the men's dormitories that bordered two of its adjacent sides. An ROTC building and a parking lot formed the other sides. The quadrangle measured approximately one hundred yards long by seventy-five yards wide.

"We've planted the grand total of fifty, count 'em, fifty cherry bombs out there. They're on cigarette fuses and staggered to go off randomly for twenty minutes. Now you just heard me call the Greenie Cops pretending to be a squealer who saw some guys fucking with fireworks out there, right? And you know

65

how bad they want to catch the 'Mad Bomber'? So we figure they'll be there in five minutes easy."

They'd be there sooner if it was humanly possible. Tom favored explosion stunts of all kinds, but he was especially fond of cherry bomb routines, and the Greenie Cops were out to collar him.

"Swede is out laying down the last series," Tom said, "and he'll finish just about the time the Greenies arrive."

Swede Olson was a third-team end who was also Tom's roommate. I peered into the darkness below and saw a tall, light-haired figure near the ROTC building. Swede.

"Here they come," Wizard said as a Greenie Cop car pulled into the parking lot. Wizard was a second-team wingback who orchestrated Tom's projects with hit-team precision.

"How's it look, Wizard?" Tom asked. Tension was beginning to clip his words.

Wizard checked his watch, "Okay, so far." From here on it was his show. He glanced up for a quick assessment of the situation below.

"Shit, they're being careful!"

Two Greenie Cops had left their car and with flashlights in hand were cautiously approaching the darkened quadrangle.

"Will they even be *on* it when the first one goes off?" Tom pressed. Everything was out of his hands now, and his frustration was showing.

Wizard's eyes were back on his watch as he shrugged. "Only thirty more seconds."

"Come on, Wizard, that's not long enough. They won't be anywhere near the middle," Tom said.

"I'm sorry, all I could get was Salem menthols, and they burn a few seconds quicker."

Wizard was a born experimenter and statistician. He'd test-burned dozens of cigarettes of every major brand in order to perfect his fuses, and now he knew the exact burn time of any length of any cigarette you could name. Last Christmas he'd cut a string that played "Jingle Bells" with cherry bomb explosions.

"Where's the first one supposed to go off?" Tom snapped. "Maybe we'll get a break there."

66

Wizard quickly rifled through the notes he compiled for each major operation.

"Skid laid that one," he said matter-of-factly. "Where'd you put it, Skid?"

"Over near the—"

Boom!

The bright flash and noise finished Skid's explanation.

"Perfect!" Tom exhulted. "Right near Swede!"

The Greenie Cops got a good look at the tall figure lurking across the quadrangle near the ROTC building and took off across the wide expanse after him. Swede quickly stepped behind the building's corner and disappeared. The Cops were ten yards from dead center when Wizard spoke again, eyes on his watch.

"Five more starting . . . now!"

Boom! . . . Boom! Boom! Boom! . . . Boom!

The Greenie Cops staggered to a halt with explosions ringing all around them.

"Got 'em!" Skid said with satisfaction.

"Three more," said Wizard as he looked up from his watch.

Boom! . . . Boom! . . . Boom!

The Greenie Cops were stranded now, unable to move. Even using flashlights they couldn't be sure of not stepping on a hidden live cherry bomb. They could only stand helplessly in the center of the quadrangle while waiting for the explosions to stop. It would be a long wait.

Students attracted by the noise began to heckle them from windows in the two adjacent dorms . . . "Hey, ya fuckin' pussies, get on outta there" . . . "Wassamatta, chickenshits, scared to take a hike?" . . .

Tom's crew didn't heckle. The complexity and precision control of it were what they cared about.

And the release from the special built-up frustrations of Redshirt football.

WHEN THE kick began to wear off, Skid and I left and went down to the snack bar. Skid was the other Redshirt tackle with

Sir Henry, but he was a special case. He'd enrolled at Cajun State when his original school dropped football and now was playing out his transfer year as a Redshirt. At six-five, two hundred fifty pounds, he was the biggest man on our team and would easily have been on the Varsity if not for his transfer status.

"You know, Sage, I've been wanting to talk to you about a little problem . . ."

"Yeah?" I mumbled through a mouthful of burger. I figured if it was "little" he wouldn't have mentioned it.

"Yeah . . ." He fingered a saltshaker for a few moments, then it poured out. "I think I'm losing my desire or ability or something. It's been downhill for me ever since they made me a Redshirt, and now I'm really getting worried about myself. I'm not sure, but I think maybe it has something to do with always having to hold back, doing less than my best . . . I'm picking up bad habits, dodging work—shit like that. It's really starting to get to me."

"It's the Redshirt dilemma," I said, offering the safest platitude I could think of. "Happens to the worst of you. You'll get over it next year when you get on the Varsity—"

"I'm not sure I want that anymore."

He *was* getting serious. Once they start questioning the system and their place in it, the process is practically irreversible.

"You see," he went on, "I've never been less than a starter wherever I was, because of my size if nothing else. I saw and got only the good things football has to offer, and there are some pretty great rewards if you're sitting topside. But Christ, man, looking from the bottom up gives you a whole new perspective!"

I nodded. "The turkeys aren't as bad as you thought, are they?"

"Right! Right! I used to think the scrubs were a bunch of lazy fuck-offs who didn't want or deserve to play because that's what the coaches always said about them. But, shit, that's not the way it is at all. They want to play as bad as anyone, and plenty of them have the ability, but someone got down on them for some reason and that's all she wrote."

68

"I know. Nothing sticks harder or longer than a bad rap on a football field."

"Yeah, once when I was at my old school, this high school all-American tackle came in as a freshman. He was a big black kid, and the first thing the coaches did was put him in the chutes with me to see what he was made of. I blew him out about ten times in a row, and it got easier and easier each time. The easier it got the more I punished him, and by the end he was dodging like a squirrel on a rifle range. It was pathetic . . . This was an eighteen-year-old kid, away from home and probably scared to death, going against an older, bigger guy for the first time in his life. But the coaches judged him once and forever on that first day's performance. He never got another chance, and he never got his confidence back. He could have been great if they'd handled him right. He was ruined in a year. I heard he became a junkie after he quit . . ."

Skid stared hard at his Coke glass. I kept my mouth shut.

"Anyway," he said, "it's bad enough I believed he was a pussy just because the coaches said so. Now I realize it's what I wanted to believe. I wanted to feel superior. Now I'm a Redshirt for the same kind of fucked-up reason that got him, and I can realize what I did to him—"

"You didn't do it to him, Skid. *They* did. They used you."

He shrugged and nodded, but I don't think he felt off the hook.

SKID AND I were just returning to the dorm when we met Tom, Swede, and Wizard on their way out.

"We were coming for you guys," Tom said without breaking stride. "Time Bomb just called to say he needs some jocks to juice a Kappa Sig rush party."

"Do you owe him a favor?"

"No, but now he owes me one. You never know when it might come in handy."

Rush parties are what fraternities use to land choice pledges. Young, and willing, women are recruited to provide companionship for an evening, and the fraternity members do their utmost to convince rushees that their frat is the off-the-wall wildest, raunchiest, goddamnedest frat in the whole fucking universe. With enough hard liquor and drugs of choice in their hands and enough pretty girls on their arms, many rushees come to believe it.

Kappa Sigs were renowned for being heavily into debauchery, and their rush parties sometimes reached postmidnight depths that were later marveled at in hushed tones. We were understandably expectant as we approached their frat house.

"Sage, Everett, all of you, come right on in," Time Bomb said, welcoming us. Time Bomb, an ex-player, was the newly elected president of Kappa Sig.

"Hey, everybody! Look who's here! The jock brigade!"

Frat members were especially glad to see us during rush week, the theory being that we lent an air of potential violence to their parties. Football players, after all, are known far and wide as the true hell-raisers on any campus, so our mere presence made the rushees think Kappa Sig was where bad-ass action *really* went down. Actually our group was bent on trashing nothing more than a few beer cans.

We stepped inside and began to drift around, enduring introductions to rushees. That was the price we paid for having the run of the house anytime we wanted it. I finally made my way to the backyard bar for a beer, and as I turned back, I got the question I hated to hear most.

"I saw you come in with the football players," a good-looking, sharp-eyed coed said. "What position do you play?"

"I'm not a player," I answered, unable to suppress the rush of shame I felt. ". . . I'm the team manager."

She looked shocked. "You're the water boy?"

I nodded. "That's another way of putting it, I guess."

"But you're so *big*, why don't you play?"

"I used to," I said a little too quickly.

"Well, what happened?"

"I got hurt."

"Oh," she said, turning away.

SHORTLY BEFORE midnight there was a slight commotion at the front door. I didn't pay much attention, but not long after, the house lights came on and the music stopped. Everyone became quiet as Time Bomb stepped up on a chair to call for attention, and when I looked over I saw Peso standing at his side. I had completely forgotten about Peso.

"Ladies and gents," Time Bomb announced, "in keeping with Kappa Sig's policy of bringing all rushees and their dates the absolute *tops* in late-night entertainment, we've contracted with this gentleman here to provide you with an experience you won't soon forget. All we have to do is walk a few blocks and the show is on. Let's go!"

As the rush-party caravan began snaking down Maple Street, I caught up with Peso to ask him what had happened.

"I found a better market," he exclaimed. "I knew these guys would go for it. I asked Time Bomb for a hundred dollars and he didn't even blink. He collected it in five minutes!"

"Son of a bitch!" I muttered in admiration.

"Fuckin' A!"

CASEY'S BAR and Grill was one of those long, narrow establishments often found in residential areas of major cities, and we all crowded into the bar's tiny back room, packed like sardines from the center pool table to the enclosing walls. Seven patrons still in the bar had joined our group—two old ladies, a drunken student, and four older men.

Mavis, the star of the upcoming show, elbowed her way through the crowd and climbed up on the pool table, then deftly tied a knot in the cord that held a naked bulb suspended overhead. The swaying light gave the room an eerie, flickering quality. She was a middle-aged redhead, lean, washed-out. She looked like she'd had to fight for every scrap of food she'd ever eaten.

"All right," she suddenly said in a voice that startled everyone with its authority, "here's how it's gonna be here tonight. I'm gonna put on a good show for you kids, you're gonna get your money's worth, but you're gonna do it *my* way or it ain't gonna be done at all. Does everybody understand?"

Most of the younger girls nodded in alarm.

"Now, first of all," Mavis continued, "I want everyone to *stay back,* and I don't want nobody sayin' nothin'. I gotta be able to concentrate to get into it. Is that clear?

Most of us just stood there waiting. Mavis checked our reaction to her instructions, then smiled in satisfaction.

"Okay, I'm ready," she said.

With that she pulled her sweater over her head and exposed the near-empty remains of what had perhaps once been so-called full, ripe breasts. A silent wave of distaste swept through the group, and Mavis picked it up.

"Don't worry, honey," she said, looking directly at one particularly well-endowed girl standing nearby, "yours will look like mine one day, 'cause mine used to look like yours."

She then tossed her skirt aside and stepped out of her panties. A caesarean scar split her abdomen from navel to crotch, laced like a football with purple tissue-tears. Even Peso winced.

"Come on, honey," she said to him as she sat down near one end of the pool table. "Go to work."

She placed her heels in the pool table's corner pockets while Peso, swallowing hard, manfully stepped forward, leaned down and began to eat her out, not even bothering to spread her pubic hair.

Almost immediately Mavis leaned back onto her elbows and began to moan. Her eyes squeezed closed while her head began to loll back and forth. Her pelvis began to twitch. Peso continued to chow down, his own eyes tightly shut.

The room temperature began to rise as we all leaned forward to get a better view. Girls felt bulges start to rise against their fannys and hips, while the guys could hear the girls starting to breathe a little more heavily. Suddenly Mavis's eyes snapped wide open and glared furiously at us.

"Goddammit!" she shouted, "I said stay back!"

We surged back against the walls en masse, but within seconds the imperceptible creeping forward had begun again.

72

Again without warning Mavis shouted. "Listen, you mother-fuckers, I need air!"

She was gasping in the supercharged atmosphere, but our surge back against the walls provided little relief from the cramped room's stuffiness. By now we were all breathing more than our individual shares.

And Mavis was finally getting into it. She opened her eyes and looked dreamily at Peso.

"Come here," she whimpered in a soft, unexpectedly feminine voice. "I need you, baby, I need you now. Come on, baby, put it in me, put it in now."

Peso was simultaneously scrambling up onto the pool table and frantically trying to unzip his jeans. Mavis reached over and expertly freed his crank, then kissed it sweetly and began guiding it between her legs. Just before penetration she came out of her reverie and noticed how closely she was surrounded by pop-eyed faces.

"Goddammit," she screamed, "this is the last time I'm saying it. *Stay the fuck back!*"

Her fury lashed us back harder than ever, and at the same time out of nowhere came the peculiar sound of something metal striking against something else with a hollow thud.

The crowd began to surge in panic, pressing and squeezing away from the wall. Suddenly a stream of thick white liquid spurted up over our heads, then another, and another. Crazy, twisting arcs of white fluid began to rain on everyone packed into the tiny room. Squeals and curses were everywhere as people struggled to get through the single door.

Finally I saw what had happened. Someone had knocked over and activated the fire extinguisher that had been on the back wall, and now the hose arm was swingly wildly from the pressure and spraying extinguishing foam all over everyone.

Peso took a direct shot in the ear.

"Don't go, baby," Mavis pleaded, "I need you—"

"Sorry, Mavis," he said as he wiped his ear and pulled his pants back up. "I just can't hack it tonight."

73

IT WAS pushing one A.M. when we returned to the Kappa Sig house thinking Time Bomb and the other members had blown it with the rushees, but soon after returning we knew we'd been wrong. The Peso-Mavis incident would live in legend. An extraordinary number of girls were allowing themselves to be "shown around the rooms upstairs," many of them more than once. Kappa Sig had more than gotten its money's worth.

Tom and I decided to leave at about one o'clock. The rest of the guys were understandably interested in sticking around to take advantage of Peso's foreplay, but Tom was faithful to his girl back home, and I had Carla. We left the others to their fun with no regrets.

"You in a rush to get home?" Tom asked as we headed back toward campus.

"Not really. I told Carla I'd try to be in before midnight, but she's asleep by now. Why?"

"Because I have to check out the Rabbit action, and I was wondering if you'd like to come along."

"Sure," I said without hesitation. Tom seldom offered sneak previews to major coming attractions.

At the dorm Tom put his hand on Rabbit's doorknob and told me to brace myself.

"What a crap-ass mess," I said when I looked inside.

Big Dick, who was also Rabbit's roommate, calmly looked up from his seat on the floor. "Yeah, but it's a beautiful, ingenious crap-ass mess."

And so it was. The room was filled with every manner of automobile parts and pieces, and those components could have come from only one car in the entire world—Rabbit's pale blue Triumph TR-6.

"That's right," Tom said as he read my mind, "Rabbit's little baby has come to visit."

"You're going to leave it like this?" I asked unbelievingly.

Grant Heape scratched his curly brown hair. "It was a toss-up after we broke it down and got all the parts up here. . . ."

Heape was the Redshirt wingback, and I knew his labor in this was more than simple loyalty to Tom. If not for Rabbit's

74

charmed existence at third-team wingback, Heape would be on the Varsity with a good chance of lettering. He made little effort to hide his feelings about Rabbit.

". . . but now we think we can reassemble it by the time he gets back," Butch Colley said, finishing Heape's sentence. Colley was a second-team safety who was also Heape's roommate, and the two of them were close as brothers.

Big Dick, Heape and Colley were the team's car and motorcycle freaks, and top mechanics as well. Heape and Colley kept an old MG running like A. J. Foyt wouldn't believe, while Big Dick could disassemble a motorcycle as fast as a Hell's Angel.

"Will it fit in here?" I asked.

"Like a glove." Heape smiled. "Right between the beds."

"Then do it," Tom said.

Big Dick shook his head. "We've got to get some sleep now and get back on it no later than nine in the morning. Can you have somebody get us up?"

Tom looked at me.

"Sure," I agreed, "I'll come over. Carla will probably sleep late anyway."

"And the girl?" Colley asked. "You're sure she's good until at least five o'clock?"

Tom smiled. "Don't worry, it's all taken care of."

"She was your doing?" I said delightedly.

"None other than," Heape said on Tom's behalf. "You don't think a jerk like Rabbit could have done that on his own, do you?"

I hadn't actually seen it happen, but I'd heard about it. It seems that when Rabbit left the dressing room after the day's scrimmage, a stunning blonde no one had ever seen before walked up to him, threw her arms around his neck and laid a tremendous, soulful kiss on him. Then she turned and led him by the hand to a waiting Corvette.

Rabbit had seemed stunned, but no more so than those who saw or heard about it. We all knew Rabbit dated around often enough, but we also knew that few girls made the same mistake twice.

"Do you mean to tell me she's sleeping with Rabbit tonight just so you can have the time to do this?" I couldn't imagine such a sacrifice, even for an old friend.

"In a way." Tom said. "She's going to pull the old 'having my period' routine, but he'll sleep at her place and keep her company tomorrow, even if he has to sleep on the floor."

"He'll do it because he'll want us to believe he scored," Big Dick said. "I bet he'd stay in a motel tonight if she wouldn't keep him."

Tom nodded. "It's locked-in all the way."

"Then let's get cleaned up and go to bed," Colley said. "We've got some major engineering work on for tomorrow."

Sunday

Carla began to stir awake as I got out of bed. I whispered to her to stay asleep, then got dressed, headed for the dorm and had the car-assembly team hard at work by nine-fifteen. As I started for the apartment, I saw the Bull being let out of an unfamiliar car. He seemed to be having difficulty staying upright on his crutches.

"Who was that?" I asked him as the car pulled away.

"Someone named Shirley," he said, and winced.

Up close his looks explained his instability. He'd over-amped on booze.

"Quite a night, huh?"

"I'm not sure," he said, "I don't remember much of it. Have you seen Quink? Maybe he knows what happened."

I doubted it. Quink and the Bull were one-two in drinking capacity but neither had an edge in drunken rationality. Quink, though, was the driving force behind their escapades. If the Bull had drunk himself into a stupor, it was certain Quink had set the pace.

"I haven't seen him, but why don't you join me for some coffee? You wouldn't believe how your eyes look."

"You ought to see 'em from *my* side."

77

He struggled up to a counter seat while I went to get two coffees, which made a clatter when I put them down on the counter top. The Bull promptly squeezed his eyes shut.

"Sorry," I said.

I let him take a few sips before I asked what happened. He took another sip, then began speaking in the slow, carefully modulated tones that distinguish a true hangover victim.

"Well, it began like usual, down at Las Ramblas . . ."

Las Ramblas was a downtown bar heavily trafficked by college students and other would-be swingers.

". . . Quink and I had a few beers and somehow they turned into boilermakers—I'm not sure how. Anyway, we started talking to this table full of raunchy-looking ladies, six or seven of them. Quink wanted to shine them on with some dumb bullshit about stealing Plymouth Rock and holding it hostage—something like that. Anyway, they were so bad that everyone else was ignoring them, so we moved in for a few laughs. I'm pretty sure we didn't intend to pick up any of them—"

"Or get yourselves picked up?"

"Whatever . . . I'm not sure either way. All I remember is going over to their table. Beyond that it's a blank."

I felt myself starting to get angry. I'd never been able to understand why Quink and the Bull would risk so much for so little. "You know, Ken," I said offhandedly, "getting that drunk could really be dangerous. I know God is supposed to watch over you and all that, but don't you think you should maybe at least meet Him halfway every now and then?"

"Yeah, I know . . . it even worries me sometimes."

Unlike Quink, the Bull wasn't beyond considering the consequences of his actions. His problem was more in judging his limits. Or admitting them.

I began to feel sorry for him but spoke without thinking. "You want something to eat?"

He looked stricken and almost gagged.

"Never mind," I quickly corrected, then changed the subject. "Was that one of the boilermaker crew who brought you in?"

"I don't think so," he said with a careful shake of his head. "She was pretty good-looking."

"Well, what did she have to say about last night?"

"She's ninety percent sure she started at Las Ramblas too, but—"

"No need to go any further. Where did you two sleep?"

"In the front seat of her car. I woke up with my nose in her twat. I tell you, Sage, you don't know what disoriented is until you wake up with your nose in someone's twat. It'll scare the hell out of you."

"You woke up with your nose in her twat?" I repeated. "How in the world did you manage that?"

"It looked like we'd been trying to get it on with each other when we passed out. You know how it is when you're drunk and lying down—you just sort of drift off. We woke up in the sixty-nine position completely nude-balls."

People were never simply nude at Cajun State. Male and female, they were always nude-balls.

"And that's how you spent the night?" I said in amazement. "Nude-balls sixty-nine in the front seat of her car?"

"Yeah," he grinned feebly. "And that's not the worst of it. She woke up first and my dong was still in her mouth. She started choking and gagging and making all kinds of horrible strangling noises, and I tell you, man, it woke me right up. We were *both* scared shitless when we first opened our eyes. I'm surprised she didn't bite it off."

That last part smacked of a put-on, but I didn't feel like calling bullshit on it. Instead, I asked where they'd been parked.

"In a Safeway parking lot across the river."

I sat stunned for a moment. There was only one way to get across the river late at night.

"What? You crossed that giant goddamn bridge blind drunk in the middle of the fucking night? Jesus, Ken! Have you got shit for brains?"

"*I* wasn't driving," he said in an effort to defend himself. "At least, I don't think I was driving. Besides, she lived over there and it was her car. What could I have done even if I'd been sober?"

"If you were sober, it wouldn't have mattered."

"Oh, yeah," he said meekly. "That's right."

79

Just then Wheeler entered the room, smiling and whistling softly to himself.

"How goes it, sports fans?" he asked cheerily, then got a close-up look at the Bull's haggard features. "Oh, you, too, huh?"

The Bull looked up. "Quink made it in already?"

Wheeler nodded. "About an hour ago."

"Did he say what he did last night after we split up?"

Wheeler shook his head. "Said he couldn't remember. Said he woke up on the floor of a girl's dorm with a big pair of blue panties stuck in one pocket and a small pair of pink ones in the other. He has no idea how they got there."

"What a fucking night," I said.

A FEW hours later, after spending the rest of the morning in bed with Carla, I met Tom and Wheeler back at the dorm so we could be at Don and Annie's apartment by two o'clock. One of our party was missing, however.

"Did the Bull have to cancel?" I asked.

Wheeler shook his head. "No, but he probably should if he looks anything like Quink. The self-indulgent son of a bitch—"

"Come on, Jimbo," Tom said, "give them a break. They stayed off it for two weeks, they're worn thin from all the crap they've been through. Their tolerance is shot and—"

"Horseshit," Wheeler shot back. "Those assholes do that every chance they get. I'll never understand how they can abuse themselves like that and still play decent football."

We stood in an uncomfortable silence. Wheeler was a good guy, but like I've said he swallowed whole what the coaches said about football success, and went along with their black-and-white mentality. Gray areas, contradictions confused and angered him. People who could break the rules and still do well shook him up.

"Speak of the devil," Wheeler said as the Bull hobbled shakily from the elevator. "How do you feel, booze-hound?"

"Kiss my ass, Wheeler."

80

"We'd better get a move on," I put in hastily, and so we set off, Wheeler sulking, the Bull grimly swinging like a pendulum between his crutches. Halfway there Tom asked Wheeler, "How about Stoner? You getting ready for him?"

"No thanks to your little inspirational messages," Wheeler snapped. "But, yes, I am getting up for him.

"How are you going to handle him?" I asked.

"The same way I handle everyone I go against, just like the coaches taught me. I'm going to stick my cage in his fucking numbers and slide my helmet right up into his chin."

"He'll knock your little ass off if you pull that kind of shit on him," Tom warned. "He's an all-American, don't forget. You better show some proper respect."

"The coaches say it'll shake him up, that no one really comes at him anymore, so it might get him off balance and make him less sure—"

"It'll only piss him off and make him murderous," Tom said.

"Look, I'm going to go all out on every play," Wheeler said. "I'm going to play good hard football and I'll do all right against him. He puts his pants on like I do, for Chrissake. He's human!"

"That's not the way I hear it," Tom said.

Wheeler kept silent for a while after that. We were nearing Don and Annie's apartment when he spoke again.

"Sage?"

"Yeah?"

"You want to play some Ping-Pong when we get back?"

"Sure, that'll be fine."

Wheeler suffered from the delusion that by increasing the speed of his hands he would magically increase the speed of his slow feet. Ping-Pong had made him fast of hand, and left him still slow afoot. Well, at least it helped him *feel* quick.

But quick enough for Stoner . . . ?

ANNIE OPENED the door and flashed a conspiratorial smile. She was a blonde pixie with the energy of a giant, and we didn't even have time to say hello before she was chattering at us nonstop.

81

"I knew it was you guys, so I beat Don to the door! Come on in and let me *fondle* you!"

She gave us all a big hug and kiss on the cheek.

"What men!" she crowed. "What men in my house! I love it! If the girls back home could only see me now!"

We hung our heads and kicked at the rug like bashful ten-year-olds. Somehow Annie always humbled us.

"Come on, you guys, take seats. Especially you, Ken. You look like something the cat drug in."

"I feel like something the cat wouldn't *have,*" the Bull said as he hobbled over to a chair with a footrest.

"Big night, huh?"

"Don't ask."

"I've got just the thing for you," Annie assured him. She went over to the refrigerator and pulled out a six-pack.

"Here's a little hair of the dog for the Bull!" she said. "Come and get it, everyone!"

"Hey, Annie!" Wheeler said, "Where's Don?"

"He's powdering his nose, dear," then lowered her eyebrows mock-serious. "But don't go in after him without a *box* of matches. We had chili last night, and I swear Don's can make your eyes sting."

Annie lacked pretension on a grand scale. No phony modesty —a straight-on, up-front woman at nineteen. We all loved her.

"No, seriously," she said, "you know how most people slip them around and then out?" She made a swimming motion with her hands. "Well, Don just drives 'em right on through." She drove a left jab at us for emphasis, which practically put us on the floor.

"What's all the laughing about?" Don said as he walked into the room.

We laughed harder and began pointing at him. He grinned sheepishly in self-defense, then he, too, began to laugh. We laughed even harder at him laughing with us *at* him, and it got totally out of hand in about ten seconds. We started holding our noses and waving imaginary matches at Don's ass, and in general acted like huge grade-school children.

The whole time Annie stood behind the kitchen counter

chugging beer and saying, "God, I love you guys! I *really* love you guys . . ."

THE MEAL itself was Annie's version of Thanksgiving dinner for ten: baked turkey with giblet dressing, cranberry sauce, fresh green beans, fried cauliflower and okra, cornbread, yams, bean salad and enough beer and wine to have us weaving over our plates by the time dessert came.

"Baked apple à la mode." Annie beamed proudly.

"Jesus, Annie," the Bull moaned, "I can't eat any more. Honest, I'm about to pop, and I was queasy when I got here."

Annie looked down at him and said, very sweetly, "Oh, you think you've had too much? Well, then, we'll just have to take it right away so you won't even be tempted."

The rest of us began to hoot as Annie took his dessert away, and the Bull tried to turtle-head into his shirt collar.

Annie quickly did a turnabout and sprang to his defense. "You boys shouldn't make fun of Kenny," she said in that same so-sweet tone. "He can't help it if he's a candy-ass."

Ah, Annie . . .

NATURALLY DON came with us to witness Rabbit's reaction to finding his car in his room. We arrived there a little before five o'clock, and found Big Dick, Heape, Colley and a dozen others loitering conspicuously in open doorways along the hall.

"How'd it go?" Tom asked Heape, the chief mechanic.

"See for yourself. We finished about an hour ago."

It was there all right, a completely assembled TR-6. Crammed into that tiny room, it looked like a whale in a fish pond.

"Oh, Christ," I couldn't help muttering, "he's gonna die when he sees it—"

Peso was standing nearby. "Fuckin' A, man. This one's for the record books."

Tom turned to Big Dick. "You got your shit together? You know what to say?"

"I've got it down cold."

We spent the time quietly exchanging accounts of the previous night. Mostly we discussed Peso's coitus interruptus, but Quink finally got around to asking Helmet what he had done. Every player was well aware of the quality breeding Helmet's dates exhibited, and there was a never-ending effort to find out where and how he got his women.

"I go to a party," Helmet replied.

"Was it an orgy?" Peso asked.

Peso maintained the enduring belief that wealth and style assured unlimited decadence, which was one of the principal reasons he wanted so desperately to become rich.

"Certainly not," Helmet answered indignantly. Then, turning to me, "What gives him this idea always?"

"Jealousy," I suggested. "Pure jealousy."

That was only partly true, but if anyone deserved to be envied, it was Helmet. His father was a German diplomat who'd been posted to eight different countries while Helmet was growing up. That rearing gave him fluency in five languages and a social development light years beyond anything the rest of us could ever hope to achieve. On top of that were his good looks matched by an inner confidence, all of which he carried without giving offense to anyone; anyone, that is, except the coaches. From their standpoint Helmet was nothing more than a Prosser who'd gotten a break.

Two years ago Helmet transferred to Cajun State from Heidelburg University, to take advantage of our Latin American studies program. He happened by a practice session one afternoon and watched our inept crew of placekickers flailing away from thirty-five yards out. He marched up to our kicking coach and announced: "This I can do."

He proceeded to lace five in a row through the uprights from forty yards out. This was in street shoes. Three days later Helmet kicked a forty-seven-yard field goal in the first American football game he'd ever seen. He also kicked two shorter ones, and from that day on he'd been the most publicized and valuable member of our team.

Unfortunately for the coaches, that debut put Helmet above

criticism, and retribution, before they fully understood the kind of person they were dealing with. In addition to his wondrous right leg, Helmet came equipped with a fully developed sense of himself, and his foreign upbringing left him with a disregard for the sanctities of football tradition. The coaches simply had no psychological leverage with him, which Helmet understood and didn't mind at times rubbing their noses in. If they'd had any notion of the problems Helmet's ability would eventually cause them, they'd have handled him like Prosser and all the others who didn't fit: dump him before knowledge of his talent expanded beyond their control. Now, though, Helmet was well established as the best we had to offer. The coaches had no alternative but to appear to accept him. They took full advantage of their eccentric "Krauthead" prodigy's skills, but otherwise ignored him as much as possible. They also tried to save face by insisting Helmet was a sort of wild-hair specialist who in no way could be considered a "real" football player, because after all, a real player could never hope to be successful with his kind of attitude.

What else could they do? Helmet was living proof they'd based their lives on total bullshit.

AT FIVE-FIFTEEN Rabbit came bopping down the hall, filled with joyous energy and pride of faked accomplishment.

"Know what I did last night, fellas? I got laid!"

"Fuck that shit," Big Dick stormed at him. "I want you to explain *that.*" He pointed dramatically at their room.

Rabbit looked puzzled, took a few halting steps toward the room, then looked back for some sign of humor in his roommate's angry features.

"Go on, asshole," Big Dick instructed. "Take a look."

Rabbit stepped into view of the room, and his jaw fell open.

Big Dick was all over him. "Now, goddammit, I just can't fucking put up with this kind of shit. I know you love that car, man, but you just can't keep the motherfucker parked in *here.*"

Rabbit could only continue staring.

"Can't you see there's no room?" Big Dick went on. "Shit, we can't even pull our beds away from the wall. Where the fuck are we gonna sleep? Did you stop to think about that?"

"But—"

"This is the *last* fucking straw. Either park that motherfucker back outside or get yourself a new roommate. I'm not gonna live with no fucking car and that's fucking *final.*"

Big Dick then stormed down the hall and out the door while we all stumbled out after him. Rabbit didn't even notice. When the last of us cleared the hall, he was still rooted to the same exact spot as when he'd first laid eyes on his car.

RABBIT'S MOMENT duly honored, we broke up and went our separate ways. I was nearly halfway to the apartment when I decided to go back and visit Sir Henry in the infirmary. I thought he'd appreciate seeing someone who could afford to sympathize openly with his bad deal. Few of his friends would have dropped by to see him. An important part of just being able to play football is keeping the possible consequences well out of your mind. It doesn't help much to see a buddy lying broken in a bed.

When I got to Sir Henry's room I found his parents already there. I'd met them briefly during freshman orientation last year. I said hello and we stood chatting colorless bullshit for several minutes. Finally I asked Sir Henry how he was feeling and if there was anything I could do for him.

"Yeah," he said, "you could explain to my parents why I have to quit."

"Now, son," his father hurriedly interjected, "there's no need to air our dirty laundry in front of strangers."

"Sage isn't a stranger, for Christ's sake, he's one of my best friends—"

"Nevertheless, Henry," his mother added, "this is a family matter and we'll settle it ourselves."

"What's to settle? I'm quitting and that's that."

"But, son, are you just going to throw away all the sacrifices we've . . . I mean you've made to put you where you are—"

You could see Sir Henry flinch.

"And what about your friends back home? What do you tell them—"

"Look, *I* told you and now Sage can tell you . . . my career is over. My shoulder is wrecked, and that means I'll never make the Varsity, or even play. Period."

"Surely he's just upset about his shoulder," his father said to me. "Won't he change his mind when it gets better?"

I looked at Sir Henry. It was clear on his face—he wouldn't.
. . .

Quitting is always a two-part process that involves first the player, and then his parents. Players come to think of themselves as among the chosen few, and parents get hooked on the reflected glory. All three have to give up some powerfully addictive status, and the sad part is that, as hard as players take it, their parents often take it harder.

"I'm afraid there's no going back, Mr. Wolf," I said. "Once you quit, you quit."

"But it's such a waste," his father said.

I figured it was time to deliver an exit speech. "Mr. and Mrs. Wolf, Hank is going through two traumatic experiences right now. His injury is bad enough, but he also has to face up to quite a few failed expectations. Please don't make it any harder on him than it has to be. You both should be very proud of him and what he's accomplished here, but now he's going to need your help and support like never before. Believe me, he gave all he had trying to live up to what you wanted out of him. It would be nice if you could do the same."

Sir Henry didn't say anything. He didn't have to. His eyes said their own thank you.

Leaving the room I heard Sir Henry's father saying, "No son of mine is quitting anything, and I don't give a goddamn what you or that wise-ass friend of yours or anybody else says . . ."

Like I said, loving parents often take it the hardest.

CARLA AND I were in the middle of supper when the phone rang. It was Tom.

"The word just came down," he said. "Special Shit Drills for Prosser after practice tomorrow."

I felt my stomach flip even though I'd expected it for days.

"Have you ever seen special Shit Drills before?" he asked.

"Yeah, once. Three years ago there was a flanker here about like Prosser, in attitude and ability."

"What happened?"

"They crushed a lung in the second drill."

There was silence on the other end of the line for several seconds, then Tom said, "I think it's time someone had a talk with Prosser. Will you come with me?"

His request caught me by surprise. "Well, I don't know . . . It's not really for us to get involved—"

"Horseshit, they could break his fucking neck tomorrow. Look, someone has to talk him out of it. You're supposed to be the old sage, it's time you started living up to your rep—"

"Okay, I'll be over as soon as I finish supper. But if Hackler finds out about it, *you* do all the explaining."

"He won't find out."

"You hope."

"What's the matter, honey?" Carla asked after I hung up.

"There's going to be special Shit Drills for Prosser tomorrow. I'm going over with Tom to try to talk him into quitting."

Carla didn't say a word. The look in her eyes as she nodded was enough.

PROSSER WAS sitting at his desk, writing a letter. We figured he'd be alone because Helmet was his roommate and, like Stanton and me, lived off-campus. The coaches believed in putting rotten eggs in the same basket, but Helmet, believing in living in the style to which he'd become accustomed, maintained an elegant townhouse apartment, which left the dorm room almost exclusively to Prosser.

"Can we disturb you for a minute?" Tom asked.

Prosser gazed at us and I felt the icy chill those pale blue eyes could generate. He seemed very very old for nineteen.

"What about?"

88

"Do you mind if we sit down?" Tom asked, still being careful. Others had found out the hard way that a wrong word or gesture could turn Prosser completely off.

He made an openhanded motion toward the empty beds. Tom and I took uneasy seats opposite each other.

Tom cleared his throat and nervously pushed the hair up off his forehead. "Have you heard anything about practice tomorrow?"

Prosser's eyes narrowed slightly. "No, I haven't, but I don't suppose you'd be here unless something important was going to happen."

"That's right. . . . Look, Pete, we know you value your privacy, but there's some bad news that concerns you and we thought you might want some time to think about it—"

"Special Shit Drills?"

We nodded.

Prosser brought his pencil to his lips and tapped it against them. "Okay," he finally said. "Thanks for telling me."

Which sounded like a dismissal.

I cleared my throat. "You're not planning on going through with it, are you?"

"Yes."

"Maybe you don't understand what special Shit Drills are like," I said. "Spring-training Shit Drills have to seem like actual drills so the coaches can at least claim they're only trying to make better players out of the marked guys, but the point of special Shit Drills is to get rid of someone quick as possible. Believe me, they don't fuck around. They start right in with all-on-one."

Prosser rubbed his eyes, ran his hands through his curiously white hair, locked his fingers behind his neck, then leaned back in his chair and stared at us.

"So you figure I should quit now, get it over with."

Tom and I nodded again, beginning to feel like a bad act.

"Well, I appreciate your concern, but that's not the way I want to handle it."

"Be reasonable, Pete," I said. "You haven't got a—"

"Look, you've both made decisions about how you want to

89

get on with the coaches, and that's your choice, your business. I'd like the same consideration."

There wasn't much else Tom or I could say to that. We looked at each other, then stood up to leave. As we got to the door, Tom turned back to face Prosser.

"You know, Pete, there's something I've always wanted to ask you. Why've you let yourself get into this situation? You could have stopped it a long time ago if you'd made any effort at all to get along with them. . . . Why didn't you?"

He didn't answer. Maybe he couldn't.

We said good-night and wished him good luck. Nobody could say we didn't try.

CARLA TURNED the television off as soon as I walked in the door.

"How did it go? Did you talk him into it?"

I shook my head and flopped down on the couch. Carla came over and curled up next to me. "What happened?"

"In effect, he politely told us to butt out."

"I don't understand."

"Join the club."

Monday

TODAY WAS the first day of the regular-season practice schedule, which meant there'd be no more early morning wake-ups for me to bother with. It was also the first day of the new fall semester, so nine o'clock found me in Romantic Poets—Keats, Byron, and Shelley—seated next to Big Dick. I asked him how he and Rabbit made out in their new accommodations last night. There was no way for them to sleep in their room with the car in it, so Don had given him the spare key to the room Stanton and I shared in absentia.

Big Dick said, "Oh, it was just about like any other night until the Greenie Cops arrived. Things picked up a little after that."

"How did *they* find out?"

He grinned. "Sometime around midnight Tom called them and said a guy had a car parked in his room. He had to use three different voices before they would believe it enough to come over and check it out. When they got there and found out it was the truth, they reacted about like you'd expect. Tom had told them we were sleeping in your room, so they came down and rousted us both out of bed. It looked for a little while like they might haul Rabbit off to the slammer."

"They blamed *him*? They thought he put his *own* car in there like that?"

Big Dick looked surprised. "Greenie Cops can't figure the instructions for a roll of toilet paper. You know that."

"Okay. So what happened then?"

"Well, when they started hollering at him, Rabbit just stood there making the same sound over and over, so they got even madder at him because they thought he was being a wise-ass. The more they hollered the more Rabbit sputtered, until finally I stepped in and explained everything."

"What did you say?"

"I told them it was all a big misunderstanding and that Rabbit's old man had arranged to have two mechanics come over from Mobile, and I assured them the car would be back on the street in a couple of days."

Rabbit's old man owned, among many other things, four or five automobile agencies in his home state of Alabama, so everyone involved in the car caper knew from the start that there'd be no real problems from it.

"Did the mechanics get here yet?"

"Not yet, but they'll be here by noon."

I thought about that for a moment, then said, "You know, maybe you could find out from those guys how Rabbit got his scholarship. There has to be some explanation for why he's here and why the coaches never fuck with him."

He nodded as the professor walked into the room.

AT LUNCH Big Dick said, "You figure they'll start with all-on-ones, huh, Sage?"

I nodded.

Big Dick's uneasiness was understandable. Shit Drills are bad enough on the receiving end, but the giving end isn't much better if there's any feeling left in you.

"Are you positive they're going to start right in with those?" Heape asked. "Some of *us* might get hurt doing them."

"Why should the coaches care about that?" Tom asked. "They want to be rid of Prosser, and that's the surest way to do it. If

92

any other Redshirts go with him, it just saves them the trouble of doing it in spring training. Besides, they'll never get rid of him with two-on-ones or three-on-ones. It's got to be all or nothing . . ."

Big Dick nodded and spoke for the defense. "That's right, Prosser's like a fucking vapor . . . you never get a solid shot on him."

"Here's something else," I pointed out. "Shit Drills started with twenty guys last spring, and they ended with most of you who finally drifted down to the Redshirts. Prosser was the only one of the original twenty who got through."

"I hadn't realized that," Heape said, surprised. "But it says a hell of a lot for him."

"Everything Prosser does says a lot for him," Tom said. "He's one tough son of a bitch."

But we all knew he wouldn't be tough enough for what was coming this afternoon.

MONDAY PRACTICE usually consists of looking over the offensive and defensive sets of Saturday's opponent, but this Monday would be devoted to work. The Varsity players had been seeing Texas sets since spring training, and by now each one of them knew every variation of every Texas formation.

A game against the defending national champions is a prestige event for second-rate hackers like us, so the entire Athletic Department especially wanted the team to make a decent showing. They felt a good effort would sell a lot of tickets in the future, and incidentally might establish some carry-over respect for our team. No one expected a victory, or even close to it, but there was a driving urgency to avoid a fiasco.

"Men," Coach Anderson said as he began his traditional Monday prepractice speech, "today's the day you have to start getting serious about Saturday night. You're going to be digging in against Number One in that game, and every football fan in this country will take the trouble to find out how well you performed. It's a golden opportunity for each of you, and I hope you don't let it slip through your fingers for lack of mental preparation. The investment you have to make is a simple one: You have to devote every waking minute to thinking about what you should do in every conceivable situation you might face. There's no way to half-ass it; you have to pay that price. If you do, you'll walk off the field Saturday night with your heads high and the crowd cheering. If you don't, I guarantee those Texas boys will shame you so badly you'll wish you'd been born in another country.

"All right, I don't think I need to say any more. Let's get after it today and start building some *momentum.* . . . Let's have a good, crisp practice with no missed snap counts, no busted plays, no dropped passes, and no fumbles! What do you say, men?"

Tense, frightened players sent up a yell that was more from relief than assent. Coach Anderson had a flair for browbeating a team into getting serious about an opponent. Actually, our players were much tougher mentally since his arrival as head coach. Unfortunately, their bodies were still the same.

"All *right,* then," Coach Anderson wound it up. "Larry, blow the horn!"

BRRAAAKK!

And so began the week-long slide toward Texas.

As MONDAY practices go, this one was an A-minus. The adrenaline Coach Anderson stirred up lasted well over an hour, and only near the end did things start to wind down. The reason, of course, was that minds were shifting off of Texas and onto Prosser, who would get his when practice was over.

Though he of course knew what lay ahead, Prosser gave no hint that he cared. He broke two fairly long runs against the Varsity defense but mostly contained himself to the Redshirt standard of into the line and onto the ground—an inauspicious ending to what might have been a great career.

The time finally came. After Coach Anderson concluded his postpractice pep talk, Hackler made the announcement.

"Redshirts stay out for some extra work. Biggs and Thompson stay out too. Everyone else take it on in."

94

Quink's name caught most by surprise, but I'd half expected them to single him out along with Big Dick. Quink *tried* to play kiss-ass like the coaches wanted, but his independent spirit had a way of coming to the surface at odd moments. This was the coaches' way of telling him that if he didn't watch himself, he would be next.

Special Shit Drills were the kind of travesty that could lead to legal problems if not handled very carefully, so only necessary and trusted people were allowed to be present. By the time Hackler was ready to address the Redshirts, only Trainer Hanson, myself and the ambulance jeep were left outside the stadium. We were like the body-disposal unit at an execution, with trainer Hanson responsible for first aid and me responsible for driving the jeep.

"Okay, men," Hackler began, "we're gonna find out who wants to play football, so let's start off with a defensive drill. Give me a defense lined up on the standing dummies."

The standing dummies were seven padded uprights that looked like canvas-covered oil drums stuck on huge springs. They stood in a row on the stadium-side goal line and represented an opposing offensive line. Eleven of the Redshirts took normal defensive positions facing the dummies.

"All right," Hackler continued as he took a position opposite the defense on the end-zone side of the dummies. "I need a running back over here with me. Prosser, you'll do."

And so it began.

Prosser deliberately walked over to Hackler rather than jogged, but Hackler only smiled tolerantly at that breach of the rules. Vengeance was about to he his, and he could afford to be magnanimous. He told Prosser to stand ten yards away from the middle dummy in a row of seven, then pointedly handed Prosser a football with his casted left arm.

"Now, son," he said, "you know the object of this drill, don't you? We want to give the defense over there a good workout. I'm going to wave my hand at them and say, 'Left,' and they'll shift left, and I'll say, 'Right!, and they'll shift right. I'll do that a few times and then say, 'Run.' When I say, 'Run,' I want you

95

to run as hard as you can in either direction and give them a good workout. Okay?"

Prosser ignored Hackler's query. He stood casually holding the ball on one hip and staring straight upfield. Hackler's expression clouded over in the silence, and he turned from Prosser to the defense.

"All right, nobody stops until everyone makes contact, everyone! Ready. . . . Left. Right. Left. Right. *Run.*"

And as Prosser took off toward right end, Hackler muttered to himself, *"Run,* you arrogant little cocksucker . . ."

Even a player of Prosser's wondrous talent had the old snowball's chance in hell of going more than a couple of yards upfield with no blockers against eleven opponents. I'd seen this drill a few times before, and the results were nearly always devastating. The runner gets straightened up by the first man to hit him, speared with helmets by the next two or three, then trampled under the cleats and crushed by the weight of the remaining seven or eight defenders.

Prosser, though, was as intelligent as he was talented. Instead of heading upfield in the normal way, he made straight for the defensive end and plowed right at his ankles. The end had no choice but to dive back at Prosser, only Prosser was lower. He wound up on the ground with the end lying on top of him, and the onrushing defenders had no choice but to pile onto their teammate's back. When it was over and the pile untangled, the defensive end was rubbing his lower back, while Prosser seemed none the worse for lying under all that weight.

Hackler was livid.

"Goddammit, Prosser, I said we wanted to give those people a workout! How the hell are they gonna get a workout if you keep diving into the ground like a fucking pussy? I want you to run! Go out for the goddamn swimming team if you want to dive! Now get up there and do it again!"

This time Prosser went left a little wider than before, but he cut back into the flow and dove into the first pursuer's ankles. The results were the same as on the other side. Prosser walked away unhurt, while one defender was left holding a sensitive wrist and another was limping slightly.

"Prosser, you're not worth shit!" Hackler yelled. "You're the most chickenshit motherfucker I've ever fucking seen. If you've got parents or friends, which I doubt, I wish they could see you now. . . . You'd make them as sick as you make me!"

"Defense!" Hackler finally shouted when Prosser failed to react. "Defense, I want you to line up in a single file right over there." He indicated an area just left of the dummies. "I want you to go over there, Prosser, and I want you to run into each man, one right after the other, and don't stop until you go through the whole fucking line! I'm going to teach your chickenshit ass how to take a lick . . ."

It was Prosser who did the teaching. Hackler's basic stupidity led him to pick a Shit Drill designed to get rid of linemen who know nothing about protecting themselves by slipping direct contact. Prosser made it through the line three times before Hackler tired of watching him get back up after each hit.

Though obviously getting tired, Prosser was holding up better than even any of us expected, but the worst was still to come. Hackler wasn't enjoying all-on-ones nearly as much as he thought he would, so he quit wasting time and got down to serious business.

"All *right,*" he finally shouted, "that's enough of that one . . . everybody come with me." He walked out to the twenty yard line and indicated a left-side hash mark. "I want you Redshirts to stand behind that hash mark." Then he walked fifteen yards farther and pointed to the thirty-five yard line's left-side hash mark. "Prosser, I want you to stand on this one." He then planted himself midfield between the two occupied hash marks, the three positions establishing a fifteen-yard equilateral triangle on the field.

"Here's the way it works, gentlemen," Hackler said as he took his place. "I want you, Prosser, to run right at me as I throw the ball at you. All you have to do is catch it. Now, those are very simple instructions, so you shouldn't have any trouble carrying them out.

"Redshirts, I want you to take turns playing pass defense. I want you to come at me in the same way Prosser will be coming from over on his side, but I want you to *stop* him from catching

97

the ball. Do you understand? *No* completions."

Hackler smiled amiably as he let the implications sink in. This was going to be the Buster Kidney drill; the number-one decimator—king of Shit Drills. Prosser would be running forward and to his right while the defenders would angle left to intercept him. The ball would always be thrown high so Prosser would be forced to fully extend himself to reach it, which would leave his right-side vital organs unprotected and directly in line with the defender's onrushing helmet.

There was no way to avoid serious injury short of refusing to do it, which meant quitting and loss of scholarship. Even Prosser must have known how hopeless his situation was.

"I want Thompson up first," Hackler commanded.

Quink stepped to the head of the line.

"All right, Thompson, show me what you can do."

Hackler was counting on Quink to try his best to stay on the Varsity by really going all-out against Prosser.

"Go!" he shouted, and the two of them began their collision course.

The ball went over Prosser's head, but he made the required leap for it. Quink could have broken him in half if he'd driven on through the tackle, but he held back and allowed Prosser simply to fall on his own left shoulder pad. He even kept his body under Prosser as they fell, cushioning Prosser's impact down to almost nothing.

"Goddammit, Thompson" Hackler screamed, "that's the worst fucking tackle I've ever seen in my whole fucking life. You're gonna be taking his place if you're not careful . . ."

Quink hung his head and jogged back to the end of the Redshirt line. Quink could only be pushed so far, sooner or later he would join Prosser. It was only a matter of time.

"Biggs," Hackler snapped. "Get your ass up there."

Big Dick hesitantly stepped to the front of the line and buckled his chin strap into place.

"And if you don't tackle like I know you can," Hackler added, "I give you my personal word that you won't even letter this year."

Big Dick clamped down on his mouthpiece, and we all knew

what was coming. It would be asking too much of him to give up his hard-won second-team position for Prosser's sake. Besides, if he didn't do it someone else would.

Prosser was fully extended in the air and reaching with both hands for the overthrown ball when Big Dick's helmet smashed into the small of his back. There was a thumping sound. Prosser screamed, and his whole upper torso snapped backward so violently that his head nearly connected with his ass. At first I thought his back might be broken, but he started twisting in pain as soon as he hit the ground. He'd lost his wind. Big Dick was immediately over him and gently lifting him by the belt to aid his breathing.

"Get away from there, Biggs," Hackler shouted. "Get back in line."

Big Dick hesitantly moved away as Hackler approached. "Get up, Prosser, you're not hurt."

Prosser somehow had the presence of mind to turn his face away so his agony couldn't be enjoyed.

"I said get *up*," Hackler repeated as he kicked Prosser in the same spot Big Dick's helmet had struck. Prosser groaned.

"All right," Hackler finally said. "That's enough for today. Good job, Biggs. Tomorrow we'll pick up where we left off. Everybody take it on in now—everybody!"

That meant Prosser had to lie where he'd fallen until he could make it in under his own power. Trainer Hanson and Hackler left in the ambulance jeep while Big Dick, Quink, and I joined the Redshirts jogging to the back dressing room. We took seats and just sat there in numb silence.

We'd all seen fuck-overs before, but that didn't make this one any easier to accept. Suddenly, a guttural roar shattered the silence. Quink stood up and grabbed his helmet by the face mask, then smashed it into the cement floor, sending pieces flying around the room.

"Take it easy, man," Skid said quietly. "There's not a fucking thing we can do about it."

Quink stepped to the middle of the room. "Why the hell not, huh? Why can't we get together and *do* something? This is making me feel like *shit*."

99

"We all feel bad, Quink," Big Dick said softly, "but Skid is right. We either do like they say or they'll kick us off the—"

"But, goddammit," Quink protested, "there *must* be something . . ." He looked at me.

I shook my head. "When you signed to play football here, they agreed to feed you and house you and give you the chance to get an education. You're bought and paid for. They own you . . ."

THOUGH A few of the guys had already stripped off all parts of their dirty uniforms, most were still half-dressed when Prosser opened the door ten minutes later. His face was whiter than its usual white and his eyes looked glazed.

"I feel sick," was all he said before he passed out, pitching forward into Skid's arms.

I went over and laid him out on the wooden bench that circled the room in front of the cubicles. He shouldn't be lying on the cold cement floor if he was in shock. Suddenly he gagged and began throwing up, and I turned his head to the side so he wouldn't breathe his own vomit. The convulsion brought him back to consciousness. He spit to clear his mouth, then asked the classic first question: "What happened?"

"You passed out for a few minutes," I told him. "How do you feel?"

He thought about it for a moment. "I hurt."

"Where?"

"All over."

"Can you get up?" Tom asked.

Prosser made an effort but couldn't. "I think I need some help."

I helped him to his feet and let him go when he stopped weaving.

"All right," I said, "you're doing fine. Now, you just stand there for a few seconds, Tom and I'll get your uniform off."

As soon as we'd lifted his jersey, everyone saw the circular red welt that covered the right side of his lower back. Nobody said a word as we continued to strip him.

"Can you get in the shower by yourself?" I asked when we'd finished.

"I think so." Some of his color had returned.

I went with him in case he fell again, but he walked into the shower-toilet area with no trouble. Instead of going into the shower, though, he stepped over to the porcelain piss-trough on the opposite wall. This part had me worried.

"Don't force it out," I instructed. "Just let it flow."

Prosser looked at me with a puzzled expression, and then his urine appeared.

"My piss is pink," he said, more to himself than us.

"I know," I said in the most casual tone I could manage. "It means you're hurt, but not too seriously. Your kidney is bruised and bleeding a little, but it's not ruptured. It should heal by itself in a few days."

"I haven't got a few days."

"I'll speak to Trainer Hanson about it."

"Don't waste your time," he said as he turned to face me and the others around him. "That would only get them down on you too."

"Jesus, man," Big Dick said, "you've proved your point. Nobody in here would have done what you just did, so why don't you hang it up while you still can?"

Prosser walked slowly over to Big Dick and, to everyone's suprise, put a hand on his shoulder. "I just can't do that," he said quietly, "but I want you to know that I hold nothing against you personally."

"Then at least go down swinging," Quink blurted. "You could beat the shit out of Hackler tomorrow. We'd give you plenty of time to get in your licks before we pulled you off."

Prosser actually smiled. "It's a tempting thought," he said, "but no, no thanks. If I were going to do that, I guess I might as well have done it a while ago."

"So that's it, huh?" Tom asked. "You're going out tomorrow to make us finish you off?"

Prosser nodded.

"Then you're just a crazy son of a bitch," Quink said in his exasperation. "And I'm through worrying about you." He left for his regular place in the Varsity dressing room.

The rest of us stood uncomfortably until Prosser said, "He's right," and then stepped into the shower.

MONDAY NIGHTS after dinner the Varsity was obliged to watch films of Saturday's performance. During the season they would be game films, but this night's were of the Saturday scrimmage.

Redshirts were excluded from these meetings. True, the coaches believed Redshirts should suffer as much tedious bullshit as could be devised for them, and two hours watching film they didn't appear in was indeed tedious bullshit, which meant there was much to be said for making them endure it. On the other hand Redshirts were also to be humiliated as much as possible. Refusing to let them attend team functions served to point out their worthlessness as players and even contributing members of the squad. Better to humiliate than merely bore them.

I was surprised to find Tom's room locked when I got to the dorm. The Redshirts almost always spent Monday nights watching Tom hoax the folks on the phone. And then I realized that if they felt anything like I did, they were all probably out getting drunk. All except one.

I knocked on his door. Prosser's voice came from inside. "Go away."

I tried the knob, it turned, I went in. He was lying face-down on the right side bed with an ice pack covering the welt on his lower back.

"I want to talk about your . . . situation, Pete," I said as I took a seat on the bed opposite. I was through being intimidated by someone half my size.

Prosser turned his head and looked at me. He seemed interested. He gingerly rolled over on his side so he could face me across the short distance that separated the two beds. The whole time he did that, I kept wondering what those icy blue dots of his were seeing.

I sat waiting, but the tension finally got to me.

"You can't fight the coaches," I said very deliberately. "Can't you see that by now? They have all the aces. Look at you. You're proof of it."

Prosser stared at me hard for a long time, then shook his head and began the laborious process of settling back onto his stomach.

A man gets tired talking to himself. I got up and left the room.

I HAD arranged to meet Carla at the Rathskeller, Cajun State's replica of an old-fashioned German beer hall. Its low, heavy-beamed ceiling, handcrafted wooden furnishings, stuffed animal heads on the walls and dark, murky atmosphere all helped make you forget you were merely in a basement section of the University Center.

As usual, Helmet was there when I arrived. Helmet's gregarious nature and German background made him a fixture in the Rathskeller, especially on Monday nights. He refused to participate in football-related activities he considered superfluous or a waste of his time, and rightfully for him, considered the Monday night film sessions to be both. Even though technically required to attend, he'd walked out of his first one, saying "Uselezz, totally uselezz," and never attended another.

I bought a pitcher of beer and found an empty table. Helmet soon joined me.

"I am glad to see you, Sagely," he said as he sat down. "I am wishing to speak with you."

"Yeah? What about?"

"About my roommate, Peter. I went to see him after dining this evening. He is in much pain."

"I know. I just saw him myself."

Helmet shook his head slowly from side to side.

"So it happens again, eh, my friend? When will they discover a more civilized way to resolve these difficulties?"

"Who knows?"

"But it is so absurd, is it not? The ruination of one such as Peter for benefit of one such as Hackler."

"I guess that's what you get when people like Hackler are put in charge of people like Pete."

"Truly," Helmet replied. "It would take the whole of tonight to explore the problems."

"Yeah, it would, but it really doesn't matter in the long run. Prosser will be gone after tomorrow, and that's a fact to live with."

"Ah, but such a talent he has. What a pity to waste it."

"He'll be better off after they get rid of him. Football just isn't the place for him."

"But he is very strong willed," Helmet said, leaning forward to speak in a conspiratorial whisper, "and also of German heritage."

I had to laugh at him. "Jesus, Helmet, is *that* all you care about?"

He grinned sheepishly. "There are, of course, many German traits of which I am not so proud."

Carla came up then. "Hi, guys," she said. "Mind if I join the fun?"

"Of course not," Helmet said as he sprang to his foot and assisted Carla into a chair. "We could hardly wish for a lovelier addition to our table."

We exchanged general bullshit for a few minutes, then I went to get Carla a glass. When I returned to the table, Helmet graciously stood to leave.

"Ah, dearest Carla," he said, taking her hand and kissing it lightly, "when will you overthrow that reprobate so we may be together always?"

"When you, my handsome young silver-tongued devil, can no longer juggle five or ten others at the same time. That should be in about fifty years at the rate you're going."

We laughed as Helmet shrugged and said, "Take care, my friends. *Ciao.*"

He turned and walked directly to a table where three girls sat huddled in serious discussion. In five minutes he had them laughing, and ten minutes later they all left together.

Carla watched them leave, turned to me, and shook her head. "Why can't more of you be like him?"

"Men in general or football players in particular?"

"What's the difference? Players, ex-players, wish-I-had-been-players; all the men I know fit in there somewhere, even my father."

"But Helmet *is* a player—"

"Oh, come on, Larry, you know what I mean. Helmet is on a football team, but he's not a football player. My father hasn't been on a football field in twenty years, but he's *still* a football player."

"I knew what you meant, I was just teasing."

"All right, so you know Helmet would be the same whether he played football or not. He doesn't need football to feel like a man—"

"Now just wait a minute, sweetheart. I grant you Helmet is one very attractive guy, but you have to remember something else about him . . . He's not part of our culture . . . We measure ourselves as men in one way and he does it in another, but we're all cut from the same cloth—"

"Really?"

"Yes, really . . . You know that boomerang-shaped scar below his cheekbone? Do you have any idea how he got it?"

She shook her head.

"Dueling."

"Dueling! How?"

"With swords. It's still very big among young Germans, especially students. A dueling scar is a prized status symbol, a sort of red badge of courage."

"Did he tell you that?" she asked warily.

"You know he'd never be that obvious, but I'm sure that's what it is. I read an article about it and saw several pictures. A sharp rapier leaves exactly that kind of scar."

"God . . . and I thought football players were crazy!"

"So does Helmet," I added. "Football makes as much sense to him as dueling does to us."

"Then what's the point of either one?"

"I don't want to get heavy with you—"

"Try me."

"All right, you asked for it . . . let's say they're part of the rites of passage into manhood. Men need ways of proving to themselves that they *are* men. Different kinds of risk seem required to make the tests valid, that's all."

"Well, I'm glad women aren't like that—"

"Maybe having children does it for you. It's hard to do, it has risk, and it sure as hell establishes credentials as a woman."

"Well, if your rites of passage are so common, how do you account for the difference between Helmet and the other players? It's like he's from another planet."

I agreed. "Helmet and others like him go for finite tests. Young Indians did things like spending three days alone on a mountaintop. Australian aborigines endure a walkabout. Helmet fought with the sword. The point is, there's a definite, limited goal for them to achieve. Once they make it they can stop trying to prove themselves and move forward as men. Their rite of passage is over and—"

"Larry," Carla interrupted, "could we—"

"Wait a minute, I'm not finished. I want you to understand this. In football, there aren't any finite goals. Instead of a few moments of swordplay or a few days of exposure, football players commit themselves to years of self-torture with no hope of ever getting to the place where someone says, 'You can stop now, you've done enough. Today you are a man.' No matter how good you do someone's always there saying, 'You could have done better, go out and prove yourself again tomorrow.' There's just no acceptable level of performance, and—"

"Larry, please!" Carla's urgency startled me. "Could we please talk about something else? You're making me feel uncomfortable with all this."

I hadn't realized how intense I'd become. "I'm sorry. I guess I'm a little upset with football right now. I'll get over it . . ."

She took my hands in hers. "Why do you stay part of it? You don't belong any more than Helmet does."

"That's where you're wrong, love. I'm a product of the system, and I'm as hooked on it as anyone."

A FULL moon was suspended directly overhead when Carla and I finally left the University Center, and late summer smells and lingering warmth filled the night air.

"Let's go for a walk," she suggested.

We'd gotten off football and talked about the hopes and dreams that two people share over drinks in darkened rooms. The outside atmosphere accelerated our closeness as I gently tightened my arm around her waist and nuzzled her ear.

"Lead the way," I whispered.

She trembled slightly. "Much more of that and I'll—"

"Never mind. Let's save it for later."

"How much later? I don't know how much longer I can last."

We took a roundabout route home. Finally the stadium's hulking silhouette came looming through the haze of street-lights and moonlight, and I had an inspiration.

"Carla, have you ever been inside the stadium at night?"

She took her head off my shoulder and looked at me to make sure I wasn't kidding. "Don't they lock it up at night?"

"Yes, they do, but I know a way to get in. Want to try it?"

"God, yes, it sounds exciting."

We quickened our pace and were soon at the secret entrance: a hidden crack in the chain-link fence near the east side ticket office. We wasted no time slipping through it.

"That was easy," Carla said, breathing faster.

"Shhh, there's a security guard who patrols this place at night. Keep your voice down or he'll hear us."

She nodded and I motioned for her to follow me up an entrance ramp that led to the top of the stadium. We made our way to the center of the south end, directly under the scoreboard, and looked out over the stadium's rim at the entire campus spread before us. The wind whipped Carla's long hair as she turned to face the field below and the city's glittering carpet of lights beyond.

"Oh, Larry, this is absolutely gorgeous!"

She was absolutely right. Eerie silence hung over the stadium's enclosed emptiness while the moon overhead provided a shimmering glow. I glanced at Carla and was mesmerized by her long black hair whipping back and forth in the breeze. I couldn't remember when she'd looked so beautiful. I took her in my arms and poured my feelings for her into a long, deeply passionate kiss. We were both trembling by the time we broke apart. "Let's go!" I urged. "We'll come back some other time—"

"Oh, yes! Let's go, let's come back—whatever!"

She started leaping down the stadium steps and I had to struggle to keep up with her bounding strides.

"Hey, take it easy! We'll get there!"

"Not soon enough," she whimpered. "For God's sake, hurry, *please . . .*"

We got down to the field and were headed across the southeast corner when Carla suddenly stopped and whirled around to face me. "Larry . . . honey . . . let's do it right here, right now . . ."

"Here? Right here on the *field?"*

"Right out on the fifty yard line, right smack in the middle!"

"Jesus, Carla, that's crazy. What if somebody comes along? What if we get caught—"

"By who? The guard? We'll just have to be quiet, that's all. Come on, it won't take long, I guarantee you."

She was already dragging me by the hand toward the center of the field. "Come *on!* Think about it. When we're old and gray and watching games here on television we'll always be able to remember the night we made love on the fifty yard line . . ."

Sold. I was already unbuttoning my shirt as we reached the center of the field.

"Just drop your pants and I'll lift my skirt," she directed as she stepped out of her panties.

"Good thinking," I mumbled through stuttering breath.

She lay down directly on top of the fifty yard line, her feet pointing toward the press box, then spread her legs and looked up at me with wide-eyed innocence.

"Am I centered?"

"Perfect!" I said as I dived down and into her.

Carla began to come almost immediately. I watched her excitement build for a few brief moments, marveling once again at how alive she became underneath me, felt the initial tinglings of my own surge . . . and then, without warning, every light in the whole goddamn stadium came on, bathing our revelry in their blinding glare.

Carla started to scream, but I acted fast. In the second she needed to emerge from the depths of orgasm, I vaulted off her with one panicky push-up and pivoted my body in the air so it landed perpendicular to hers. While suspended in the air I shoved my still-stiff crank to one side with my right hand so it wouldn't be crushed when I landed on my stomach, and simultaneously clamped my left hand over Carla's just-opening mouth. The flurry of movement positioned us so that my face was near her left ear, our bodies forming a right angle joined at our heads.

"Be quiet and don't move," I said in a tight whisper.

I was already scanning the field's four ground-level corner exits to discover where the guards would make their entrance. Meanwhile Carla lay paralyzed on her back, with her recently uplifted skirt jammed tight between her legs. When no one appeared I checked each exit a second time. Finally a movement caught my eye in the upper reaches of the stadium's west side, just below the press box.

"Don't panic," I said, panicking.

A lone figure stepped out of an upper-middle entranceway with a clipboard in his hand.

"Jesus H. Christ, it's Soupbone!"

Carla yanked my hand away from her mouth.

"Soupbone! What's he doing here, what does he want—"

One of Soupbone's duties was to check the stadium's lighting system before every home game, listing and then reporting every extinguished bulb to the maintenance crew so the crew could replace them before game time.

"I can't explain now," I told her quietly. "Just don't move and maybe he won't notice us."

Her eyes followed mine up to Soupbone's position.

"What do we do if he sees us?" she whispered. She was apparently gaining control of herself.

"Hell if I know," I whispered back. "Let's worry about that if it happens."

Soupbone slowly examined each bank of lights that stood towering above the stadium's upper edges. Occasionally his head would move down toward the clipboard to note a bulb to be replaced, but his face always went right back up to the lights. Five minutes later he turned and walked back down the entranceway, and two minutes after that the lights went back out. As far as I could tell, he'd never even bothered to look down at the field.

We lay trembling in the covering darkness until we were sure the coast was clear. Finally I got to my feet and began to pull my pants back on.

"Oh, Larry," Carla said as she covered her mouth to suppress a giggle. "Look at yourself!"

My crank had diminished to its absolute smallest.

"Fear will do that to you," I said with a nervous laugh.

"Don't feel too bad," she said. "I feel like I just had an alum douche!"

We both began to laugh and soon were damn near hysterics.

By the time we reached the apartment, though, we'd sufficiently recovered to finish what we'd started.

SEPTEMBER 18

Tuesday

I SLEPT poorly that night. The frustrations and anticipating Prosser's upcoming day combined to fray my nerves, and as if that wasn't enough Carla woke me up with a rotten weather report.

"It must have rained really hard last night after we went to sleep."

I moaned in disgust and asked how it looked outside now.

"Big puddles and it's still drizzling."

I moaned again as Carla went into the kitchen to start breakfast. I seriously considered staying in bed all day, then reluctantly began to drag myself out.

Rain meant Stanton and I had to work our asses off at practice. The main problem would be keeping the footballs and the football handlers' hands reasonably free of mud, and though we always did our best to maintain a steady supply of towels, we could never quite satisfy the demand. Rain practices were always an exercise in futility for managers, and I hated the shit out of them.

Of course, there was always the possibility that the coaches would decide to hold practice indoors in Holt Field House. It all depended on how they felt the team was coming along in its preparations for Texas. If they felt the players needed more physical toughening, then they'd send them out in the slop to pound on each other. If they felt the team was more in need of mental sharpening, they'd send them inside to work on execution.

I felt pretty sure we'd stay outside. Texas was a big, physically aggressive team that did nothing fancy, and we'd need all the toughening we could get just to stay on the field with them.

Too bad, and for more than one reason: Going inside would also have given Prosser a stay of execution.

THE DECISION was posted on the bulletin board at lunch: Practice as usual, on the field.

"Jesus," Big Dick said as we sat down with our trays, "you think they'll have Shit Drills in this weather?" He still hadn't come to grips with his part in yesterday's fuck-over, and the prospect of participating in another one clearly disturbed him.

"They won't let him slip the hook now," I said.

"Besides," Tom added, "Thursday is only two days away. They can't risk having him here for two-minute drills."

The only serious hitting done on Thursday is a series of two-minute drills held at the very end of practice, in which the Redshirt offense goes against the Varsity defense in simulated last-minute drives. It's the only time Redshirts get to play real football because there's no stopping to run a play over. The ball and the clock keep moving.

Last year Tom guided a truly inferior Redshirt team to several last-second scoring drives against Hackler's finest. He may have lacked option-running ability, but Tom was a superb tactician and an excellent passer, the two qualities most needed by a successful two-minute quarterback. In fact, when he was allowed to call his own plays Tom was the best quarterback we had at using personnel, the clock, and field position. It was a shame he didn't play for a pro-spread team, he'd have been a starter for sure.

This year's Redshirt squad was considerably stronger than last year's, even with the loss of Sir Henry. Skid was a good blocker,

Heape was an excellent receiver. Of course, Prosser was the *real* difference and everyone knew it. If he wanted he could run absolutely wild in a wide-open exercise like Thursday's two-minute drill. The coaches had to get rid of him before then or he could make the Varsity look like stomped shit two days before the game.

"Maybe he'll have a better chance in the mud," Peso suggested. "It'll be harder to get a solid shot at him."

"Don't kid yourself," I said. "His footing will be gone and he won't be able to dodge hits like he usually does. Face it, his number's up."

"Fuck 'em!" Quink said. "If they make me hit him, I'm going to brother-in-law like I did yesterday. I don't give a shit what they do to me . . ."

Others began muttering agreement and I suddenly found myself saying, "What the hell's the matter with you, Quink? What the hell's the matter with *all* of you? Why can't anybody just accept this for what it is and get it over with? Why keep beating the same dead horse over and over . . ."

I was on my feet and shouting by then, shouting into a dining room that had become uncomfortably silent.

"C'mon, Sage," Tom said, "ease up. You know Quink didn't mean anything. He was just blowing off. Isn't that right, Quink?"

"Yeah, sure," Quink said nervously. "Don't listen to me."

I looked around the room. Each face staring up at me belonged to somebody I liked, yet in a few hours some of them would commit mayhem on one of their own. And I'd be part of it.

"I'm sorry. It's just that I . . . lately I've . . ."

There was no way to tell them.

"Excuse me," I said as I turned to leave.

WORD OF my outburst had gotten around by the time I reported to the stadium. I knew it was going to take a hell of an acting job to repair the damage.

"Heard you got a little upset at lunch today," Cap'n said as

I entered the equipment shed. "It's not 'cause old Soupbone caught you diddlin' your gal on the field last night, is it?"

I winced in mock exasperation. "You just can't keep a secret around here, can you?" I said, smiling bravely at having been found out.

Cap'n smiled. "I told 'em that's prob'ly what it was. I knew there wasn't nothin' wrong with you."

Nevertheless, everyone was noticeably subdued around me during preparations for practice. Stanton quietly arranged my share of the equipment when I had to run an errand and got behind schedule. There was no bullshit kidding anywhere near me. Emotional control is the ticket at every level of football, except when directed at opponents. Any loss of that control makes everyone nervous, as if they too might be affected by an individual's show of weakness. Anger is acceptable only if directed in prescribed channels.

As I did my taping in virtual silence, Coach Anderson came into the training room and conferred with Trainer Hanson about Don's knee and the Bull's ankle, then ambled over to where I was working. "Hi, Larry, how's it going?"

"Fine, coach, just fine."

"Good, glad to hear it." Then, with a knowing smile, "Heard you had a little trouble with the lights last night."

Last night's indiscretion fit well with the accepted jock image and would be favorably viewed as a clear indication that I was still a football player at heart.

"Yes, sir," I said, grinning appropriately and ducking my head in expected fashion. "I guess I did."

"Well, I guess we'll just have to make Soupbone post his schedule from now on," he said, raising his voice so the whole room could enjoy his wit. "That way you both can do your business without getting in each other's way!"

Everyone laughed, nervously. Then Coach Anderson switched to his sincerely serious tone of voice.

"You're doing a hell of a job for us, son," he said as he placed a fatherly hand on my shoulder. "Keep up the good work."

I said I would.

It was only the second time he'd spoken to me as a person in the two years I'd worked for him, but that wasn't at all unusual. Coaches go out of their way to avoid relating with players on a personal basis, figuring such familiarity weakens their authority—a policy that extends even to minor hangers-on like me.

PRACTICE WAS about what I'd expected. The rain stopped an hour before the opening horn, but the field was soaked and soon became a quagmire. Players caromed off each other, giant mud-covered blobs; footballs squirted around like greased pigs, and Stanton and I wiped away like crazy at everything in sight. Finally, Coach Anderson whistled everyone to the tower as a prelude to the final stage of practice. As we were all gathering at the center of the field, I noticed Prosser slowly jogging along.

He'd had a relatively easy practice—so far. It was impossible to tell he was hurt until he tried to pull up after a run, and even then he seemed only slightly stiff. He'd been able to keep a low profile all day because Hackler had completely laid off him. There wasn't much point in calling attention to him during practice, considering what was going to happen when it was over.

"All right, men," Coach Anderson intoned, "we've had a decent practice considering the conditions, and I want you to keep up the good work through this last drill. It's going to be a twenty-minute Varsity scrimmage that we're going to hold over on the baseball outfield so you can have a chance to dig in against each other. I know you've had a hard time doing that in this mud, but the grass over there is fresh and strong and you'll be able to get good traction on it even though it's wet.

"Now, remember—especially you backs and ends—when you hear a whistle, stop! We don't want any late-hit injuries when we're tired, and we don't want anyone piling up into those bleachers. Also, if you see yourself going into the fence, make a fist—*don't* grab it. It can cut your hands if you're not careful? All clear? All right, then, get on over there before you cool off."

As I sloshed along through the mud my worry about Prosser began to fade. My duties during the upcoming drill demanded total concentration. I'd be handling ball cleaning and placement plus keeping track of down and distance, but practice on the baseball outfield also meant an additional responsibility . . . to stay very aware of those two sideline hazards Coach Anderson had mentioned.

Whenever wet weather forced us to scrimmage on the baseball outfield, we kept the sessions short and confined to the smallest possible area—football cleats tear wet grass runners out by the roots. The athletic director felt that since we weren't forced to dodge line drives when we practiced we shouldn't make the baseball team work out on bare ground. So we held our scrimmages in the far corner of left field, running plays from fifteen yards inside the left field foul line through foul territory and toward the track beyond. That gave us forty unobstructed yards to work in, which is all we needed when long passes weren't allowed, and we tore up only a fifteen-yard strip inside the left field foul line.

Such restrictions, though, were minor compared to the ones that lay just outside both our sideline boundaries. Ten yards beyond the left sideline markers and twenty-five yards upfield from the initial line of scrimmage was a wood-and-metal bleacher that extended along the left field foul line. Any player running into it at high speed would almost surely break something—football pads offer little protection against hard edges. As a result anyone heading that way got quick-whistled to a stop by me or the assistant coaches.

The outfield boundary was a ten-foot-high chain-link fence that stood five yards beyond and ran parallel to our right sideline. We were less worried about the fence because there was give in its fishnet construction and players just bounced off when they ran into it. Their pads also gave effective protection even when they hit the circular brace poles.

The fence's only serious threat was the one Coach Anderson cautioned about. Its diamond-shaped holes had crusted zinc coating at the connecting joints, and those rough spots could cut. They were nothing like the jagged, inch-long bottom prongs that kept freeloaders from sneaking underneath into games, but we couldn't afford even small hand injuries just four days before a game.

Fortunately, nearly all plays ended before reaching either danger zone. . . .

I spotted the ball. "First play, twenty-five to go."

In this drill the first-team offense had five plays to go twenty-five yards against the second-team defense. Then the teams switched: second-team offense against first-team defense. To be successful, the quarterbacks had to make fairly daring play selections . . . a close-to-the-vest series usually failed to score. A mix of traps, flares, sweeps and play-action passes was needed to get anywhere. We often played some of our best football during this exercise.

The first-team offense broke its huddle and got set to run its opening play. I took my usual position straddling the line of scrimmage ten yards outside Denny O'Toole, the right end. O'Toole cheated out a yard as he took his stance, which put Loop Watson, the second-team left defensive end, on the alert for something coming his way.

Sure enough, at the snap Gil Travers, the starting wingback, cracked down on Watson while O'Toole cut out on Big Dick's cornerback position. Even though the two defenders sensed what was coming, the cross-blocking end and wingback had superior angles of attack. Don moved between the four prostrate bodies on a fullback slant and picked up seven yards.

When the play was whistled dead I ran to retrieve the ball from the pileup where Don had been tackled. He was still pinned beneath a couple of players when I reached him, but his mud-spattered face was beaming as he handed up the ball to me.

"How'd it look, Sage?" he mumbled through his mouthpiece.

"Sharp," I said as he got to his feet. "You picked the hole perfectly."

I gave him a quick pat on the rump as he headed back for his huddle, then wiped the ball and respotted it.

"Second play, eighteen to go."

The second play started off looking exactly like the first, but it turned out to be a play-action pass instead. After O'Toole and Travers crossed and delivered brush blocks on Watson and Big Dick, they both took off downfield. Unfortunately, wet grass can be just as slippery as mud. They lost their footing making down-and-out cuts, which left Ronnie Davis, the quarterback, with no choice but to dump a flare pass to Don in the right flat.

Don tucked it away and headed straight upfield near the right sideline, where Big Dick was coming up from covering Travers. Big Dick delivered his usual hard shot when they met, but Don's straight-ahead momentum carried him right through that tackle and two more solid shots before he fell twelve yards downfield. It was a beautifully powerful run.

"Goddammit, Slade!" Coach Marshall bellowed, "that's the way to *run* that fucking ball! Way to cram it down their throats!"

"Need some stick, defense! Need some *stick!*"

"Third play, six to go."

The next play was a fullback dive off the right cheek of Wheeler's ass. Wheeler threw a crunching forearm into the nose guard and Don cut off his block for a score.

"All right, big offense! Bring on those Longhorn pussies!"

I was surprised at how strong we looked on that drive without the Bull in there at fullback—one of the hardest things to over-come when you lose a starter is the lack of faith in his substitute. Don had apparently taken care of that problem. He was show-ing his teammates that he could hold his own against anyone, and they were responding. I'd seldom seen it happen so quickly.

The first-team defense looked equally impressive on the next series. They allowed the second-team offense two incomple-tions, two short runs, and a sack that totaled up to minus four yards in five plays. Then the first-team offense came out for its second series and lost no time taking up where it left off. John Lawrence, the tailback, swept left end for eight yards outside another good crackback block by Travers.

"Goddammit, defense," Hackler screamed, "get your fucking heads out of your asses and *hit* somebody . . ."

The second-team defense started chattering and slapping each other on the helmets. They'd try to ring some bells on the next few plays.

"Second play, seventeen to go."

I glanced behind my back at the players standing along the

sideline in front of the fence. I knew they'd be pleased at Hackler's aggravation. I looked for Prosser, but couldn't single him out from the row of mud-covered look-alikes.

By that time the ball had been snapped for the next play and a fullback sweep was already in progress. Don had taken a short pitchout from Davis and was heading my way behind Lawrence's escort. I immediately started backpedaling out of their way, then noticed two thin streamers of tape fluttering around Don's right knee as he ran, which meant the dampness had soaked through his leg bandage enough to loosen it. I made a hasty mental note to caution him about it after this play was over.

As the sweep continued to develop, Big Dick and Watson began a fight to maintain outside positions. Their combined responsibility was to force Don inside toward the defensive pursuit, and they both knew Hackler would have their asses in traction if they failed. Watson started off with a hand-fight against O'Toole's scrambling crab-block, but he got completely wiped out by a double-team crackback from Travers.

That left Big Dick alone outside. He backpedaled until he thought he had the proper angle, then dug in and blasted Lawrence with a forearm shiver. Lawrence lost his balance trying to recover, forcing Don to give ground in order to negotiate around Lawrence's sprawled body, and giving Big Dick time to regain his outside position.

Don now had the option of waiting for a pulling guard to come help out, or heading upfield alone and hoping to beat Big Dick one-to-one. His previous success on the safety-valve pass must have made him think he could go it alone. He cut upfield without waiting for help and tried to run over Big Dick.

As I said before, Big Dick was a damn tough defensive back. He drove forward like a rutting Bighorn sheep and blasted his face mask square into Don's chest. Don's straight-ahead momentum neutralized the impact and left neither man with a clear-cut advantage. They both continued to sweep outside, struggling for leverage.

It's great to watch two studs go after each other like that. Their legs churn and drive against each other while their upper

119

bodies remain welded together, and it seems as if they can only fall sideways from exhaustion. In this case, though, a closely staggered line of defenders was rapidly closing in to finish Don off.

I was still backpedaling away from the flow when the second defender hit into both men somewhere behind Big Dick. All three remained on their feet, moving laterally toward the sideline. Another pursuer added his weight to the rear, but Don obstinately kept his head high and refused to go down.

I should have started blowing my whistle right then and there, but I held off in the hope that Don might luck out and break free. I'd seen pursuers knock their own men off runners many times before, and it usually happened in exactly this kind of side-sweeping situation. Suddenly I heard a frantic shout from behind my back.

"The fence! Watch out for the fence!"

I blew my whistle as soon as the warning registered, then I stopped moving backward and spun around to gauge where the fence was fifteen yards and closing fast. It wasn't a critical distance yet, but substitute players along the sidelines were already scrambling away from the hurtling group of bodies. Whistles began to shrill all over the field, but nothing stopped . . . it all just went into a kind of slow-motion sequence.

I looked back at the combatants and saw that they'd drawn alongside me a few yards downfield. My new angle allowed a view of two more pursuers running in close tandem. They were so covered with mud I couldn't tell who they were even at close range, but I could see their eyes. Their eyes told me they would neither hear nor react to our whistles. Those two were listening to the inner voices of all their coaches' preachings of the football gospel—GO FOR THE BALL! PUNISH THE RUNNER! DON'T STOP TILL HE'S DOWN!—and they were beyond all else.

Tiny globs of mud flew out from the moving stack of bodies as those fourth and fifth defenders smashed into it. Don staggered as the first impact traveled into him through the three people already clinging to his body. Though still in Big Dick's tight grasp from the waist up, Don had managed to keep his legs free and churning until the fifth man delivered his blow. I saw, heard, and almost felt it happen, and my first thought, strangely enough, was of Annie.

It was nothing more than a misstep on the wet ground. Don's left foot hit a slippery patch and failed to hold, which threw all the weight massed against him squarely over his bad right knee. It sounded like a short-shot .22 rifle when it snapped under the strain, breaking so cleanly and completely that his right hip nearly hit his right ankle when they all fell. I knew in that instant that Don would never play football, or walk normally, again.

Don and Big Dick hit the ground together, with Big Dick's face mask still flush against Don's chest. Their fall sent a splash of water almost to where I stood. The other defenders swept forward and up over their bodies with a rolling motion that could only mean trouble for Don.

When a knee goes like that, any twisting of the lower leg does even more damage to the joint and makes decent repair extremely difficult. Knowing that, I was running toward them and shouting before the last man left his feet.

"Don't move, don't move! Slade's hurt . . . I'll untangle you! Get up *slow!*"

I didn't gain much on them at first because their combined mass skimmed along the wet grass like a ball-bearing over oil. Still, those last two hits generated enough momentum to shift their motion from laterally along the line of scrimmage to somewhat parallel with the sideline. That put them moving more toward me than away from me, which meant I'd reach them that much sooner. And then the whole pileup slammed into the base of the fence.

I'd been so intent on reaching them quickly I'd failed to notice how far they were sliding. Their abrupt stop caught me by surprise. The two top bodies were catapulted off the stack and into the fence while the bottom four skidded only a couple more yards before stopping. A fine pink mist went up as they slid those last few feet, but the significance of it didn't register on me right away. What struck me first was that Don wasn't screaming in pain from his shattered knee. I assumed he'd had

121

the wind knocked out of him when they hit the ground.

I was two strides away when they stopped moving and one stride away when I saw and heard it. Just as I was about to repeat my warning to get up slow and easy, a bright red plume spurted up into the air accompanied by a sharp hissing noise, something like steam escaping from an iron. Someone had cut an artery on the fence.

The pileup still had to unstack itself carefully to protect Don's knee, but I also had to find that cut and get pressure on it. The blood had spurted from beneath the far side of the pile, apparently near the fence line, but I couldn't tell exactly where it came from. All that weight slamming into the fence had bent it out of shape.

A second plume shot up just as I reached the pile, smaller than the first. A third and fourth came up as I yanked the topmost body away. Their level continued to drop. I was clutching the final man by the jersey when the fifth spurt came up only enough to clear his helmet. I threw him aside like a rag doll and saw what had happened.

"Oh, Jesus God!" I screamed. "Help me, for God's sake, somebody help me!"

Don's head had been jammed underneath the fence on impact as his hard, smooth helmet neatly burrowed below the serrated bottom edge. His shoulder pads had prevented him from sliding through any further. He'd been trapped at the neck like a fish in a gill net. He'd slid like that those last few feet beneath the fence, and now his throat was hanging in shreds along those jagged bottom prongs.

Don was blinking the blood from his eyes as I jerked Big Dick off of him, staring at me from the other side of the fence as I dropped to my knees and straddled his chest. In a total panic now, I tried to reach his wound by jamming my fingers into the fence holes to rip them apart. Don could see the futility of my efforts and tried to say something to me, but no words came out of his mouth. His severed carotids were barely spurting by then, and only a pathetic gurgle came up from the ugly, blood-filled hole where his throat had been. Then his eyes blinked again, opened wider then ever, and rolled up into his head.

"He's dying, for God's sake!" I began sobbing. "Somebody *help* me!"

Big Dick tried to help me lift the fence, but its tension had stretched as far as it would go. I was straddling Don's chest and yanking blindly at the prongs when I felt his body start to twitch, and then lay quiet. We both knew then that he was dead.

"No!" I was screaming. And I couldn't stop.

Big Dick grabbed me in a bear hug to pin my flailing arms. "Stop it, Sage! You're tearing your hands up! There's nothing more you can do!"

The rest of them arrived as we kneeled there in our bloody embrace.

"Oh, Jesus," someone muttered at the sight of Don lying there. Someone else gagged.

I don't remember much of what happened from then on. All I can remember is looking down at my own shredded hands and seeing the look in Don's eyes when he saw the look in mine.

SEPTEMBER 19

Wednesday

MY FIRST dim awareness was of how tired and confused I felt. I opened my eyes and saw a bottle of clear fluid suspended above me to my left; a long plastic tube extended from the bottle to the crook of my left elbow. From my elbow I noticed my hands. They were covered with gauze boxing gloves and were lying on top of a white sheet that stretched across my legs. I began to realize that I was in a hospital room, but I couldn't understand what I was doing there. As I continued to groggily survey my surroundings, I was surprised to find Carla and Dr. Wade Yarbrough, our team physician, talking at the right side of my bed.

My initial efforts to speak were futile because my tongue felt swollen and heavy, and my mouth was incredibly dry. After several failed attempts, though, I was able to squeak out a few words.

Carla hurried to me. "Thank God," was all she could say.

"How do you feel, Larry?" Dr. Yarbrough asked as Carla reached out and touched my cheek.

"I'm a little . . . dizzy." Also completely fucked-up.

"We had to put you under for a few hours, but you'll feel better soon."

I nodded. "I need water . . . to make . . . my mouth work."
Carla took care of it.

"Feel better now?"

"I have to take a leak."

Carla reached down under the bed and pulled out a large plastic bottle. While I was pissing into it I began to remember bits and pieces of what had happened . . . and those fragmented memories made me shiver.

"Whoops!" Carla said as she got a better grip on my crank, "almost lost you that time."

I looked up at Dr. Yarbrough. "Don . . . he's dead, isn't he?"

My stupefied brain still saw it as a bad dream, but somewhere deep inside I knew it was true.

He nodded.

"And Annie?"

"Her parents came and got her as soon as they heard the news."

My eyes focused on my hands. "What about these?" I said as I lifted them and noticed they were completely numb beneath the bandages.

"Not bad, all things considered. The flesh was ripped instead of cut, and several wounds had foreign matter, dirt and such, embedded in them, but on the whole I'd say you were damn lucky. I think we got all the severed parts back together. With good care and therapy, both hands should be like new in a year or two—"

"A *year*? Or *two*?"

"It takes a while, Larry, for nerves to regenerate."

"Oh, Jesus!" I muttered as I began to understand exactly what I'd done to myself . . . like somebody would have to wipe my ass when I took a dump . . . and then something else hit me . . . no more being a manager, a part of the team. For the second time in my life I felt the gut-twisting jolt of what life would be like without football . . . well, I wasn't ready to deal with that . . . and somehow forced it from my mind. . . . "How's Biggs?" I asked Dr. Yarbrough. "He got cut up, too, didn't he?"

"No problem at all. Six stitches on his left hand, nine on his right. He's already back in the dorm."

"How many stitches did I have?"

"Numbers don't mean much in your case, Larry . . . we had to do a lot of double-layer stitching—"

"How many?"

"Seventy-three on the left, a hundred and twelve on the right," he said quickly.

"Holy shit!"

"Let me say again that those numbers don't mean much. We used extremely fine stitches to make sure your palms retain their proper shape. Not only that, you have large hands, nearly twice as large as Biggs. Believe me, you're going to be all right."

"Okay," I said, trying to believe him. "You're the doctor."

"That I am," he said, "and as a doctor I'm ordering myself to get some sleep. It's past my bedtime. I'll drop in and see you first thing tomorrow morning."

When we were alone Carla came to the bedside and stood looking down at me the way my mother looked at me when I had appendicitis in the seventh grade.

"What about Mom and Dad? Did you talk to them?"

She nodded. "I called them as soon as I found out about your hands. They said to give you their love and asked you to call as soon as you feel up to it."

"Will they be coming down to see us?"

Both my parents had jobs that would be difficult to leave at a moment's notice unless the emergency was extreme.

"They can't get off right away, but they're going to try to work it out to come down in a week or ten days."

I was glad about that. I needed time.

"Where are we?" I suddenly thought to ask. "Memorial?"

Carla nodded. Memorial Hospital was where they always brought guys who needed surgery.

"What time is it?"

She checked her watch. "A little after two A.M."

That meant a long time since the accident, and that the word had probably gotten around by now.

"Do many people know what happened? Outside the team, I mean?"

"Do many people know? The whole country knows! It's been

126

on every major news program—local and national—since six tonight."

It took me a while to digest that. Then a thought struck me. "How did Annie find out?"

For the first time since I'd been awake, Carla's composure showed visible cracks. "I told her," she said in a shaky voice.

"Oh. Can you tell me how it went?"

She closed her eyes. "Not without crying," she said, "and I've promised myself I won't cry anymore. Give me a few days, Larry."

I shifted the subject back to the news program. "What did they say about Don?"

"Just what a horrible tragedy it was. Mostly they talked about you."

"*Me?* Why . . .?" Then I remembered, and I looked away from Carla. How could I even face her? Dear God, how could I face *anyone* again? I'd helped kill a man and they put it on the goddamn national news—

"You're a hero, Larry," Carla was saying.

I looked up at her. "*What?*"

She seemed surprised by my reaction. "You're a hero, you sacrificed your hands trying to save Don's life. I hear the switchboard here lit up like a Christmas tree right after the national news. Calls came in from all over . . ."

I heard her words, but all I could think about was Don's last seconds, every chilling detail—including my not blowing my whistle when I should have . . .

I tried to hold back my tears the way all good men are supposed to do, but I didn't make it.

Carla sat down on the edge of the bed and cradled me in her arms. "There, there, honey, don't you worry about it . . ." And then she couldn't hold the tears back any longer either, and we cried together as she rocked me, and I drifted back to sleep in her arms.

WHEN I woke up the second time, the bottle of fluid and the plastic tube were gone and a young nurse had replaced Carla.

She was sitting in a chair at the right side of my bed, and as soon as she noticed me looking at her she got to her feet and pressed a button on a console at the head of the bed.

"Hello there, hero," she said, "how do you feel?"

Her well-intentioned words reminded me of how rotten I actually did feel, but there was no reason to take it out on her.

"Fine," I answered on my first attempt. The anaesthetic seemed to be wearing off. "Where's Carla?"

"She didn't get much sleep last night so we talked her into going home early this morning. She said to tell you she'll be back soon."

"What time is it now?"

"Almost nine. I just rang for your breakfast. You are hungry, aren't you?"

Now that she mentioned it, I realized that I was and told her so. I'd thrown up just before I passed out after the accident and had had nothing but a few sips of water since.

"Is there anything else I can do for you while we wait?"

"Well . . . if it wouldn't be too much trouble . . ."

She smiled and reached for a bedpan.

It had begun.

NURSE KELLEY had almost finished feeding me breakfast when Dr. Yarbrough walked into the room. She started to get up but he waved her down.

"Keep your seat, I'll only be a minute. How do you feel this morning, Larry?"

"Mentally or physically?" I sounded belligerent without meaning to.

Dr. Yarbrough stiffened at my tone. "Whichever you prefer."

"Mentally, I wish I'd never been born. Physically, I'm well rested and nearly fed."

He gazed steadily over his half-shell glasses. "Are you always so irritable in the morning?"

"I'm sorry, Dr. Yarbrough, I owe you better than that. I guess I'm still upset by the whole thing."

"Well, try to pull yourself together. Coach Anderson is here and he wants to see you as soon as you finish eating. I think it's important."

That suited me because I had intended to ask to see him. Since waking up, I'd gone over every detail of the accident a dozen different ways, but every replay came out the same: Don's death was my fault. I could have prevented it. . . . The "hero" had fucked up.

NURSE KELLEY left with my tray as Coach Anderson came in.

"Hello, son," he said somberly, "how're you feeling this morning?"

"Fine, coach," I said, responding with those automatic words, "just fine."

"Good, good, glad to hear it."

There was a pause, a brief moment of discomfort while he chose the tack he wanted in this unfamiliar situation. "A lot of people heard about what you did yesterday," he began, "and you can't imagine how many calls we've had since last night. All of them want to know about you, how you're doing. We have a stack of telegrams this high."

He indicated the width between his thumb and forefinger.

"Yes, sir," he went on, allowing himself a slight smile, *"Time, Newsweek, Sports Illustrated, Sporting News;* they've all called about you. You're the biggest thing to happen around here in a *long* time."

"What about Don? What do they say about *him?*"

He seemed uneasy. "Well, they all mention him first, naturally, but they all mention you too."

He made it sound like he thought that was what I wanted to hear.

"It's my fault Don is dead! And you think I care who's asking about me?"

"Now, wait a minute, son," Anderson said as he moved back a step. "You don't know what you're saying. Don's death was an accident, pure and simple. Nobody's to blame for a thing like that."

The discharge of adrenaline somehow soothed me. I lay back

129

against my pillow. "I late-whistled them. I forgot about that lousy fence and blew my whistle too late."

He came forward and sat on the foot of my bed. We'd both dropped our masks.

"Well, hell," he finally said, looking right at me, "if that's the way you want to look at it, I never should have had us out in that weather. Or I should have kept us on the practice field. That makes me as much to blame as anyone. And it's Davis's fault, too. He never should have called that play. And it's Biggs's fault for not turning the flow back inside. Shit, son, if you want to fix blame, I can get you a goddamn list!"

"But it's not right to pretend—"

"Son, yesterday afternoon you did one of the most courageous things I've ever seen, and it's one of the most courageous things a lot of people have heard about in a long time. Don't cheapen what it means to them. What I'm saying is that there's damn little dignity in dying, but what you did trying to save Don can at least give his death a lasting value. . . . I'd hate to see you piss that away."

Maybe he was right . . . maybe it *would* be stupid to reduce Don's death to a dumb mistake.

"Listen to me, Larry," he commanded quietly, "that accident was either nobody's fault or a lot of people's fault, but no one person is entitled to all the blame. You'll wind up right alongside Don if you try to take it alone."

I felt tears starting.

"That's the way she goes, son . . . you can blame yourself to death for all the bad things in life, or you can take your lumps and move on."

He was getting to me, no question, and finally I nodded.

"Good," he said, clapping his hands and getting to his feet. "Now, how do you feel, seriously? Are you up to a little excitement?"

"What do you mean?"

"Remember I told you how all those people want to know about you—how you are and so forth?"

I nodded again.

"Well, I didn't mean just people around here. I meant people all over the country. Reporters and television crews have flown in from everywhere. We've called a press conference for you at ten this morning. Think you can handle it?"

Jesus! "Could we do it a little later?" I wanted some time to gather myself and talk to Carla, and it was already almost nine-thirty.

"We can't wait," he said emphatically. "The evening editions of the east coast newspapers get left out if we do that. It has to be at ten."

I didn't like it but I also felt too weak to argue against it.

"Fine," he said, heading for the door. "They're setting up the lights and cameras in a big room down the hall. Stay here and rest until they're ready to prep you."

I lay there in a daze, trying to figure out what was happening to me and wondering if it wasn't another of Tom's crazy scams. When the makeup lady arrived, I knew it was for real.

A FEW minutes before ten I asked Nurse Kelley to dress me in the clean clothes Stanton had brought over from the stadium last night—probably his first official act as the new senior manager. Not long after, a small, bald, sweating little man arrived in a highly agitated state.

"Absolutely not," he began, "you simply can *not* appear before the nation dressed like that. We're set up around a bed, for heaven's sake, and America expects you to *be* in a bed, hands all destroyed. Can't you see what being dressed will do to your image?"

"Who the hell are you?" I asked him.

"My firm has been retained to handle publicity for your team," he snapped, "so you'd do well to follow my advice."

"But I'm fine now," I protested. I'd nearly fallen off the bed when I first sat up, but the initial dizziness had passed.

"That's not the point," he insisted. "The point is that we don't want to look contrived, now do we? Everything is set up around a hospital bed, and people will expect to see a hospital *patient* sitting in that bed, not some strapping brute with 'Manager, Cajun State Football' written across his chest, for God's sake!"

131

I looked down at the tiny green lettering above my pocket.

"So will you just let the nurse and me put this gown over your clothes? No one in that room will care, but we have to think of your public. Image, dear boy, image, image, image!"

I couldn't *believe* the guy. He was fruity as a Popsicle, but I could see he meant business. I let them put the gown back on.

THE ENTIRE floor was filled with people when I stepped out into the hall. Flashbulbs started popping and everyone started clapping, and I couldn't find a familiar face in the whole crowd. It reminded me of our charter flights to away games when all those strange faces come to lick the gravy while Freshmen, Redshirts and the injured were kept down on the farm.

Coach Anderson grabbed my arm and hustled me down a hallway lined with more people congratulating me and patting me on the back. He brought me into a brightly lit wardroom with six beds in it. The bright lights sat on top of a forest of thin poles that extended around the foot of the right-side-center bed. Four television cameras were set up outside that perimeter, two at the foot and one on each side. They were small, portable models like the ones used to film interviews at practice.

I began to pick out familiar faces in the room, mostly local sports commentators and a couple of sports reporters. Then I saw Randall. I went over to him and spoke in a low voice.

"Man, am I glad to see you. I feel like a freak."

"You're doing great, kid," he said softly. "I'll talk to you later."

A hand gently turned me around. "Larry," the familiar voice said, "we haven't met. I'm Stan Jefferies." Jefferies was a big-time roving correspondent for one of the major networks.

"Hi," was all I could manage.

"We're about ready to begin the interview, so could we ask you to get in bed now? We have to get a light-meter reading."

I got into the bed like a good little hero.

"Now, Larry," he went on, "Coach Anderson assures us

you're an articulate young man, so we're not going to waste time rehearsing. We're only going to ask simple, basic questions about the accident, and all we want is simple, basic answers. If you have any problems or make any mistakes, we'll cut them out of the tape, so don't be nervous. Okay?"

"Okay."

He smiled and said, "Fine," then turned around, reached for a microphone and said to one of the cameramen, "How do I look?"

The cameraman nodded an A-okay and Stan Jefferies said, "Roll it!"

THE INTERVIEWS went more or less like Jefferies said they would. None of the interviewers were ghoulish or maudlin and the whole affair seemed to come off surprisingly well. When it was over everyone thanked me and gave me a small ovation, and then Nurse Kelley escorted me back to my room.

The crowd was much thinner on the way back, and many of those remaining stopped in briefly to offer personal regards and sympathies. After several minutes of that, Nurse Kelley ordered everyone out so I could get some rest. When they were all gone I thanked her and sent her to get Randall. I was back in bed by the time he came in.

"Well?" I asked him, "what'd you think?"

He shrugged and stuffed his pudgy hands into his pockets.

"What does *that* mean?" I asked, suspecting I knew.

"It means I'm not sure. I don't know what to make of it."

"Make of what?"

Randall nervously scratched at his ear as he moved over to the chair beside the bed. "This whole publicity bit," he said as he sank down, "is giving me some nasty vibes."

"Nasty like how?" Knowing the answer as I asked it.

"Nasty like exploitative. Right now it's all very correct, but I think it could build into something a little ugly. It has the makings . . ."

"Go on."

He got up and paced around the room for a few moments, then went to look out the window. "You know what's outside that window, don't you?"

"What?"

"A great big couldn't-care-less town as far as Cajun State football is concerned, that's what. You've got an eighty-thousand-seat stadium that packs them in the aisles for pro games, but your guys can't draw flies. Right?"

"Right."

"So what you have is a team with potentially vast financial resources that it's never been able to tap. The school emphasizes academics and the team plays basically shitty football, so the football program is barely able to pull its own weight. You follow?"

"You're saying the coaches and the Athletic Department might just be tempted to exploit Don's death to sell tickets, that they're already beginning."

He turned around to face me. "Well?"

"Jesus, Randall, don't you think that's occurred to me? Anderson came in and told me people wanted to know what happened. That *sounded* reasonable enough, so I went out and told them what happened. Still . . . you'd know more about what they're up to than I would lying here—"

"Well, I have to admit nothing has looked out of line so far. It's certainly a national-level news story, so there's no problem explaining all the attention it's getting." He paused a moment. "All I'm really saying, I guess, is that the *potential* for some ugly exploitation is lying right there. It'll take some pretty noble types not to pick it up and make the most of it."

I sank back in bed. "I think we both know about the nobility of coaches," I said.

I'D BEEN alone less than an hour when Carla arrived. Obviously upset, she rushed over to hug me, or be hugged by me.

I wrapped my arms around her as well as the clumsy hand bandages would allow. "What's the matter, honey?"

134

"Oh, Larry!" She began to cry. "It's so awful. Annie lost the baby this morning!"

I held her until she quieted, then guided her to the bedside chair.

"I'm sorry," she said quietly. "They only told me a few minutes ago. I'm all right now."

"Sure, honey, we'll talk about it," I said, "but right now I'd like to check out of here."

"Will they let you out so soon?"

"I don't see why not. I feel up to it, and I can't be held against my will."

"Don't bet on it," she said bitterly. "The entire team has been confined to the dorm just like on game days. The coaches sealed it off this morning so only authorized personnel can get in."

"What the hell is that all about?"

"I don't know. Classes were called off for a day of mourning, and that's supposedly what they're doing—mourning."

"Couldn't it be voluntary?" I wondered. "Enforced mourning sounds a little strange to me."

"Well, considering all you've told me about how the coaches operate—"

"Yeah, you're right. It's par for them."

"So, anyway, they might not want you out either."

"Look, I'm going to walk out of here *now*." And we did.

THE ASSISTANT trainers were monitoring the team's dorm lobbies, Bud covering the sixth floor and Raymond the seventh, but two minutes of bullshitting got me past Bud. Watson and Travers saw me first.

"Hey, man," Loop exclaimed, "you're lookin' good!"

"We all wanted to come see you this morning," Gil added, "but the coaches—"

"Yeah, I heard about it. Come on down to Tom's room and we'll talk."

We picked up a trail of others as we moved along. Everyone wanted to know about my hands and was as confused as I was about what was going down. We ended up filling Tom's room to overflowing, with several people left standing in the hall.

"Why are they holing you up here like this?" was my first question.

"We don't know," Tom said. "They told us it was to help keep our minds on Texas, but that's bullshit."

"Yeah," Wizard said, "there's got to be more to it than that."

"Maybe they don't want you talking to reporters," I suggested. "The old 'no comment' routine." We were discouraged from talking to anyone about team business because of supposed gambling influences.

"That could be it," Tom said. "They brought reporters around to our tables at lunch and let them ask us questions but—"

"The coaches were standing right there at all times," I said, finishing his sentence.

Everyone nodded. "Whatever it is," Tom said, "they're taking it pretty damn seriously."

"What about practice?" I asked. "Did they cancel it yet?"

"You're not ready for this," Peso said. "We voted to have it."

"You can't be serious!"

"It's true," Heape said. "They made us vote at lunch. Anderson gave a phony little speech about how it was entirely up to us, but he asked us to consider what Don would have wanted."

"Shades of Kennedy," Swede mumbled, recalling how most scheduled football games were played the weekend of the assassination. Everyone justified their money-grubbing by saying it was what Kennedy would have wanted.

"You mean you actually voted to have practice anyway?"

They all smiled funny little smiles.

"We were told to vote on it because of all those media people eating with the coaches," Wizard explained. "Hackler went out with the ballots and came back ten minutes later to announce the count."

"Don't tell me," I said. "Let me guess."

"You got it," Heape said. "Unanimous."

"To sound better on the tube and in the papers," I said. "A split vote makes it look like there's some chickenshit assholes on the team who don't want to honor Don's memory with a practice."

"I'm one," Tom said, followed by a chorus of "me too's."

But the coaches had called the tune.

I STAYED with them about forty-five minutes, during which players would drop by to say a few words and then move on to let someone else in. I'd especially wanted to see Big Dick, but they said he was napping so I decided not to wake him.

I left when they started getting nervous about the upcoming practice. The accident would make it a doubly-tough mental strain, and each of them needed to go through his own preparations for it. I took a back route to the stadium and stayed with Cap'n in the equipment shed until just before time to take the field. The injured aren't exactly encouraged to hang around displaying serious wounds, and I didn't want to seem like a martyr looking for sympathy. You're expected to keep a certain distance once you lose your active status, which is another method of isolating the unfit, the losers from the winners.

Coach Anderson called the team together for a prepractice speech, and I noticed a group of unfamiliar journalists and cameramen busily recording his words from outside the team perimeter. Their presence clearly inspired him.

"Men," he began, "yesterday we went through a tragedy that will stay with each of us for as long as we live. There's no point in my moralizing about what happened beyond saying that it's hardest to accept when you're young and strong and healthy. But now it's over and we have to put it behind us, and this practice is where we have to start.

"Now, we'll expect some dropped passes and missed snap counts today, that's only natural. But we still have a game to play come Saturday night, and we can't use Don Slade's death as an excuse for giving up. *He* wouldn't give up *one inch* without a fight. . . ."

Anderson's tone had risen, the hint of tears glistened, and suddenly his voice dropped to a near-whisper. ". . . and we all know—every one of us who saw it happen—we all know that's

137

why he died. Because he wouldn't quit when the average person would have. That's the kind of man he was, and that's the kind of men you'll have to be to honor his memory on Saturday night."

Dramatically, he searched the faces of those crowded around him as he drove his message home. He let the silence build for several long seconds, then spoke out again, voice rising. "Goddammit, men, the University of Texas Longhorns are coming here to whip your asses! Are you gonna let 'em do it?"

A chorus of "Fuck no!"'s.

"Then get out there and show me something!

Anderson's speech had been masterful and for a crazy moment even I felt like the team could beat anyone. It was only when practice started that we all came back to reality.

IT WAS strange watching Stanton blow the starting horn. An injured freshman had been assigned to help him, but it was clear Stanton had assumed my duties, with or without second thoughts. I wondered who my permanent replacement would be.

The spark was missing from the moment calisthenics began. Everything looked exactly the same on the surface, uniformed bodies performing routine exercises, but I knew the spirits inside those bodies, and I could see they'd been damaged. Each player has his own natural rhythm, and the rhythms were no longer the same.

I don't know if they were gun-shy or heartbroken, but practice was bad, even for us. They tackled like pussies, ran like sleepwalkers, blocked like clowns, but the coaches kept up a constant patter of compliments and encouragement. I'd been watching about twenty minutes when Big Dick ambled over my way. He was dressed in shorts and a jersey, like all the other injured players, and his palms were covered with tape.

"Sage," he said evenly, "I heard you wanted to see me."

"Sure did. I wanted to see how you're doing."

"I'm okay," he said, folding his arms across his chest. "I'll dress out for the game."

He stared hard out over the field.

"Have you got something to say to me?" I asked, forcing the issue.

"Yeah, buddy, I do. I'd like to know why everybody's making such a big fucking deal about what you did, but nobody mentions how you didn't blow the whistle when I stopped him—"

"Now, hold on," I said. "I told Anderson that first thing this morning. He said if it was my fault for blowing a late whistle, it was your fault for not turning the flow back inside." I was still trying to believe it.

He came off it then. "Oh, shit!" he muttered. "First Prosser and now this! How fucking bad can it get . . . ? Hey, look, Sage, I'm sorry I said those things to you—"

"Forget it."

"No hard feelings?"

"Nah, I'm glad you got it off your chest."

Besides, I more than half agreed with him.

Reporters and photographers had begun clustering around us. At first they only stared and took pictures, as if we were some strange animals in a zoo. Then one of them from the morning's interview session stepped forward.

"Pat Roder, UPI," he said. "I overheard some of the players call you 'Sage' a while ago, and I'd like to ask what that means. None of the coaches seem to know."

"It means he's the Old Sage who's been around a long time and knows all the answers," Big Dick said.

Roder and the others started to write in their notepads.

"Come on, Big Dick, I don't know all the answers." Then, turning to the reporters, "Don't put that down about me."

"And don't try to explain *my* name, either," Big Dick said with a straight face.

By now Coach Anderson had hurried over into the center of our group.

"Hey, you guys," he said with a winning smile, "didn't we give you enough material already today? These boys have been through a hell of an ordeal, so why don't you just let them enjoy practice now? Later on we'll make more interview time available if you need it. What do you say?"

Some looks passed between the reporters, but they finally went along. After they'd drifted out of hearing range, he wheeled around to face us.

"What'd they want?" he asked bluntly.

"They, um, wanted to know why the players call me Sage."

"That's all?"

"Yes, sir," Big Dick assured him. "That's *all.*"

That seemed to satisfy him. "Okay, now, listen to me. There's going to be reporters hanging around here asking questions and getting underfoot from now till game time. Well, that's basically a good thing for the team and I'm all for it, but it can work against us if we're not careful. Some of them might try to trip you up with misleading questions and put words in your mouth that you don't mean. You understand?"

"Why would they do something like that, coach?" I asked innocently.

"I don't know why!" he snapped. "Reporters are just like that sometimes. They just won't let a story sit the way it is. They'll play with it and twist it till you can't even recognize the truth of it. You boys read the sports pages, you know how inaccurate those stories can be."

Big Dick started to open his mouth and got it shut.

"I don't want you two talking to the press unless a coach is present, and that's an order. We have more experience at this sort of thing, and we can tell if it starts to get out of line. Do I make myself clear?"

Too clear.

WHEN WE were alone again on the sideline, Big Dick began to imitate a radio announcer. "And so once again, sports fans, censorship rears its ugly head on the Cajun State campus. What's the reason? Nobody knows, but you can be sure of one thing: This reporter will be keeping his eyes and ears open in an effort to find out—"

"Goddammit, Jensen!" Hackler shouted, delivering the first harsh word of the day, "play to the outside, don't get sucked in like that!"

Prosser had stutter-stepped Jensen inside on a slant and skirted around him, but then, in typical Redshirt fashion, he'd cut back into Ames's pursuit and let himself be nailed for only a three-yard gain.

"What do you think Prosser will do now?" Big Dick asked.

Ironically, Don's death had given Prosser, literally, a new lease on life. At least temporarily. There'd be no Shit Drills as long as media heavyweights and stray fans were hanging around, not even to get rid of someone like Prosser. Consequently, he had a license to steal until the media heat died down. We all wondered if he'd take advantage of it.

I shrugged. "We'll know after tomorrow's two-minute drill."

Big Dick nodded solemnly and then said what had been on everyone's mind. "You know, those fucking coaches would have been happy to see Prosser under that fence. Hackler would've danced a jig."

BIG DICK rejoined the defensive backs for a skeleton drill about ten minutes before Randall showed up. I tried to wave him off before he got to me, but he ignored my signal.

"I just got warned to stay away from truth-twisting reporters like you," I said. "You'll be covering pinball tournaments if you're not careful."

"Hey," Randall said, "what the hell's the matter with you? You're not part of this anymore, my friend. Your career, face it, is *over.*"

I knew he was right, but I wasn't up to accepting it yet. It was like with Don—I knew he was dead, but so far it only seemed like he wasn't around. . . .

"Orders from Anderson himself," I said, resisting reality as best I could.

"So what? I'm not impressed by shit like that."

"I'll still be part of things around here," I said as I glanced at my bandaged hands. "For a while, anyway."

"You're going to be out on your ass as soon as this game is over," he said, squaring off in front of me in his bantam-rooster stance. "Face it, for God's sakes. For your own good."

He was right, of course. "All right, you're right . . . but I still don't want any showdown with Anderson. Not now. I'll tell him we're talking politics if he comes over here—"

"Look, Larry, you don't owe these turkeys anything. You paid your dues, man; you gave good service. Take your gold watch and go home."

"I wish it was that easy," I said quietly.

WE'D DRIFTED over near a three-quarter-speed half-line drill. There was no tackling, and Prosser was doing nothing unusual, but little moves here and there indicated his true abilities.

"Is there any chance they'd move him up now that Slade is gone and Rowley's ankle won't be much by game time?" Randall asked.

"No way," I said. "Ordinarily they might be tempted, but Hackler has made a personal deal out of it. It's the blackball system: If one coach gets down on you, the others are obliged to get down on you just as hard. They almost never override each other about who to get rid of."

"So even if the others wanted to use him, Hackler's vote would keep him down?"

I nodded. "That's the way it usually works. Of course, Anderson's not subject to that, but he's not likely to undermine coaching principles or loyalties."

"It sounds like a closed case to me."

"More or less. I don't think Prosser has any supporters on the coaching staff, but even if he did, it probably wouldn't help. Only Anderson and Marshall carry any weight against Hackler."

"I'd sure like to see what Prosser could do in a game, but if it's hopeless . . . By the way, I'd like you to ride with me to Don's funeral."

The word funeral jolted me. Images flooded through my mind . . . Don's eyes, his throat, the pool of blood underneath his head . . .

"Sure," I managed to get out, "when is it?"

"Two tomorrow afternoon. I got it from the A.P. We should

leave around noon so we can get there a little early. I'm sure his family will want to talk to you."

I nodded, then realized I had someone else to consider. "Do you mind if Carla comes along? She's a close friend of Don's wife."

"I know," Randall said. "I talked to her for a little while last night at the hospital."

"You did? She didn't mention it to me."

"She must have talked to a hundred people she didn't know last night. You should have seen how she took charge of that madhouse. You'd have been proud of her."

"I'm *always* proud of her."

AT THE end of practice Coach Anderson announced the next day's tentative plans.

"We had a good practice today, men," he lied, "and I'm damn proud of you. It shows the kind of character we have on this team. We're going to surprise a lot of folks Saturday. Now, I hate to bring up this subject, but it's something we all have to face. Don Slade is going to be buried up in Libertyville tomorrow, and I think we all should attend as a group. Does anyone here have any objections to that?"

Silence.

"Good, then it's settled. Right now the services are scheduled for two o'clock, but there may be a change in that arrangement. We'll give you the final word some time tonight. Dress will be gray slacks and team blazers. Any questions?"

Again no one spoke.

"All right, we're going to have one minute of silent prayer now, then take it on in."

We all stood with heads bowed until Anderson clapped his hands and sent everyone to the showers.

I WAS standing behind a large concrete pillar outside the back dressing room door talking with Tom about Prosser when Anderson and Marshall came drifting by. We heard them coming and shut up. They didn't see us and continued talking as they passed us, ". . . so all I'm saying, T.K., is that it might make one hell of a big difference. We'd be crazy to go in without that kind of insurance."

"I understand how you feel, Paul, but it's still something I'd like to avoid if there's any way we can work around it."

"Look, I went along with everyone before because it didn't make that much difference, but now the pressure is really on us. Think of the crowd, T.K., just *think* about it . . ."

When they'd passed out of hearing range, Tom said, "What do you make of that?"

"I think I know."

"Really?"

"Yeah. Marshall is trying to convince Anderson to get Don's funeral moved up to ten o'clock tomorrow morning."

"How in the hell did you get that?"

"Because a while ago Anderson said there might be a change in the funeral time, and just now Marshall mentioned the crowd."

"So?"

"So the funeral gets maximum media coverage if it's held at ten o'clock instead of two."

"You're sure?"

"I'm sure. Coach Anderson explained it to me this morning. And *that* would hype the attendance."

Tom shook his head. "Assuming they're into something like that, why would Anderson hesitate to ask for a time change?"

"Good question. I have a hard time picturing him with a guilty conscience about it."

"Not only that, Marshall's the last coach I'd figure to push for it. Well, we'll find out soon enough what they're up to."

I WENT home and watched myself talk about Don on every major news program. Carla kept switching channels so we could see how each handled the story. One local sports announcer insinuated that Don's death might fire us up enough to beat Texas. It would have bothered me more if the announcer hadn't been a low-brow jerk who spent most of his program reporting horse racing results.

After cooking and feeding me supper, Carla drove me to the infirmary to meet Dr. Yarbrough. A small blood spot had seeped through the bandage on my right hand, and when Carla'd called him about it he'd told her to bring me over.

"Ah hah," he exclaimed when the bandage came off, "there's the culprit."

I almost gagged when I saw my hand. "It looks horrible. Are you sure you fixed it?"

"Except for this stitch right here," he said, pointing to a broken black string at the base of my thumb.

My hand was a bloated purple and yellow. Ugly red gashes ran in twisting patterns all over the palm and fingers, and thick black thread held them all together like the stitching on a baseball. All but one of those stitches seemed to be cutting through the surrounding skin. Carla turned away.

I could only stare numbly as Dr. Yarbrough resewed the broken stitch and then rewrapped my whole hand. The hero and his wounds.

The phone was ringing when we got back to the apartment, and Carla rushed in to grab it. It was Tom, so she held the phone up to my ear so I could talk.

"Where you been?" he asked. "I've been trying to get you for an hour."

"I popped a stitch and had to get it fixed. What's up?"

"I wanted to congratulate you for calling it on the nose this afternoon. Anderson drove to Libertyville after practice and talked Don's family into moving the funeral up to ten o'clock. It'll be announced on television tonight and be in the papers tomorrow morning. Not only that, there's a rumor going out that we'll dedicate the game to Don and be high enough to beat Texas. Did you hear it on the evening news?"

"Yeah. What does Peso have to say about it?"

Peso, in keeping with his consuming interest in things financial, was wired into every underground money market. For obvious reasons, football betting systems were his specialty. He could read a point spread like a road map and chart fluctuations like a seismograph. He'd be one of the first to know if people were taking us seriously.

"He says they opened at thirty-seven," Tom said, which meant bookies were accepting bets with Texas as 37-point favorites over us. "But they jumped off the board last night and came back on at thirty-five this afternoon. He says that kind of movement could mean anything, but it's not really out of line considering what's happened. He'll know a lot more tomorrow night."

"What if people buy that shit about us winning?" I asked.

"The spread drops and people betting on Texas clean up."

"No, I mean what will happen at the gate?"

"Oh. We'll probably break the attendance record. It looks like you were right about the coaches."

Thursday

LIBERTYVILLE WAS about an hour's drive from the city, and Carla and I used the time to get to know Randall better. We found him to be good company. We arrived before the buses carrying the team, but not before a small crowd of reporters and television camera crews that had apparently been waiting for some time. They swarmed around the car asking for comments, and I answered as best I could. Finally Carla and I left Randall to cope with them while we went inside.

For me, and I suspect for Carla as well, Don's death finally became reality when we glimpsed his body in the half-opened casket. His skin was bone-white, his scattered freckles had somehow disappeared. His closed eyes were sunk deep in their sockets, and they were ringed by large, dark circles. Only his reddish-blond hair looked the same as two days ago.

I glanced down at his hands to avoid looking at the terrible place below his chin. They were neatly folded across his stomach, and were as white as his face. I noticed a scraped knuckle on his left hand. The skin had been knocked off during that last practice, and the wound had stayed raw.

Finally I got up the nerve to look at the turtleneck sweater that covered what used to be his throat. I remember wondering what they had stuffed the hole with because the concealment was perfect. I think that sweater was a pale yellow color, but my eyes kept filling with what I'd seen under the fence and, finally, there were too many tears to see any more. I turned away and went into the small antechamber that had been set aside for Don's family.

The first person I noticed was Annie. She was sitting in a wheelchair, which startled me at first, but then I remembered yesterday's miscarriage. She was staring vacantly past me as I stepped through the room's entrance, but her hands went to her mouth when she recognized me. She got unsteadily to her feet while two girlfriends tried to make her stay seated, but she shook them off and weaved toward me. I stepped forward to meet her in a state of near-shock myself. She looked more wretched than I could ever have imagined, nearly as changed as Don. Her face was drawn and pale like his, but her eyes were red and puffy. When she spoke to me I knew she'd been heavily sedated. "Oh, Luurie," she slurred, "it's so . . . I'm so . . ."

She fell into my clumsy embrace and we stood holding to each other for a long minute as people in the room glanced away and I watched Annie trying to fight through the haze of drugs.

"What hap . . . happened?" she mumbled, "can you . . . tell me?"

"It was an accident, Annie," I whispered, repeating the same useless words she'd heard countless times by then. "An accident."

". . . everyone says . . ."

Suddenly Carla was at my side, and gently but firmly took Annie into her own embrace, steering her back to the wheelchair. Annie directed a few incoherent words at Carla before sinking back into the stupor I'd found her in, eyes vacant, staring.

A large, ruddy, middle-aged man approached me, and I recognized him as Don's father. "Son," he began very quietly, "I want to thank you for what you tried to do for Donnie. Mrs. Slade and I want to . . . we want to . . ." And then he just let it go and turned away.

It was devastating to watch this powerful-looking man literally reduced to tears. I said quietly, "Don would have done as much for any of us, Mr. Slade." It was banal, but it was all I could manage.

My mind was nearly a cinder by the time I found myself standing in front of Mrs. Slade. She was a small gray-haired woman who sat staring straight ahead while tightly clutching a white rose in her lap.

"Mrs. Slade, I can't tell you how I feel . . ."

"That's quite all right," she said as a little smile twisted across her face. "I understand perfectly, perfectly. Have you met my other sons?"

She motioned to her left side where a young man older than Don and two younger boys sat with bowed heads. "That's Doug and Mike and Steven," she went on. "Say hello, boys."

They all looked up at me and nodded. Then the oldest, the one she called Steven, put his arm around her and said, "Take it easy, Mom, take it easy . . ."

Oh, Jesus.

AFTER THE funeral we all stood around and talked quietly for about a half hour, then the buses pulled out to take the team home. Carla wanted to stay behind with Annie, but I convinced her to come back the next afternoon when Annie would be more lucid.

On the way back Randall said, "How do you think the funeral's going to effect the team? I saw some pretty shook-up people when they lowered him into the ground."

"If it makes them feel anything like the way I feel," I said, "I doubt they'll be able to dress out this afternoon."

"They *better* be able to dress out. All the real heavyweights are moving in to cover this one. *Sports Illustrated* and *Sporting News* are both planning cover stories on the game, and their men are due in town sometime today. I heard they made a courtesy stopover in Austin yesterday, but it's your guys they have to figure out. It isn't everyday a runt school like Cajun State challenges the national champions."

We rode in uncomfortable silence for a while. Finally I said, "What do you think about the rumor the coaches put out about us winning?"

Randall looked at me. "How do you know it was *your* coaches?"

"Got to be, you said it yesterday. If they put out that line about us winning and then hype it right—they fill the stadium."

"But there's a risk in it for them."

"How do you figure?"

"They put Texas on their guard against you. If they come in here expecting a tough game they'll take you seriously, and if *that* happens you guys can grab your asses with both hands and kiss them good-bye. Your coaches ought to be poor-mouthing and begging for mercy—"

"Except nobody will turn out for the game if they poor-mouth too much about how bad our chances are."

"Sure they will. Maybe not a stadium full, but enough to make a difference. Hell, there'll be twenty or thirty thousand extra just curious to see what Don's death will do to the team. But even if there were no extra fans the strategy should be the same: keep the score as close as possible. A close score will eventually bring out a crowd and get recognition, but a rout will destroy all the sympathy Don's death has created. Look at it this way, would you rather have a stadium full of fair-weather fans see you get the shit kicked out of you by a fired-up Texas team, or would you rather have millions read and hear that you played a decent game?"

He was beginning to make sense. "I see your point, but who does that leave to put out the rumor about us winning?"

"We came up with two better choices at the office last night. Either gamblers or Texas sympathizers could be behind it. Gamblers make an absolute killing if money starts flowing in on Cajun State because they'll cover every penny of it and clean up."

"Yeah, but what if we beat the spread? Wouldn't the syndicate bosses ventilate the guys who backed Texas? Some very heavy bread is going to go down around this one, and high rollers won't take that kind of bath without making someone pretty goddamn sorry about it."

Randall shrugged. "That's why they're called gamblers. Anyway, I'd go for that risk. Your people don't have a chance, even if the spread stays where it is."

"What about the Texas supporters? Where do they fit in?"

"Long shots, but don't count them out entirely. Dirty pool is the name of the game, and it might be that they've decided to make your guys sound like real fire-eaters because of Don's death. If that stirs the Longhorns up enough to flatten your asses, then the lopsided score puts a whammy on the rest of their schedule."

"So our coaches don't figure into it at all?"

"I didn't say that. They just might be so blinded by the immediate gain of filling the stadium that they'd start the rumor. Also, gamblers don't usually make serious moves this far in advance of game time, so they might not be behind it. And on top of that the Texas coaches may have decided not to look like assholes for stomping you poor turkeys into the ground, figuring it could hurt their image more than a big score would help."

"Then what are you trying to say?" I asked, properly confused by now. "No one is behind it? It just made itself up?"

"Someone is behind it, all right. The problem is figuring out who."

WE TRIED to stop off for a hamburger when we got back to the city but made the mistake of going to a place off-campus. I was immediately recognized and surrounded by people wanting to hear all the grisly details about Don. Which turned our stomachs. We went home without eating.

As Randall dropped us off at the apartment he said, "You want me to pick you up for practice?"

"No, I'll walk, but thanks just the same. See you there."

I was quiet while Carla fixed and fed me a sandwich. She didn't push me to talk. Afterward as she washed the dishes I stayed at the kitchen table, feeling numb. Finally she came over and straddled my lap so she could face me and drape her arms across my shoulders.

"Funeral got you down, right?"

"Yeah, but those people back at the burger joint really got to me too." I held up my bandaged hands. "These things are like walking around with a Kotex on my head."

She didn't smile. "They'll be gone before you know it, and you'll slip right back into your well-deserved obscurity."

She was right and I knew it. But there was more to my problem than that.

Carla was looking intently at me. "How about some dessert?"

She started unbuttoning her blouse, and blood shot from my stomach to my head and back down to my crotch.

"What did you have in mind?"

She stood up and dropped her panties, then unbuckled my pants and restraddled me as I stayed sitting in the chair. And then she proceeded—wordlessly, lovingly—to smooth out all my knotted emotions.

When we were finished and she was still sitting on me, she looked directly into my eyes and cut to the unspoken reason I was so depressed.

"Please don't feel guilty anymore, darling," she said softly. "You did all anyone possibly could have done."

I looked back at her and realized exactly what and how much she meant to me.

"Carla, will you marry me?"

She didn't miss a beat.

"God, I thought you'd never ask!"

I HAD just punched the sixth-floor elevator button with my elbow when I heard someone shout, "Hold the 'vator!" I quickly pressed the "hold" button and the already-closing doors snapped back open. Heape and Colley stepped in with me, nodded solemnly.

"Still bummed out about this morning?" I asked as the doors slid shut.

"Nah," Heape replied. "I mean, sure, we're still bummed out

about that, but we just got some fucked-up news about Rabbit."

"Yeah," Heape added as the doors slid open. "Come on down to Tom's room and we'll fill you in."

Peso came by and swung the door open to reveal Swede in bed trying to salvage his nap. "Hey, what the hell?" He winced as Peso flicked on the lights and walked through the room to open the blinds.

"Rise and shine," Peso said, "there's supposed to be some hot copy going down."

"It *better* be hot," Swede grumbled.

Others shuffled in, followed by Tom and Wizard. Tom said, "I have the dubious pleasure to announce that tomorrow night at the stadium's south entrance, Cajun State is going to hold its first bonfire and pep rally in over a decade. Now," he added, glancing at Heape, "what's this all about?"

Heape and Colley looked at each other, but something in Colley's manner gave Heape the floor.

"We just got the goods on Rabbit," he began.

Everyone in the room became attentive.

"You know those two mechanics who've been working on the car?" Heape went on. "You know how they've been blowing us off every time one of us asked about Rabbit? Well, they just finished putting it back together out on the street, and Butch and I got a chance to talk to Danny, the young one, alone. Ralph —the old one—was a real hard-leg, but he had to go call Rabbit's old man to tell him they were finished and to get final instructions and all that. Butch and I happened by just after he left, so we struck up a conversation with Danny and it turns out he played ball with Rabbit in high school so he knew the whole story. Naturally he swore us to secrecy because he said they'd sack his ass if anyone found out he told, but he felt he could trust us not to get him in trouble. Right, Butch?"

Colley nodded solemnly. "He may know his cars, but he can't judge character for shit."

"So, anyway," Heape went on, "Danny confirmed what we always suspected about Rabbit being a little wacko. It's for sure now. He was under psychiatric care for years as a kid. Danny said Rabbit's two older brothers were absolute bona fide studs in high school, and both played college ball on scholarship at Alabama. He said Rabbit got overpowered by their reps and cracked up in junior high trying to be like them. He's supposedly never been the same since."

"He tried to kill himself with pills," Colley added.

"Right. So the psychiatrists told the old man that before Rabbit could form his own identity or some shit like that he had to come to grips with his brothers and what they represented to him. I guess it has something to do with all that ego and id shit. Anyway, it turned out that all Rabbit *really* wanted was to be a football star like his brothers'd been. The psychiatrists found out that the reason he tried to kill himself in junior high was because he was afraid he'd disgrace the bigshot reputations of his brothers. So, the old man solved his problem the way any smart rich man would. He bought his way out of it. He practically owns the area where Rabbit went to high school, so he was able to get the local offense structured around Rabbit. Danny said that no one ever found out exactly what strings the old man pulled, but he did make Rabbit the big deal on his team. Of course Rabbit was never a star like his brothers, but it got him through high school."

"Which brings us to the interesting part," Colley said.

"Yeah, what about a college career for our budding young psycho?" Heape asked rhetorically. "Well, the old man had no choice because both older brothers had played at Alabama. Neither one ever started because they were injured a lot, but they were both on the Varsity, which meant Rabbit had to do at least that much. So, the old man put out feelers about buying Rabbit's way in but he found that money wasn't the answer at big-time schools like 'Bama and Auburn. They blew him off and told him to find a smaller program, which brought him here."

"Exactly how come?" I asked.

"Apparently the coaching change two years ago tipped him off to an opportunity here," Heape said. "He got wind that the Athletic Department wanted to go all-out to hire a top-flight coach like Anderson, but they were short on inducements. The old man offered to help out if the department would sign Rabbit to a scholarship and keep him on the Varsity as long as he stayed uninjured and wanted to be on the team. He asked that the coaches play Rabbit in games if they could—which explains them putting him at safety on our kickoff team—but beyond that he made no demands. It's a straight trade-off—the coaches keep Rabbit around and stay off his case, and the old man keeps his part of the bargain."

"Which is those fine brand-new Pontiacs the coaches get each year," Colley added. "Those little numbers come courtesy of Rabbit's old man."

"Hey, wait a minute," Peso interrupted. "Those cars are loaned to the coaches for promotional considerations. Hell, you've all seen the ads they do for that agency here in town. Coaches everywhere get in on shit like that."

"Coaches at the major schools may get in on it," Skid said, "but not at places like Cajun State. I had a cousin who played at the University of Detroit before their football program folded, and even they never had a car deal like that."

"I think Skid's right," I said. "The old staff here didn't have them either. Those cars arrived when Rabbit arrived, but I never put the two together."

"It makes sense," Peso said. "All the old man would have to do is juggle his books a little and have those cars come out of his Alabama agencies with no one the wiser. The local agency plays along to get all that free advertising, and it's sweet for everyone. Son of a bitch, the old man really put one together!"

"Well," Tom said, "we either expose what happened and make a tremendous stink, or we sit on it and let nature take its course."

He paused for feedback, got none. Finally he looked at Heape, since Rabbit was all that stood between Heape and his dreams of glory as a Varsity wingback.

"What do you say, Grant? You're the one who'll be most affected by what we decide."

Heape thought it over for about five seconds. "Well-l-l, if it was anything other than committing suicide, I wouldn't hesitate to lower the boom on his scrawny little ass. But since it *is* that kind of risk . . . let's lay off him and see what happens for me next year."

Everyone in the room breathed with relief. Nobody wanted another death.

THE BACK dressing room is always loose before a Thursday practice because the week's hard work is nearly over. The only serious hitting exercise is the two-minute drill held at the very end of the session.

Ordinarily Redshirts prepare themselves for those last-minute drives the same way Varsity players prepare for Saturday games, which explains why they often make the Varsity look inept. The Redshirts peak for two-minute drill while the Varsity just wants to get off the field and take a shower.

Today, however, was no ordinary Thursday. Today the Redshirts would perform for a dozen or so media heavyweights and dozens of fans. They all recognized it as perhaps the only time in their careers when a good performance might have some value. Except for Prosser, I'd never seen them so keyed up. Typically, Prosser seemed to have no interest in what was going on around him.

"Are you going to give Prosser his shot this afternoon?" I asked Tom.

In a way, Tom controlled what would happen. If he didn't call Prosser's number, there'd be no chance for him to do his stuff.

"I thought about holding him down," Tom admitted. "I figured that since they were getting low on running backs, they might keep him around if he gave them a break."

"But you decided against it?"

"Yeah, there's no point in it. Even if all the other coaches would agree to let him stay, Hackler's vote would still sink him. But the clincher was when I thought back over all the shit they've put him through. So I'll tell you what I'm going to do. I'm going to get the ball to him every way but on a silver platter, and I just hope he runs it right up their asses—"

He was interrupted by Teekay Junior bursting into the room. We kept quiet as he snapped his clipboard up where he could read it. The motion was the same one Coach Anderson often used, and when Teekay Junior spoke, his voice was a bizarre

156

imitation of his father's authoritative tones.

"I have some announcements to make," he said, "and I want your undivided attention for a few minutes."

We all managed to keep straight faces. I pretended respect out of habit, and the Redshirts did so out of fear. Teekay Junior called nearly all plays. He could make life miserable for anyone who bothered him.

"First of all," he began, "it's been decided that every eligible team member—Redshirts included—will dress out for Saturday's game. This is a one-time honor, a part of our tribute to Don Slade . . ."

He paused for the expected cheer. Silence was what he got.

Realizing applause was not in the cards, Junior finally went on. "All Redshirts will be allowed two free tickets to the game. Ask a Varsity player how to go about picking them up if you're not familiar with the procedure."

More silence. Everybody knew the Varsity players were allowed four tickets per game. NCAA rules allowed athletes only fifteen dollars per month for laundry money and pocket change, so most Athletic Departments—ours included—got around that restriction legally by utilizing the ticket exchange. Players were given tickets with the option of promptly selling them back to the ticket office for face value, and most did exactly that. Being able to pick up that extra cash was one of the side benefits of making the Varsity. The Redshirts rightfully viewed those two tickets as one more insult to swallow.

"Finally," Teekay Junior concluded, now understandably anxious to get out of the room, "you can keep the usual Friday night movie passes if you want them. Any questions?"

Whenever Coach Anderson said, "Any questions?" nobody ever asked any, but Teekay Junior was always bombarded. Several Redshirts started chattering at once until Tom stood up to speak for the room.

"Are you saying the Friday night practice and meeting are optional for us this week? We can go to that or to a movie?"

"Uh, no," he said, flushing slightly, "that's not what I meant. You're still not allowed to practice tomorrow night or go to the meeting, so you might as well take the passes and go to a movie.

You're allowed to dress out for the game, nothing else."

"What about uniforms?" Tom said, "and where will we dress out? You know the visiting team always uses these back rooms to dress out, so where does that leave us?"

"All that will be worked out later," Teekay Junior said, becoming more flustered. "You'll be notified about everything. Just do what you're told and you'll be all right." With that he got the hell out of the room.

We sat in silence for a minute, then suddenly the tension broke, and a slowly rising tide of laughter began until everyone was whooping it up at Teekay's inanity. Suddenly the door cracked back open and his scarlet face appeared.

"By the way," he gushed in a nervous bleat, "I forgot to mention one thing—there'll be no two-minute drill this afternoon. The coaches don't want to risk any more injuries before the game."

This time there was no laughter when he left. We all sat stunned as the message sank in.

"'They're *afraid* of us,'" Tom finally said. "'They know what we can do and they're cutting us off at the pass. You've got to hand it to 'em, they don't miss a dirty trick."

REDSHIRT CONSENSUS was that they'd been outflanked and, as usual, there wasn't a damn thing to do about it. Still, even Tom, the most militant, realized the coaches were doing the right thing. Ordinarily a poor Varsity showing against the Redshirts was at worst a slight embarrassment, any number of rationalizations being open to them. Not so to the reporters and fans who would be on hand today.

"You know," Tom said as he sat down with me, "I can understand what the coaches are trying to do and in a way I can't blame them, but I sure wish there was some way we could pressure them into having the drill anyway. I'd love to see Prosser put their feet to the fire."

"Yeah," I agreed as I leaned over to look at the wall clock in the freshman room, "but practice starts in twenty minutes. I think you're a little late."

"It doesn't matter. We could have had twenty *days* and it wouldn't have made any difference."

"Wait a minute," I said, surprised I was still capable of any original thinking, "I just had an idea. . . . It's a pretty long shot but . . . Let me get out of here and see what I can do."

"Hold on a second," Tom said, grabbing my arm as I got up to leave. "What's on your mind?"

"Something I've learned watching you operate on them," I said, and turned to start looking for Randall.

RANDALL WAS already out on the practice field when I got there, but so were about two hundred other people. Most were just curious rubbernecks responding to all the recent publicity, but I knew a substantial number had to be reporters, TV people and dedicated gamblers. When I spotted Randall talking with a small group, I thought it would be a simple matter to walk over and unobtrusively attract his attention. I was wrong.

"Hey, look! There he is!"

"Yeah! That's the guy!"

"Christ's sake, wouldja lookit those hands?"

"Hey, buddy, come over here a sec, meet a pal of mine. . . ."

I froze, but fortunately Randall had been attracted by the commotion.

"Randall," I shouted when I picked his face out of the crowd, "I want to talk to you!"

"Sure thing," he said, elbowing his way past the rubbernecks. He grabbed my arm, spun me around and steered me back through the turnstile gate I'd walked through moments before.

"There you are, my man," he said when we'd finally made it into the shadows under the stadium ramps. "The price of fame, Larry. Now, tell me, what's up?"

"Oh, yeah, well . . . do you know anything about Thursday's two-minute drill? I mean, its significance and all . . . ."

"No . . . can't say that I do."

We sat in an empty concession both and I filled him in on the

Redshirts' desire to embarrass the coaches by upstaging the Varsity.

"Where do I come in?" he asked.

"Do you know the *Sports Illustrated* or *Sporting News* guy?"

"Well, I met them when they dropped by the office this afternoon, and I was talking with Glenn Novak when you came out just now. He's the one from *Sporting News*. But I can't say I know either of them very well. Why?"

"Because if they asked Coach Anderson to see some hitting, he might decide to hold the two-minute drill after all."

"Do you really think that's a possibility?"

"It's a long shot. What do you say? Want to take a crack at it?"

"Might as well. Like the song says, When you ain't got nothin', you got nothin' to lose."

PRACTICE HAD started by the time we got back out on the field.

"How do you want to handle it?" Randall asked as we approached our first target.

"Introduce me and then try to work it into the conversation. Play it by ear. Nice and easy."

He nodded and walked up to a frizzy-haired middle-aged man. "Glenn? There's someone here I think you ought to meet."

Glenn spun around with a wary look that brightened when he saw my hands. "I'd recognize *those* bandages anywhere. It's a real honor to meet you, Larry."

"I'll let you two chat while I go round up Dave," Randall said. "I'm sure he'll want to talk to Larry, too."

"Who's Dave?" I asked as Randall headed away.

"Friend of mine from New York, works for *Sports Illustrated*."

"Oh?" I said, trying my best to sound casual.

"Yeah, he'll be anxious to meet you, all right. You're all he's been talking about since we got together yesterday in Austin. We're both knocked out by what you did for Slade."

"Actually I panicked, really . . ."

"Look, son," he said, "cut the bullshit. I'm an old man and I

160

can smell it a mile away. We know what you did and how you did it, so can the false modesty."

Dave Moorehouse came up then and gave me the same hero's rush. He looked to be in his early thirties and seemed less jaded than Glenn.

"Can't wait to see your people tangle with those Longhorns," he said, to my astonishment.

"How did they look when you saw them yesterday?" Randall jumped in.

"Ready to play." Glenn said. "Stoner's lost about ten pounds, looks even quicker than last year."

I thought of Wheeler and winced for him.

"You think these guys can stay on the field with them?" Randall asked. He was still carrying the ball for me.

"Hard to say, you can't tell much about people by watching them run through a few plays."

"Yeah, well, according to Larry here, you won't be seeing them in action until Saturday night."

"Why not?" Dave said. "Afraid we'll spill some big secrets?"

Randall's face lit up. "Matter of fact, they *are* afraid of tipping their secret weapon in front of all these people."

"Secret weapon?" Dave said warily. "Okay, I'll bite. What kind of 'secret weapon'?"

"You guys haven't heard about *Prosser?*" Randall said. "Where have you been, for crying out loud?"

"Don't get cute with me, boy," Glenn said. "I was at this before you were born."

"Aw, come on, Glenn, I was only kidding. I'm just surprised you haven't heard about Prosser, that's all."

"Well, who the hell is he?"

Things had gotten out of hand. Randall was supposed to in-trigue these guys, get them to ask Anderson for two-minute drills, not make them sore with his grandstanding or actually mention Prosser. Jesus . . . all they had to do was ask Anderson about Prosser and there'd for sure be no chance. And now I spotted Anderson staring at me from the coaching tower. I decided to take off.

"If you gentlemen will excuse me," I said, "I have to be going now. It was a pleasure meeting both of you, and I hope we'll see some more of each other before game time."

"Yeah, sure," Glenn said, hardly aware of me.

"You can count on it," Dave said.

"And I want to talk to you later when you find some time, Randall," I said.

"Right," he nodded excitedly, not bothering to look at me. "See you later."

As I walked away I heard Glenn's voice fading . . . "Now, tell us all about this Prosser character . . ."

I DRIFTED along the sideline for awhile. The morning's sadness, if anything, seemed to have sharpened concentration. It looked as though Anderson's gung-ho strategy was working. Execution was precise and there were remarkably few mental lapses. Emotions were still subdued, though, so the cheer that rose from near the standing dummies was a surprise.

I glanced at the defensive line's work area and saw them clapping and raising clenched fists. The nearby defensive backs joined in the ruckus, and soon the commotion had spread to all the groups as a lone figure trotted into view and headed directly across the field to report to the offensive backfield unit. Even with a noticeable limp in his stride, the Bull left little doubt that he intended to play.

He spoke briefly with Coach Mayhue, the offensive backfield coach, while everyone returned to work and spirits seemed to lift over the entire field. . . . Shouts of ridicule, encouragement, frustration began to pepper the air.

The Bull watched his group drill for a few minutes, then jogged onto the track and began slowly, carefully, to make his way around it. He completed a lap and a half before coming back onto the field near where I was standing.

"How about it?" he said, puffing hard. "How do I look?"

"Like you're already out of shape."

"Never was in shape . . . to run that far. . . ."

"Look, just be thankful you can run at all. How's it feel?"

"Not bad . . . considering."

He took one last deep breath, exhaled loudly. "Man, I needed that." We stood side by side near the field's northeast corner and watched the double line of rubbernecks winding along the west sideline, some drifting one way and some the other.

"They're all sneaking over to see the fence," the Bull said as he nodded to our right on the field's opposite side. Thirty yards beyond the track was the place where it had happened. "They're probably looking for a puddle of blood or something."

"I know."

"Just look at those damned ghouls! Disappointed as hell that all they can see is a goddamn fence bent out of shape." He stood silent for a moment. "Fuck 'em," he finally said. "And how about you? How're your hands?"

"Doc says they'll come around, in a year or two."

"My ankle should be okay in a day or two. You're right, I'm lucky. . . ."

"How'd it feel out on the track just now?"

"Okay on the straights, murder in the turns. I'll try some low-speed cuts tomorrow and see how it goes. I've been practically *living* in the fucking training room. If it doesn't hold up it won't be from lack of trying. Diathermy, whirlpool, elevation, ice; diathermy, whirlpool, elevation, ice. Man, I'm *sick* of it."

"I don't blame you."

We stood in silence for a few moments while he flexed his injured ankles, he looked up and smiled. "Still, not bad, considering."

The Bull was back.

PRACTICE ENDED with extended skeleton drill sessions and work on the kicking game, which meant I'd let the Redshirts down. The two-minute drill was normally sandwiched between those two phases of practice, so it was obvious my plan had failed. I was walking off the field with my head down, wondering what I was going to say to Tom, when Randall appeared at my side, bubbling like an idiot.

"Am I a genius?" he asked. "Seriously, am I a *genius*?"

"Seriously, I don't know which of us needs his ass kicked the hardest, but I vote for you—"

"What do you mean?"

I realized he really didn't understand what had happened. "We blew getting Glenn and Dave to pressure Anderson into holding the two-minute drill. What in hell made you get off on that 'secret weapon' bullshit?"

"That's where I'm a genius. It couldn't have turned out better if we'd planned it. You heard it with your own ears. I told Glenn and Dave that Prosser's the secret weapon Anderson is going to unload on Texas."

"And you're telling me they bought it?"

"Enough to check it out," he said with satisfaction. "I stuck to facts, told them if they didn't mention my name they could verify with anybody they wanted. I even told them about the Texas coaches who saw the scrimmage—"

"But what did it accomplish?"

"I'll tell you, it at least made some important people aware that Prosser *exists*. He can make a difference against Texas, and now the word is going out about him."

We had stopped under the ramps adjoining the Redshirt dressing room.

"I mean," he went on, "who *knows* what they might say, and what the talk will do? One thing I can guarantee . . . those two guys will let a hell of a lot of people know about Prosser before game time. We've set some pretty big wheels in motion on this one, Larry, *powerful* wheels. It's hard to imagine what the consequences could be."

"You sound like a commercial."

"I'm not kidding, Larry. There's already question marks about this game, but we've just dropped the biggest one of all. I hope you understand the possibilities."

"I'm not so sure I do," I said. "You make it sound almost *ominous.*"

Randall's excitement was evident as he moved up closer to me and lowered his voice.

"There's going to be millions of dollars riding on this game.

The word at the office puts it at five or ten, maybe more. Prosser is a new element, an unknown factor, and he upsets everyone's strategy. *Now* do you see what I mean?"

"I think so," I said, "but I wonder if he can really have that much effect. . . ."

"That's the beauty of it! It doesn't matter what he *can* do. What matters now is what people think he *might* do. Look, suppose they'd had that fucking drill this afternoon the way you wanted and he'd made a few nice runs. Okay, everyone would say, 'Wow, the kid is pretty good.' Even Glenn and Dave would have been impressed, but they wouldn't have made an issue of it. They don't push one-shots like that. They're here for the *game,* and some obscure Redshirt who gets lucky in practice isn't going to interest them very much. Face it."

"But now that he's some kind of mystery man—"

"Exactly! He's capable of *anything!* Sky's the limit!"

"So where does that leave us?"

"We wait, along with everyone else. If the coaches dress him out for the game, we'll know we got to 'em."

"He's already dressing out for the game, they announced before practice that *all* the Redshirts are dressing out."

"No shit?" he said, momentarily put off balance by the new development in his scenario. "All right, so we probably won't know what the coaches are thinking until the game starts."

"Do you really think there's any way they could be forced to use him?"

"Jesus, Larry! You still don't see it, do you?" He shook his head in exasperation. "It doesn't matter whether they use him or not. What matters is that they *might* use him. The possibility is more important than the reality."

I TOLD Randall I wanted him to meet with Tom and Peso later that night, then went to the Redshirt dressing room.

Tom was drying off from his shower. "Couldn't pull it off, eh?"

"Not exactly . . . but you remember Randall Webber, the reporter you met the other night?"

"Yeah, nice guy. Feisty. I like him."

"Well, I think he started something out there this afternoon. I'm not sure I like it either."

Tom looked up at me in anticipation.

"No, not here," I said. Postpractice quiet had set in, and only the shower room noise prevented even our subdued voices from being overheard. "It's a long story. Meet me later at the U.C."

I stopped by the equipment shed on the way to the front dressing rooms to check with Cap'n about what the Redshirts were going to wear and where they were going to dress out.

"It's a problem," he agreed. "I got five spare uniforms and fifteen extra people, so somebody gets left out. The ones that do have to wear the uniforms from two years ago."

"Those shitty-looking green satin pants?"

"I don't pick 'em, son, I just hand 'em out."

"I know. It's just that the light blue ones we wear now will make quite a contrast, won't they?"

"I 'xpect so, but you can ask Soupbone. Them old green ones is all we got besides the new ones."

"What about jerseys?" I asked, giving the pants up for lost.

"We got plenty white jerseys. Only difference will be numbers and stripes."

The old jerseys had green numbers with two green bicep stripes, while the new ones had blue numbers with blue and green UCLA shoulder stripes. Cap'n had understated the contrast.

"Who'll get the new uniforms and who'll get the old?"

"Don't know that right now," he said. "They gonna send me a list later on."

"Why don't they put *all* the Redshirts in old uniforms instead of only ten. That way they'll at least look like a unit."

"I don't reckon the coaches'll think of somethin' that simple" —he winked—"but if they get all busy and forget to send a list, then that's what I'll do."

"Thanks, Cap'n, I'd appreciate it." I had already started to turn away when I remembered my final question. "By the way, where do you suppose they'll dress out?"

"No one told me yet, but I'm bettin' it'll be the weight room. Ain't no place else to put 'em."

The weight room was a cramped anteroom adjacent to the training room, and it was the only unused place in the whole area on game days. A perfect place for the outcasts to dress out.

They thought of everything.

I MOVED on to the half-empty Varsity dressing room and confronted the usual postpractice effluvia: odors of tape remover, deodorant, sweat, talcum powder and antiseptic mingled with steam from the shower; damp twisted towels, tape cutters, tape and gauze bandage shreds, orange rinds and dirty uniforms lay scattered on the floor; weary players positioned around the room in various stages of dress and undress. Mostly the habitual stragglers were left behind by now, and I spoke to a few as I moved along.

"How's it going, Quink? You doing all right?" Don's death and Prosser's reprieve had left Quink safely on the Varsity.

"Yeah, I'm okay. You?"

"I'll get by."

I moved on down to Wheeler. "How about it, Jimbo? You feeling pretty good?"

"I'm ready," he said. "I'm *really* ready for that big son of a bitch."

"Some reporters saw him yesterday and said he's lost ten pounds."

"No shit? Stoner lost ten? Was he sick or something?"

"They didn't say." I knew enough to let him find out for himself about Stoner's increased quickness.

I continued down the line until I got to my main target. "Peso, my man, how's it going?"

"What do you need, Sage?"

The con artist suspecting the con. "I need to talk to you later tonight about a few things going down around this game. Meeting in Tom's room about nine. And by the way, find out what you can about the point spread before you come."

He nodded.

"And, Peso?"

"Yeah?"

"Don't mention it to anyone."

T OM WAS reading the afternoon paper when I joined him in the University Center's upstairs music lounge, a good place to meet because our people hardly ever went up there.

"It says here our game's 'been thrust into the national spotlight,' and it also says the Bull is 'extremely doubtful.' I hope the guy who wrote that was at practice when he came out onto the field this afternoon. Do the coaches really believe that 'extremely doubtful' bullshit will put Texas off guard?"

"They'd say he had terminal blue-balls if they thought it would give them an edge."

Tom shrugged, put away the paper. "What'd you want to talk about?"

I filled him in on the afternoon's events. "So what are we going to do with it?" I asked. "Spread it around or wait and see what develops?"

"I think we should wait until we get some hard evidence the coaches are feeling some heat about Prosser. I mean, just because a few people start talking about Pete doesn't necessarily mean the coaches will respond. Look at it this way . . . if rumors go out about Prosser being some kind of secret weapon and then they don't even *use* him, he comes off looking like a geek and your friend Randall's credibility gets blown up his ass. Even worse, what if by some incredible miracle they actually put him in the game? If his performance is anything less than outasight, it's a bust. As much as I've seen him work, I'm not sure he's *that* good."

My energy drained out onto the floor. "Great . . . it looks like Prosser's no closer to playing, and I've got to tell Randall he could be in shit up to his neck for trying to do me a favor."

"Well, he did blow the drill," Tom said, then changed the subject, which had come down to a wait-and-see thing. "Where do you suppose we'll dress out?" he asked.

"I talked to Cap'n. You guys dress out in the weight room and wear the old uniforms."

"You mean those green pieces of shit? We have to wear *those?*"

"Maybe not all of you. Cap'n has five extra Varsity uniforms, some of you may get those."

"I'd rather see us all wear the green."

"That's what I thought you'd say, and that's what you'll get unless the coaches say otherwise. I fixed it with Cap'n."

"Thanks," he said. "If we have to look like yard-wide assholes, I guess it's best to do it as a unit."

"Like old Emperor Augustus said, *Sic semper tyrannis, e pluribus unum.*"

"Translation?"

"Fuck the fuckers, and hang together."

He laughed. "We'll do our best."

"I'm sure you will . . . by the way, I've called a meeting about our little problems at your place, nine. Okay?" He nodded and as we headed for the stairs noted a black wreath still hanging on the music room door.

"Does it seem to you like only this morning when they put him in the ground?"

I shook my head.

More like forever, and in another way never at all . . .

I WAS surprised to find Helmet at our apartment when I got home. He was his usual polite self, but Carla looked tight. After a few minutes of small talk she came to the point.

"Helmet got a threatening phone call this afternoon, Larry, and he doesn't know what to do about it."

Neither, for Christ's sakes, did I. I sat down and asked for a beer.

"Did you hear what I *said*, Larry? Helmet got a threatening phone call today—"

"I heard what you said," and turned to Helmet. "Okay, tell me about it."

"The person say to me, 'Muddle'—he does not say my name

correctly—'Muddle, you must not kick so well Saturday night. You will make many people very unhappy.' Then he hang up. That is all."

"You think it was serious, or just some sick joke? We're going to be targets for a lot of weirdo stuff until things settle down around here."

"But you're also going to be targets for gamblers, according to what I've heard at school this afternoon," Carla said.

She seemed more upset than Helmet.

"I worry not so much the intention of the caller," Helmet said. "I am asking what my response should be. You are my good friends and—"

"Go to the police," Carla said. "That's what I'd do."

"Now hold on a minute," I said. "Let's not go off half-cocked. It could cause more trouble than we've got if cops start swarming all around us."

"Then at least tell the coaches," she said. "You've got to do something—"

"We will do something, honey. Tom and Peso and Randall and I are getting together in a couple of hours over at Tom's room. Helmet will stay here and have supper with us, then we'll talk it out and do whatever the group decides. Okay, Helmet?"

Helmet smiled cheerfully. "I do not like coaches and coaches do not like me. This way is much better."

PESO, AS usual, was late, but the time was well spent on Helmet's problem.

"I can't believe a professional gambler would do something that might bring in federal agents," Randall said.

"I agree with Randall," Tom said. "We're hardly the favorite in this game, even with the hype from Don's death and the so-called secret weapon . . . sorry, Randall . . . no, I think it's some kook getting his jollies."

"So what's the consensus?" I asked, suspecting that Randall and Tom were at least partly downplaying the whole thing for Helmet's benefit. "Forget it?"

"Not exactly . . ." Tom said. "Helmet, let's wait and see what

170

develops . . . there're two more days for us to get help if it starts to look like you really need it. A move right now would be premature, but any more calls and we'll bring in the police. Okay?"

Helmet slapped his palms on his knees and got to his feet. "If that is what you feel, then that is what I shall do. I will leave you to your own affairs now, but I thank you sincerely for your help. I will, as you say, keep you posted."

As soon as Helmet was out the door Randall turned on Tom. "What do you *really* think?"

"I'm worried, but I still doubt he's in any real danger."

"Why not?" Randall pressed. "He's the only consistent point maker on your team, and they only need to get to him to affect the outcome, the point spread, at least."

"Randall's right," I said. "A hell of a lot is riding on Helmet, and I don't think serious gamblers worry about the law at any level. Way I hear it, they got a lot of it on the payroll."

"True," Tom admitted, "but I still think it's too early to make a move that would freak him out."

"But what if you're wrong?" Randall persisted.

"Look, they'll call Helmet again, or they'll call Davis or Wheeler or one of the others who handle the ball a lot. We'll *know* if it's a serious threat. Right now we're just guessing."

Peso made his entrance then. "Sorry I'm late, fellas," he said as he straddled the back of Swede's desk chair. "Did I miss anything?"

"Fill you in later, lover boy," Tom said. "Now . . . did you get anything new on the point spread?"

"It's down to Texas by four," he said casually.

"What!" All together.

"Touchdowns!" Peso quickly added. "Four touchdowns—twenty-eight points."

"That's more like it," I said with relief, "but it still means the spread is dropping."

"There's nothing else it *can* do right now," Peso said. "Since that rumor went out about us winning, the betting action has been unreal. The spread will probably get down around twenty before things stabilize."

"We shouldn't even be on the board with those monsters," Tom said.

"You know that, I know that, and every serious gambler in the country knows that," Peso agreed, "but the great sea of fish out there doesn't know that. All the fish know is what they read in the papers and see on the tube."

"And so the suckers are going for it?" Randall asked.

Peso nodded. "By the millions. It looks like a sure bet to them. Twenty, thirty points is a hell of an edge for a team that's supposed to be psyched-up enough to play nearly even. As long as money keeps flowing in on us and the spread keeps dropping, the gamblers' kitty gets larger and the bets get surer. They're gonna clean up!"

"And the better Cajun State's chances seem, the better things get for them, right?" Randall said.

"You're right, Mr. Reporter."

"Then I really fucked-up this afternoon," Randall said flatly. "I played Prosser right into their hands."

Friday

THE MORNING went about like I expected. Instructors, along
with showing appropriate concern for my condition, made a
point of what a hardship the new semester was going to be
without use of my hands. I couldn't write, I could expect depres-
sion and frustration to set in . . . nobody said I couldn't pass their
course, graduate on schedule, but all indicated my grade-point
average was likely to suffer and suggested dropping out a term,
then coming back when I'd regained at least partial use of my
hands, and so forth and so forth.

Carla was her usual supportive self at lunch, assuring me that
we'd work things out. After lunch she left to visit Annie. I stayed
behind to get a handle on my new wonderful life.

The Friday afternoon before any home game was structured
by the coaches to be as boring and uneventful as possible. The
team was isolated in the dorm under the same procedure as
Wednesday, so that Bud and Raymond could keep unwanted
"friends" and "cousins" away from the players. At the same
time players had to give legitimate reasons for leaving the
dorm. Keep the horses in the paddock until the big race—and
no fillies allowed.

Naturally Redshirts were subject to those Varsity restrictions even when they weren't dressing out for the game. It was all in keeping with the coaches' philosophy of making them suffer as much inconvenience and tedium as possible. Tom's counter-philosophy consisted of subverting every such coaching strategy by making the best of each bad situation. Which was why he often spent those empty Friday afternoons entertaining the troops with dumb hoaxes and pranks, at least keeping them distracted from their lowly status and the approaching game.

Normally I spent home-game Friday afternoons in the dorm with Tom and the rest, but I no longer felt a part of that routine. An invisible curtain had dropped between me and all but my closest friends on the team, and very soon even they would be forced to abandon me. I'd lost my functional status the moment I'd wrecked my hands.

After Carla left I spent a couple of hours wandering around a park adjacent to the Cajun State campus. It's a serene, beautifully manicured area, ideal for trying to cope with a troubled psyche. The loss of so many familiar patterns and routines was causing the same numbing disorientations I'd experienced when I hurt my knee, and the same sensation of imminent disaster went with it.

It's difficult to describe the experience of being washed up on the beach of football has-beens. You're suddenly sprung from a comfortably rigid world, from a frozen one-dimensional lifestyle that though occasionally difficult to maintain is seductive as all hell. You can call it born again, but it hurts like the devil. It makes you want to crawl in a hole and hide. The scars run deep. How deep usually depends on when you get knocked into the real world. If a guy taps out after high school or early in college, he's more likely to reorient himself to get a degree and prepare for some other life in the real world. The later you tap out the more disadvantaged you're likely to be with your peers outside football . . . and end up selling cars or insurance even though you've got the brains for something better. What counts is you *think* you're good for nothing else. Football, they say, builds character. It can also cook your brain.

Fortunately I'd been through the separation, courtesy of a wrecked knee, four years ago, and now I knew pretty well what

174

to expect of myself, and the system. I made up my mind, took a deep breath and headed for Dr. Westrum's office in the University Center.

When I arrived at the counseling office Dr. Westrum's secretary told me Sir Henry was already inside signing his scholarship-release papers. It's a nasty business that gets dumped on Westrum because our athletic director, whose job it normally would be, has no stomach for it. Westrum does. Even so, it must be difficult to watch a young man sign away a significant part of his past, and future.

I went back into the hall to wait for Sir Henry so we could meet without being watched or overheard. He'd gone home for a few days of recuperation after Sunday's quitting trauma, and I was glad to know he was back on campus.

"Looks like we're both out of a job now, doesn't it?" I said from behind his back as he came through the door.

He turned awkwardly and I thought it was because his arm was still strapped to his side, but then I saw the tears in his eyes. He looked back at me. "Fuck it, Sage, you've seen me cry before."

"Hey, what's to cry about?" said I with fake cheer. "The worst is over, old buddy. I divorce thee, I divorce thee, I divorce thee. Simple."

"Oh, *man,*" he said, then managed a half-smile. "How're your hands? You know, I've been really fucked up sitting there at home wondering how you guys were doing. . . ."

He seemed determined to get off his own case and I was happy to let him do it. "The hands are going to be fine, but otherwise things have been a six-ten, two-eighty bummer. Be glad you weren't here."

"That bad, huh?"

I nodded solemnly. "The worst. Look, I have to talk to Westrum right now, but why don't you go upstairs and get us a booth? I'll join up soon as I can."

"Fine. Can I get you anything while I'm waiting?"

"A Coke," I said. And then, holding up my hands, "Don't forget a straw!" Joke.

DR. WESTRUM greeted me with his usual vaseline. If he felt anything about what he'd just done to Sir Henry, he didn't show it.

"So tell me, Larry, what can I do for you?"

"I need to know where I'd stand with the Athletic Department if I dropped out this semester and finished up later on. Could I count on any financial help, and if so, how much?"

"I was afraid it might come to that," he said smoothly. "What are you getting now? The usual?"

"Right. Half-tuition, room, books, and meals."

"Well, I have to be honest with you . . . your timing on this isn't too good, Larry. The tuition money you've paid will be refunded if you pull out now, but the Athletic Department money won't. I don't think the director would authorize you coming back under the present arrangement. Maybe we could negotiate for room, books, and meals if you pick up the tuition."

I expected it. The only *real* money the Athletic Department shelled out for an individual was the cost of tuition paid in a lump sum at the beginning of each semester. Dorm rooms were permanently reserved, books came from a common stockpile, and they threw away enough food each day to feed a battalion.

"That's very kind of you, Dr. Westrum, but it's not going to do me much good. I'm going to be getting married soon and what I'm really going to need is a marriage allowance. In addition to the books and meals. Do you think there's any way I could get that if I agreed to pick up the whole tuition?"

That was pushing them and I knew it, but I also knew they knew they'd be roasted alive by the press if word got out that they'd screwed me. I was in the catbird seat just like Sutherland had been when he'd gotten kicked in the balls, and I felt I had to press my advantage.

Westrum nervously cleared his throat. "Well, we haven't really considered you for quite that much compensation—"

"Well, maybe I should point out that one semester's marriage allowance is a small amount of money compared to the goodwill such a charitable act might generate."

"Yes, well . . . let me just check with the director and Coach Anderson about this matter, Larry. Would you mind waiting outside while I see if we can work something out for you?"

"Not at all," I said as I stood up to leave. "And would you check on my rehabilitation while you're at it? I want to make sure there's no confusion about that."

He nodded as he dialed the phone, and I stepped out of the room. I knew my rehabilitation would be no problem for them because insurance policies cover all such therapies. Still, I didn't want to leave it unmentioned. They get forgetful.

I shot the shit with Bernice, the secretary, for about ten minutes before Westrum came out to join us. He was all smiles, so I figured I had it sacked.

"No problem," he began. "I talked to the director and he says he'll be glad to approve your request. He says he'd like to give you the tuition as well, but he doesn't think he could ever get it past the board of directors. He hopes you understand his position."

Fuck him and his position, which was what he'd have liked to do to me and mine. "That's fine with me." I smiled back. "Next time you talk with him, tell him I appreciate his generosity."

I got up and started to leave, but Westrum spoke before I got out the door. "One more thing, Larry. Coach Anderson wants to talk to you. Can you go right over?"

"Not right this minute. Something I have to do first. Tell him I'll be there in an hour."

I spent most of that hour filling in Sir Henry on the week's business.

"It really sucks," he said, "everyone scrambling for bucks over Don's dead body."

"Well, you can be glad you're getting out of it."

"Except I could have used it to get an education. I'm not glad to be losing out on that."

"So where from here?"

"I don't know. They gave me the usual deal—the rest of this semester and all the therapy I need for my shoulder—then bye-bye. My old man dumped me because I quit, I guess I'll get a job and hack it that way. . . . What about you? Where do you go from here?"

"I go directly to Coach Anderson's office without passing Go and without collecting two hundred dollars."

He must have noticed my evasion of a straight answer, but let it pass.

"He wants to talk to me," I added.

"Anderson himself? Any idea what he wants?"

"Could be about Prosser. Yesterday afternoon he saw me talking to those New York reporters I told you about, and a simpleton could put two and two together if he's getting any heat about Prosser."

"Sounds like your ass might be in a sling, old buddy. Want me to go along with you?"

"Nah," I said, getting up. "I just got made a civilian too. Today I am a man."

BY THE TIME I got to Coach Anderson's office I wasn't nearly as cocky as I'd pretended.

"Hi, Larry, good to see you. Have a seat. I hope it wasn't much trouble for you to stop by."

"No, sir," I said as I sat in the proffered chair. "No trouble at all."

"Good, good." Dead air for a moment, then, "How're the hands?"

"Fine, coach, just fine."

"Good, good, glad to hear it . . . say, did you see yourself on television? We all felt as though you did a hell of a job."

"Thank you."

He picked up a pen from his desk top and began rolling it between his hands. Somehow it all reminded me of Captain Queeg and his little steel balls. "Did you get to talk to those journalists enough yesterday?" he finally asked in a still friendly, unaccusatory tone.

My cheeks began to burn as I struggled to the defense.

"Um, yessir, I did talk to them a little, but there really wasn't much I could do without being downright rude. I know you warned us against it, and I'm sorry it happened—"

"No *problem*, Larry, I gave those orders for Dick Biggs's

benefit more than yours. You're intelligent and mature, and I trust your judgment. Biggs is a sincere young man, but I'm afraid he can be manipulated. I didn't want to take any chances."

"Oh."

"Besides, I've known Glenn Novak for years, trust him like a brother. He'd never try to give you a hard time."

They were friends . . . Coach Anderson might as well have been standing right alongside Randall when he tried to snowball those guys about Prosser. . . .

"So I wanted to make sure they had enough time with you," he went on. "They're doing important stories on our game, and I want them to have our full cooperation."

"Yessir," I brilliantly managed.

"Now, speaking of the game . . . did you know we're expecting one of the largest crowds ever to witness a nighttime sporting event in this country? Maybe even in the world?"

What did that have to do with Prosser? I wondered.

"No, sir, I didn't."

"Well, it's true. Now, I understand you've already made some plans to watch the game from the student section with your girlfriend. Is that correct?"

"She's my fiancée now, sir, and yessir, that's true."

I was surprised that he could already know that. Carla and I had only briefly discussed the matter last night, and I'd barely mentioned it to the guys.

"Well, son, we've got a hell of a big problem on our hands if you do that."

I stared.

"Those people are coming to see the ball game first and foremost, but a hell of a lot of them will be wanting to see you too. They'll be very disappointed folk if you're not on the field with us. Not only that, we surely don't want it to seem like you're not still part of the family. You're kind of a symbol to the team now, Larry, and I know you don't want to let them down after all we've been through together this week."

"No, sir, I guess not." I was beginning to get the drift of this and with it was rapidly recovering my composure.

"Good! Now, I'd like to offer my personal invitation to you to take part in everything leading up to and including the game, just as if nothing had happened to your hands. Can we count on you to do that for us?"

I twisted my face into what I hoped looked like a mask of indecision. "Well, I don't know . . ."

"If there's some problem with your hands, I'm sure we can work out anything you need."

"It's not that," I said, still trying to sound worried. "I promised Carla that she wouldn't have to sit alone for this game, and now I have to break my word to her—"

"Would it help if I talked with her?"

"No, I don't think that's necessary. She'll just have to make the best of it and I'll try to make it up to her some other way."

Actually Carla had a clutch of friends she enjoyed sitting with, and *I* was the one not looking forward to watching from the stands.

"Well, I hate to cause any problems for you two young people, but I'm sure you see how important your presence is to the team and the fans. I'm being frank with you about this matter, Larry, and I hope you understand my position."

"Yes, sir, I believe I do."

"Fine. Then I guess that's about all I have for now." He put the pen back in its holder. "Do you have anything you'd like to talk about? The extension of your aid or your therapy or anything?"

I decided to push my luck. "Yes, sir, Coach Anderson," I said in my new civilian voice. "There *is* a personal favor I was going to ask as soon as some of this excitement died down, but I suppose I might as well ask you now."

I thought his smiling features sagged just a bit and that he stiffened slightly in his chair. He was rarely on the receiving end of obligations to someone like me, and the situation must have made him edgy.

"Yes?"

"I'd like you to give Hank Wolf the assistant manager's job behind Stanton. It's the only way he'll be able to stay here, and

I think he'd do a first-rate job for you. . . . I'd really appreciate it."

Anderson smiled at the simplicity of my request, but his natural deviousness made him hedge. "That doesn't sound like too much to ask, but I'd like to think about it for a few days."

"I know what you mean," I said pointedly. "I'm already having second thoughts about facing Carla with the bad news."

"Yes, well . . ." He cleared his throat decisively. "I wanted to ask Cap'n how he felt about it, but I'm sure there's no personality conflict between those two. Tell Wolf the job's his if he wants it. Have him report when his shoulder permits."

"Yes, *sir!* Thank you, sir!" Civilians can afford to be sassy. Especially heroes.

"All right, then," he said, obviously tired of the unnatural exchange. "I guess that's it, Larry," and pretended to absorb himself in some papers on his desk.

I got up, started to leave, then turned back. "One more favor, sir . . ."

His smile went to a scowl, as though to say, Don't mess up a good thing, kid, but all he actually said was, "Yes?"

"Could you open the door for me, coach?"

SIR HENRY was still sitting in the booth where I'd left him, idly tossing sugar packs into a cup and no doubt contemplating his less than bright future. He was flabbergasted by my news.

"Me? A manager?"

"It's not as bad as it sounds, I like to think I've upgraded the profession around here."

"Aw, hey! Fuck me! What am I saying? This is *great!* Sage, how can I ever thank you? Ten minutes ago I could look up at an ant's belly. I'm flying, man . . . really."

"Well, what do you say we fly on over to the dorm and introduce the team to its new assistant manager?"

"Great," he said. "Now I can at least go back over there. I've got a reason."

I envied him. Whether he knew it or not, his best days with

181

the team were just beginning, while mine were clearly numbered.

SIR HENRY and I were halfway to the dorm before I remembered that when Randall dropped me off after the meeting the previous night he and Carla and I had arranged to meet at the Red Lion for supper and then go over to the evening practice session. I hurriedly explained my situation and headed away, leaving Sir Henry to go on happily to the dorm.

Every Friday before a home game, practice was held in the stadium under the lights to familiarize everyone with nighttime conditions. It always started at eight, and consisted of little more than breaking a sweat doing routine things like running down under punts and kickoffs. Our opponents usually arrived at midafternoon and then went through a similar light workout at eight forty-five, so our routine seldom lasted more than thirty-five minutes. If a team wasn't ready to play by the day before a game, additional work wouldn't make much difference.

I figured Carla and Randall must already be inside the Red Lion by the time I got there, but it took several seconds for my eyes to adjust to the restaurant's dimness. Randall was getting up to come lead me to their table when I finally spotted them and waved him back down.

"Hello, love," I said as I leaned over to kiss Carla. "Sorry I'm late. How'd it go with Annie today?"

Randall was helping me into my chair at that moment, and gave me a sharp poke in the ribs. Carla stared down at her plate and said quietly, "I don't want to talk about it right now."

I was familiar enough with that tone of voice to let the matter drop.

Randall changed the subject with, "Hey, what happened to you? You're fifteen minutes late."

"I had a meeting with Coach Anderson."

Randall grinned. "Anderson, eh? Is he already feeling some heat about Prosser?"

Since things were off on a sour note anyway, I decided to give it to him straight-out. "I'm afraid there won't be much heat developing about Prosser. I hate to be the one to tell you, Randall, but Coach Anderson is close friends with Glenn. His exact words were: 'I trust him like a brother.' The only heat to come out of that will probably be directed your way."

"Oh, shit!" Randall said, and then to Carla, "Pardon my French, not to mention my mouth." He slumped back in his chair and stared at the flickering candle in the table's center-piece.

"Would one of you mind telling me what's going on?" Carla asked.

I filled her in as best I could in front of Randall, avoiding laying on any blame.

"It seemed like a great idea at the moment," he said weakly, "but I guess I should have figured they might know each other. Anderson wasn't exactly a slouch before he came here. . . . Aw, what the hell . . . it's only a job, and if I have to kiss that much ass to keep it, they can have the damn thing. Bring on the food! The condemned man ate a hearty meal."

WHEN WE arrived at the stadium at a quarter to seven Sir Henry and several of the Redshirts were already there, having skipped the usual Friday night movie so as not to miss the first pep rally at Cajun in over ten years—rallies are mostly for winners, which we hadn't exactly been.

I quickly got some uneasy-making news from Tom . . . Helmet and Davis *both* had gotten calls toward the end of the afternoon saying their arms and legs wouldn't work too well if they had good games Saturday night. . . . The feds had been immediately called and had gotten together with them after dinner.

"Helmet's taking it pretty good, but we don't know about Davis," Tom said. "You know, I don't think Helmet really understands the implications of this thing—"

Carla started to say something, then held off, clearly biting back an I-told-you-so.

"Well," Tom said, "all we can do is wait and see what the feds say. We should know more after practice . . ."

It was about eight when our team began gathering in the southwest corner exit chute, which was just below and to our right. Yelling and carrying on to psyche themselves up, they finally got themselves together and sprinted out onto the field.

"They sure do sound ferocious," Carla remarked when we could hear ourselves again.

"They always sound like that before they get a look at the other guys," Heape said.

"They look kind of strange too," Carla said, "like something's missing."

"It is," I said, and explained they'd dressed out in regular uniforms but without the shoulder, hip and other padding, which accounted for the big billowy jerseys and baggy wrinkled pants. "It isn't how they look but how they feel—the uniforms give them a sense of game reality even though there's no hitting in the final practice, helps set the tone of having passed the point of no return. Texas, for sure, is going to show up tomorrow night."

Calisthenics were ending, and we settled back to watch the workout, which started badly. Davis and Wheeler bunglod the exchange on the first snap from center. Even though something like that was hardly news under the circumstances, there were several muted "oh, shit"'s from the watchers. Davis was a steady, reliable performer who, even though he lacked exceptional size, arm or speed, handled our roll-out offense better than anybody else that we had. It was questionable whether his back-up, Dee Kimberly, could do the job if Davis somehow got too rattled.

We felt a little better after that, though, when Davis didn't mess up during the rest of the workout, and in fact it now seemed that that first fumbled snap was the center's, Wheeler's, fault. Wheeler was far more high-strung than Davis, and, come to think of it, whoever made those calls to Helmet and Davis showed a lack of knowledge about our team by not working on Wheeler. They couldn't know, of course, that Wheeler was already more shook by the persistent specter of Stoner than he could be by a few threatening phone calls.

Helmet was in typically good form, thank God, booming kick-

184

offs and field goals in stylish fashion, seemingly unaffected by the phone threats. Somehow I didn't quite go along with Tom that Helmet didn't understand what was going down, but it certainly looked as though he wasn't about to let it get to him.

We especially focused on the Bull. His ankle would make all the difference in our ground game the next night, and the ground game—such as it was—had to consistently keep the ball away from Texas to give us any chance of holding the score down. Ball control, with an occasional third-and-long pass, was our only hope of preventing a rout.

The Bull ran like a champ. He had a not surprisingly hard time going left, but he fired out of his stance reasonably well and seemed to have little trouble moving to his right. The Bull was indeed back, and that was good.

"Looks like his ankle's gonna hold up," Tom said.

"Now if they only had Prosser," Randall muttered.

AFTER SOME thirty-five minutes Coach Anderson gathered the team around him. We couldn't hear his words from our position in the stands but it wasn't hard to imagine the gist of them. Last year Anderson fell into the habit of telling the players to go out and "stand like tall pines." One day Helmet suggested, "Coach An-dare-son, should we not for a change be like the stout oaks instead of the tall pines? We are knocked down too easily when we stand as the pines."

We'd stifled our giggles. The coaches looked on Helmet as a disrespectful Kraut water-head, but because of his ability and popularity they let him get away with cracks like that. Anderson had glared at him for a heavy moment and then continued on as if he'd never spoken. In a peculiar way I sometimes even felt sorry for Coach Anderson—Helmet . . . in fact much of the world outside the stadium . . . was such alien territory.

BIG DICK hadn't dressed out with the others and he headed our way immediately after the team left the field.

"What's the word from inside?" Tom asked him.

"You're not ready for it," Big Dick replied with a shake of his head. "Those calls? The feds say it's strictly routine around big games where a lot of money rides. They cover hundreds of threats every year in college and pro ball and no one's ever been hurt for playing full out. They don't publicize the calls for obvious reasons. Don't want to give people ideas. . . . Not only that, the feds got Stoner to come over and tell Helmet and Davis about all the threats *he's* gotten. Davis said he was a nice guy and really put them at ease about it."

"It's enough to make you believe in the tooth fairy, isn't it?" Heape said.

WE STAYED in the stands to watch the Longhorns work out. We should have left when we were ahead. As they began to gather in the northwest-corner exit before taking the field we could see several who filled their uniforms without benefit of pads. Stoner's number "50" stretched across his back without a wrinkle—an awesome presence. When they stormed onto the field with a roar that seemed to vibrate the wooden planks we were sitting on, we looked away.

"I don't want to watch this," Randall finally said as he stood up and headed away.

He spoke for us all.

AFTER THE pep rally we all split up. Tom, Heape, Skid, Sir Henry and the others headed back to the dorm with the Varsity because Redshirts were under Friday's eleven o'clock curfew even when they weren't dressing out for the game. Tonight, of course, they were and went back without complaint.

A senior reporter had been assigned to cover the night's practice sessions, but Randall went along with him to file his story. Carla and I declined the offer of a ride, deciding to walk back to our apartment.

As we started home I realized that this was the same kind of warm, late-summer evening we'd strolled along in a few nights earlier. Carla must have been thinking the same thing, because as the stadium passed on our right she gazed almost wistfully at it.

"Can it only be four days ago that we were in there . . . making love . . . it seems more like four years . . ."

She was silent for a while, then glanced over at me. "Larry, did you notice that nobody mentioned Don tonight? It was almost as though he never existed . . ."

I nodded. "Yeah . . . well, I guess they didn't have to . . . his death is always going to be with us . . . not much point in being reminded of it . . . besides, there's not much call to sell tickets at a pep rally for your own team—"

"You sound bitter," she said.

"Who? Me? No, just something I ate." And couldn't swallow. Carla looked at me, and we walked along in silence for a while. Finally I asked her about Annie.

"Well, in your mood, Larry, maybe I shouldn't, but okay. . . . Do you remember Annie talking about her twin sister Gwen? The one who lives in San Francisco?"

"Yeah, I remember. She and Annie were close, weren't they?"

"The closest. So naturally after the accident Annie wanted Gwen with her. The only problem was that Gwen was back-packing in the Sierras and couldn't get here before Thursday around noon . . . that was why Don's funeral was originally set at two in the afternoon. Well, Annie had the miscarriage early Wednesday morning, but by Wednesday night she was recovering. Then she was told that your precious Coach Anderson had talked Don's father and her own father into moving the funeral up to ten in the morning. He'd told them it would help the team, that it was what Don would have wanted. Can you *believe* he'd have the nerve to say a thing like that?"

"Yeah."

"Well, Annie got terribly upset. She told them no, they couldn't change the funeral time, they had to wait for Gwen, but nobody would listen to her. She got so upset she started hemorrhaging again, and that's when they doped her up so badly. It makes me sick to think about it."

Carla was trembling and wiping away with the backs of her

tightly clenched fists the tears coming down her cheeks.

"How's Annie now?" I asked, carefully placing an arm around her shoulders. "Gwen's there with her, isn't she?"

"It's not enough," she said. "Annie will never forget what they did to her . . . neither will I."

Saturday

I SPENT the morning watching cartoons on television because there was nothing else for me to do, ... and besides I like them. Carla had to teach, and most of the players had to attend classes, so I was left with an empty dance card.

About lunchtime there was a knock on the apartment door.

"Come in," I shouted, "it's open."

Randall. "Hi, pal," he said in a dispirited voice. "How's it going?"

I took one look at him and turned the TV off. He looked like he'd either been up all night or slept in his clothes.

"What's the matter?"

"I've been wandering around most of the night, that's all. They're letting me go."

I steered him to a seat at the kitchen table. "What happened?"

"They're dumping me, that's all. I got the word last night. My try-out period ends in two weeks, and they're not picking up my option. Joke."

"Did they say why?"

"Wrong attitude. Unprofessional . . ."

"You think talking to those guys about Prosser had anything to do with it?"

"I'm sure that's part of it, but what the hell . . . I don't fit in there. It's just a kind of shock to strike out my first time at bat." He smiled. "Jesus, I'm even mixing up my sports metaphors. I'm going to stick with politics from now on. At least you get what you pay for."

"I'm sorry I turned you on to those guys—"

"Hey, forget it . . . it was bound to happen sooner or later."

"Any idea where you'll be going?"

He took a deep breath. "I'm going back home," he finally said. "I'm a fish out of water down here."

"How long before you leave? Not right away, huh?"

"A week or two. No sense putting it off."

I looked at him and realized how much I'd come to like him in the past few days.

"I'm going to miss you," I said. "You're a good man, Charlie Brown."

Ho risked a smile. "You're right, goddammit, I am! It's their loss, right?"

"Fuckin' A, Jack."

I MADE arrangements for Randall to watch the game with Carla and her friends, using the ticket I'd gotten for myself. He went home to get some sleep, and Carla and I went to bed, but not for sleep. Afterward I left for the mid-afternoon pregame meal, the official starting point of the pressurized ritual that leads up to kickoff. Usually only players dressing out for the game are allowed to attend, so my invitation from Coach Anderson was something special.

It begins with a short wait in the lobby area outside the dining hall. Everyone stands around while the food is laid out on the tables inside, then the doors are opened when everything is ready. The pre-game meal is the only one served this way—all others are cafeteria style—because it's the only meal where a set number of people eat at a specified time.

Ordinarily I'd have been inside helping the cooks set the tables and lay out the food, but that was Stanton's job now. Today I stood with the Redshirts in a far corner of the waiting area, feeling as lost and out of place as most of them. With the exception of Heape and possibly Prosser, none of us felt we deserved to be there. We tried a few jokes to loosen up, but only in hushed tones so the somber Varsity players wouldn't hear our irreverence and be offended.

We froze, though, when the coaches strode into the lobby and Coach Anderson spotted us across the room and pointed a finger in our direction.

Without saying a word, Hackler nodded at Coach Anderson's commanding digit and walked over to us. "What are you assholes doing here?"

I knew the others would be even more afraid to speak up than I was, so I gave it a try . . .

"Not you, Larry," Hackler interrupted, "you're supposed to be here. I'm talking about these other ungrateful pussies who take a mile when you give them an inch."

The Redshirts stood around, momentarily stunned into inaction, but Prosser didn't miss a beat. He was on his way out the door by the time Hackler finished speaking, and the others quickly followed. Tom did try with, "No one told us not to come," but Hackler roared back, "Well, who the hell told you *to* come?"

Tom turned and followed the rest.

The rest of the team, of course, saw what had happened, but made the required effort to pretend it hadn't. Redshirts got fucked-over like that all the time.

When Tom finally was out of sight Hackler turned to me, a shit-eating smile on his porcine face, and said, "You're keeping bad company lately, old stick, but you're still welcome at our table."

"Well, thanks just the same," I said politely, "but I seem to have lost my appetite."

Then I did an about-face and walked out after Tom and the others.

NOT KNOWING what else to do then, we all went to the UC for burgers and Cokes. "Goddammit!" Heape said, "they're setting us up."

Skid shook his head. "They couldn't do much more than they've already done."

"The hell they can't, they can let us get over there and then tell us it's all a big mistake, we're not dressing out after all—"

Tom shook his head. "I doubt it. In a way what happened back there was our fault, we took too much for granted. I mean, Don's death may have forced them to dress us out, but it didn't force them to treat us like human beings. We're still Redshirts, gentlemen, and we shouldn't have been stupid enough to forget it."

"Yeah," I said, "the coaches have more important things to do than dream up exotic ways to fuck over a few Redshirts. Their asses are hanging way out for this game, and the pressure on them must be tremendous. I think you guys just got in their way at the wrong time—"

"You really think they're under the gun?" Skid asked.

"Sure. They're caught in their own publicity. They wanted to hype a big crowd and a lot of media coverage out of Don's death, but now it's a double-edged thing . . . they actually have to *produce* something now that they've got everybody's attention."

"But nobody *really* expects us to win, do they?"

"It isn't a matter of just losing," Tom pointed out. "It's more a question of *how* we lose. Put it this way—the coaches have got the whole goddamn sports establishment looking straight up their assholes. If all that comes out is shit . . . well, I wouldn't want to be in their shoes."

Well and colorfully put, I thought. Tom fed me the last couple of bites of my hamburger, then said, "Tell you what, Sage, just to put all our minds at ease, why don't you mosey on over to the equipment shed and make sure we *are* dressing out? Cap'n will know by now."

"What if he says you aren't? You just going to stay here and not report for the game?"

Tom shook his head emphatically. "We've got to report in and give them the satisfaction of screwing us or we'll risk losing our scholarships, but we'll do it on our own terms. If Cap'n says they're going to stick it to us, we'll break out Swede's bottle of Johnnie Walker and go over there bombed out of our fucking minds. The coaches will be too freaked-out over the game to even notice."

As I left for the equipment shed, I half-hoped Cap'n would deliver bad news.

THE GAME crowd was already beginning to gather on campus, so it took quite a while to wade through all the people hassling me about my hands, but I finally made it to the equipment shed. "Cap'n, are the Redshirts dressing out for sure?"

He nodded matter-of-factly. "Yep."

"Did the coaches ever send you a list on the Redshirts?"

"Yeah, they sent it down this mornin'. Quarterback, wingback, and tailback dress out like the Varsity, everyone else wears the old uniforms. I'm sorry, Larry, but there wasn't nothin' I could do for you."

"Hey, that's okay, Cap'n, I know you did your best . . . you got any idea why those three backs are dressing out but not any linemen? Won't you have two Varsity uniforms going unused?"

Cap'n nodded. "That's right, but I got no idea what they're thinkin' up front. All I know is it's gonna be a problem for Tom Everett."

"What kind of problem?"

"Well, when I saw that list I called Coach Anderson and told him I got only two spare backfield uniforms to put on three backs. I asked if he wanted to name a lineman instead of one of those backs, but he said no, put Everett in a line uniform. He gets number 67."

I was standing there trying to make sense out of what Cap'n was saying when I noticed Don's number 42 pinned up and spread out across the back wall like a giant white and blue butterfly.

"Who's gonna wear that one, Cap'n? Heape or Prosser?"

"Neither. That's the one they're gonna be givin' his family at the pregame ceremony."

FOR THE Varsity, the period after the pregame meal and meeting is one of quiet reflection and routine tape jobs. The quiet reflection comes from realizing the game will start in less than three hours, and the routine taping cuts down on training-room traffic once the players start dressing out. It also gives everyone an early taste of preparing for combat.

The taping had already begun in the study lounge by the time I got back to the dorm. Wheeler saw me leave the elevator and left the taping line to come over.

"How's it look outside?" he asked nervously.

"People all over everywhere," I said, "and underneath the stadium is just like at kickoff—kids and vendors running around like ants. They say there's a sellout of 83,000, which would be the largest crowd ever to witness a nighttime sporting event in this country."

Wheeler nodded vacantly and reentered his place in the taping line while I headed down to Tom's room.

"It doesn't make much sense, does it?" Tom said after I told him and Swede what I'd found out. "Except for the part about giving away Don's jersey. I'm surprised they had brains enough to think of that."

"Good ink," Swede pointed out, "they'll get damn good ink for doing it."

"But why do Heape and Prosser dress out for real," Tom went on, "and why do I wind up in a fucking lineman's uniform? Why not dress all of us the same, or at least put a lineman in the lineman's uniform?"

"Why not *three* linemen in the three linemen's uniforms?" I added. "Or you and Heape in the good uniforms instead of Heape and Prosser?"

"Maybe since we're weak at running back and Davis might be shook up," Swede said, "they might be dressing out a couple extra just in case. People get hurt against teams like Texas."

"You've got to be kidding," Tom said. "They're not going to use a quarterback wearing a lineman's number 67. . . . Look, even if Davis did get rattled by that phone call there's still two guys ahead of me. Same with Prosser and Heape. The odds on any of us playing are like the sun rising in the west."

AT SIX o'clock the team and its attending personnel gathered in the dormitory's ground-floor lobby for the traditional quarter-mile walk to the stadium. Lined up like a small military unit —twenty ranks of four abreast—we moved out across campus for what was usually a six or seven minute trip, but today it was very different. An incredible number of fans and well-wishers lined the route, pounding us on the back, offering advice and encouragement ("Give 'em hell, son!" "Kick some Longhorn ass!"), until finally I had to protect my hands by bracing my elbows against Skid's shoulders to form a pocket between his back and my chest.

"Son of a bitch!" Skid muttered as we squirted into the fenced-off area near the locker room. "Your hands okay?"

"Fine." I nodded, "they're just fine." They'd been bumped several times, but the pain hadn't been too bad. I did notice, though, that the bandages felt loose on the backs, which meant the swelling was probably starting to go down. I made a mental note to contact Dr. Yarbrough tomorrow to have them checked and rewrapped.

Skid went over and got in the Redshirt equipment line while Varsity players poured into their dressing room. Varsity uniforms are laid out in the player's cubicles before a game, including the "roll" of towel, T-shirt, socks, and jock. The displaced Redshirts had to pick up their own rolls and uniforms before going to get dressed in the weight room.

I went into the Varsity dressing room and looked around. Even though there was still plenty of time left to get ready, the disrupted schedule seemed to have panicked everyone. An important part of a player's pregame preparation was the half-

195

hour wait before Coach Anderson's order to "strap it on," and they all seemed to be hurrying out of their clothes in order to start waiting that much sooner.

I eased back out, conscious that I was the only person in the room without a specific reason for being there, and felt a new sense of isolation as I watched Cap'n and Stanton scurrying around in the equipment shed. I knew they were gathering and arranging the spare-part tray that would be carried to the sideline for the game. Preparing that tray used to be one of my jobs.

Then I remembered there was somewhere I could go and not feel so out of place. Turning, I walked the fifty-odd feet to the weight-room door and rapped on it with my elbow. Someone pushed it open and I stepped into the dim room and asked what seemed a reasonable question.

"What happened to the lights?"

"There's no lights in this fucking hole," Heape snapped in obvious frustration.

The weight room was a converted storage area with no lights of any kind. I was surprised I'd forgotten that.

"We can make do with the outside light coming in through the windows," Skid said quietly. "It's not so bad once your eyes get used to it."

Other than having no lights, the weight room was a small, barren area with two Universal weight machines bolted into the dirty concrete floor. A phalanx of mirrors lined the walls, making lights unnecessary on even the cloudiest days. The top two feet of the western wall were windowed, so reflected sunshine provided all the light needed for *daytime* workouts. Since the stadium was always locked at night, nighttime facilities weren't normally an issue.

As my eyes adjusted to the dimness I began to see that most of the Redshirts were standing motionless with blank looks on their faces, apparently not yet reconciled to the baseness of their temporary quarters.

"Standing there staring at it isn't going to change anything," I said. "Why don't you all just go ahead and start dressing out?"

Some of them made shuffling, aimless movements then, and another problem quickly became apparent. There were small piles of equipment scattered around the room—helmets, shoulder pads, hip and girdle pads, knee and thigh pads, and shoes —but no indication who owned what pile.

"Hey, Brenner," a voice called from a far corner, "this looks like your stuff over here. Don't you have a torn decal on the left side of your helmet?"

"Doesn't Morton wear a size 34 girdle?" another asked. "I think this is his."

"Who has peace symbols in his thigh pads?" Chuckles. Weak ones.

And so it went until Vin Newbert, the first to remove his shirt, announced angrily, "There's no fucking hooks in this place, we have to leave our clothes on this filthy goddamn floor—"

"Just fold them neat and put them on your shoes," Skid advised smartly.

"Jesus, Skid," Heape snapped, "you can make me sick, you know that?"

Most of the other Redshirts were reaching Heape's level of frustration, and I couldn't blame them . . . whether by design or not, they were being humiliated to the point where dressing out lost damn near all its value.

"What's the drill after we get dressed, Sage?" Tom asked, wisely trying to move beyond the immediate situation. "We sit in the Varsity room or stay here or what?"

I was surprised they hadn't at least been told that much, but I was grateful for the opportunity it gave me to be of some use.

"I don't know," I said, "but I can go back up front and try to find out."

"Good, old buddy," Tom said, "and if you see the concierge up there, tell him I want a word with him about the accomodations."

THERE WERE still no coaches in the Varsity dressing room so I decided to stay until one appeared. I looked around, noting the various stages of pregame preparation, and wondered if the atmosphere had ever been more nerve-racking.

Step one: putting on the jock, socks and T-shirt from the roll.

Next hip pads, whether the old strap-on kind (favored by line-men), girdle pads (running backs), or two additional knee pads over the hip bones and held in place by the jock strap's waist band (wide receivers and defensive backs). Pants followed, complete with knee and thigh pads in position. Few players have the nerve to play without thigh protection, but a lot of defensive backs disdain knee pads. I've never understood that, but then I'm particular about knees. . . . Shoes come next, together with the ritual that goes with them. A football player's shoes are one of his few safe outlets for a little individualism. Players cling to individual taping patterns, or shining methods, or lacing techniques as mute self-reassurance that they still exist as human beings in their otherwise look-alike uniforms. . . . The final piece of basic pregame waiting uniform was the game jersey, put on as in the Friday practice without shoulder pads underneath. The players stayed that way until forty minutes before kickoff, when Coach Anderson came in and told them to "strap it on." Which meant to put on the shoulder pads and helmets and get ready to take the field for warmup drills.

The sound of someone throwing up in the toilet area meant The Wait had begun for real. . . .

The Varsity dressing room is long and relatively narrow, with the toilet and shower area jutting off the side wall opposite the player's cubicles. There are two alcoves on either end of the shower toilet complex, with quarterbacks and tailbacks in the one nearest the training room and marginal players in the far one. A portable blackboard is always placed in the quarterback alcove, and I was standing near it when Coach Merritt, the receiver coach, came out of the adjacent training room.

"Coach Merritt," I said, moving to block his path, "what are the Redshirts supposed to do when they get dressed? Do they come in here, or what?"

He looked puzzled for a moment, then said, "Can I get back to you on that, Larry? I don't know a thing about it."

Merritt wasn't the worst of coaches, so I said "Okay, fine, I'll check with you later."

I rejoined the Redshirts in the weight room and reported what had happened.

"Great," Heape said, "I bet those fuckers forget about us and we spend the whole goddamn game sitting on our asses in this dump. . . ."

SEVERAL REDSHIRTS were dressed and ready to go by the time I went back up front. There was now less than an hour before kickoff, and I knew three or four assistant coaches would be in the quarterback alcove going over last-minute details on the blackboard. Sure enough, Coach Merritt was there with three others, and I had no trouble catching his attention.

"Go tell the Redshirts not to worry about warming up," he began. "Coach Anderson doesn't think they're familiar enough with the routine, and he doesn't want those old uniforms making it look like a Chinese fire drill out there. Tell them we'll send for them just before we take the field for the kickoff."

The first reason was pure bullshit—every player is familiar with warmup routines—but the Chinese fire drill angle seemed fairly legitimate. Two different uniforms *were* going to look strange, so it made sense to minimize their exposure.

"What about the guys dressed in the Varsity uniforms?" I asked. "They're dressed out like the others."

Merritt shrugged in exasperation. "That was mostly Coach Marshall's idea. If he wants them out there, I'm sure he'll let them know. Now, is that all?"

It was obvious I was pushing him too far, so I said, "Yes, sir," and left.

THE REDSHIRTS were not really surprised or even disappointed at having to miss the pregame warmups, but they did wonder about Coach Marshall's reasons for dressing out Tom and Heape and Prosser like the Varsity.

"I think Grant's case is pretty easy to understand," Tom began.

"Is that so?" Heape said. "Then explain it to me."

"Marshall does respect talent. Everyone knows if it wasn't for Rabbit you'd be on the Varsity right now, and I'm sure he plans

199

to give you a shot next year after Travers graduates."

"So he's dressing you out as a gesture of encouragement," Skid added. "He wants to be sure you don't quit on him."

Tom nodded. "That's what I'd do if I was him."

"Okay, then," I said, "so that explains Grant. Now, how about you, Tom? No offense, but I doubt you figure too large in their plans for the future—"

"In a way I do, I made myself sort of useful . . . maybe it's paying off."

We all knew what he meant. It's not easy to find an ex-high school star who's willing to submerge his own style to imitate accurately each week's opposing quarterback. And even when the coaches *do* find someone like that, it's almost impossible to keep him around. Nearly everyone gets discouraged and quits after a year of that kind of thankless work.

"All right, then, that leaves Pete," I said. "Again, no offense, Pete, but I guess you're the least likely candidate of all."

Prosser was sitting against a wall, eyes closed, in that sometimes infuriatingly relaxed way of his, and, typically, said nothing.

"This may sound crazy," I said, "but could Marshall be throwing his weight around to get back at Hackler for fucking up the Bull's ankle?"

"Makes sense. Marshall's not the kind to let something like that pass without a counter-punch," Skid said.

"And there sure as hell's not much that could piss Hackler off more than seeing Pete get a break," Heape finished.

Everyone, except Prosser, nodded in agreement.

We decided I should spend the pregame warm-up period with the Varsity and make sure the Redshirts weren't accidentally left behind. Ten minutes before kickoff, the last thing a coach was likely to think of was a handful of misplaced, ragtag-looking scrubs.

Tom stood up and spoke for them all. "Look at this fucking clown suit."

He was right. His lineman's uniform was designed for a two-hundred-pound-plus body, and Tom was a skinny-looking one seventy. The pants went down to the middle of his calves, the jersey fit like a tent. Maybe in his case the coaches did mean well, but they'd have done better to give him a decent fitting old uniform instead.

"Sweets to the sweet," somebody said, and nobody laughed.

ANDERSON, HACKLER and Marshall spent the pregame waiting period in Trainer Hanson's office at the back of the training room. At this point the only worthwhile function they served was staying out of everyone's way.

Unlike the Redshirts, Varsity players were still without shoulder pads when I got back up front, but I knew Anderson would soon leave Trainer Hanson's office to tell them to get ready, so I made a last quick tour of the room.

"How about it, Ken? How's the ankle?"

The Bull looked up and nodded. This wasn't exactly a time for heavy conversation.

"Quink? How's it going?"

"I'm taking Don's place in the wedge, man," he said gloomily. "Mother-crammer . . ."

Which meant he'd be one of three up-backs on the kickoff receiving team, lining up between the six front linemen and the two deep-backs. It was trench duty on the bomb squad.

"Who's in the center?" I asked. The center man of the three was the point of attack, and he usually got the holy shit knocked out of him by opposing linemen trying to break up the wedge.

"Duggan, thank God."

Dave Duggan had been moved up off the Redshirts to third-team fullback after the accident. He was a good choice for center man on the wedge—burly, a good blocker, slow and totally expendable.

"There's always a silver lining," I said as I turned away. "Swede, Peso . . . you guys ready?"

"Fuckin' A," Peso said firmly, and then in a whisper, "as long as we don't get sent in."

Swede started a tight-lipped grin, but it died fast.

Wheeler, like most of the others, was lying on his back on the floor below his locker.

"How about it, Jimbo?" Of all the players to be tested tonight, everyone knew Wheeler faced the roughest challenge. His efforts against Stoner would largely decide our success up the middle, and if we didn't control some of the middle . . .

Wheeler looked up at me with dilated pupils. "I took some speed," he said.

Oh, shit! I thought, then squatted down beside him so no one could hear us.

"Have you ever done it before?"

I knew lots of guys who took amphetamines for a boost, but they always got the feel of the drug at practice before they tried it out in a game. I'd never known Wheeler to take anything stronger than coffee.

He shook his head. "I just couldn't stand the thought of facing him without some help, Sage. He'll rape me!"

"Do you know what to expect from it?"

"They say I'll feel real strong and won't get tired, but I may be a little confused at first. Is that the way it is?"

I nodded. "That's it." Jesus

He took a deep, shuddering breath and said, "Wish me luck."

I gave him a tap on the shoulder.

"You got it."

And then Coach Anderson's voice rang out behind me.

"All right, men, strap it on!"

WITHIN FIVE minutes everyone was dressed for war. Players were banging on each other's shoulders and heads, all the while emitting prehistoric roars and growls of intimidation. A terrifying scene if you don't recognize it as simple posturing.

Players pushed and shoved and crowded together at the exit door, as if unable to wait another second before leaping out to devastate everything in their path. The whole display was orchestrated for the benefit of the coaches who, after spending nearly an hour in that tiny back room, needed reassurance that their team was "ready." As soon as Anderson said, "All right, everybody outside!," the volume level dropped to near-zero and the players politely filed out the single door.

The walk from the dressing room to the entrance chute
. . . the cool, clean evening air strikes you first, then the noise
of steel cleat-caps scraping on concrete drowns out everything
else. You round the corner and enter the area under the stands,
and the fans down there begin to notice and cheer, some call
out your name, others encouragement. . . .

As the first players enter the chute people in the stands begin
to notice. A small cheer goes up followed by more as more and
more people realize what's happening. You look up from the
chute and see thousands of people, an ocean of them, and you
stand awash in the warm sound. You soak it up and swell with
it and you feel you're at the core of whatever brought them
together. To be part of that core—no matter how insignificant
your role—only football gives you that. Take away those heady
moments of swollen self-satisfaction and you couldn't get
lobotomized gorillas to take part. *With* those moments you
have every man (and probably many women) in the stands
wishing there was some way he (or she) could be down there
with you.

Standing there in the chute, looking around and feeling that
familiar supercharging adrenalin rush, I realized how much I
was going to miss all of it.

AT COACH Anderson's signal the team streamed from the
chute, into the end zone, under the goal post and onto the field.
Anderson hadn't been far off the mark when he'd predicted a
record crowd. As I walked out onto the field behind the team
I tried to spot empty seats in the stadium's upper reaches; there
were none to be seen. And the crowd noise! Not even pro games
produced that kind of pandemonium here.

I took up a position next to Trainer Hanson as the team lined
up for the calisthenics. He began to shout something up at me,
so I bent down to put my ear close to his mouth. I still couldn't
hear above the crowd's roar. Suddenly he grabbed my wrists
and pushed my hands up over my head, and the noise level
went even higher. Then I understood what he was trying to say
. . . a lot of the noise was for *me*. . . .

I felt stripped naked, nearly overcome by a crazy urge to run out of there. Finally Hanson dropped my hands and the noise subsided. And then within seconds there was another roar, and my heart began to race again with that strange sensation I'd just experienced as I spotted the Longhorns making their own entrance down at the northwest chute, and I was taken over by a chilling realization: my own shot at the brass ring was past me now. This was the last of it.

DURING THE warmup drills Davis looked sharp and confident in his movements, Wheeler showed no ill effects from the upper he'd taken, the Bull refused to limp in front of his opponents, and Helmet boomed kicks while the Longhorns stole secret glances at him. Our players spent their free time tracking Stoner and McElwee, Texas' all-American split-end, and whichever other individuals they knew for certain they'd face head to head. The drills ended at seven forty-five, and both teams quickly went back to their respective locker rooms.

That final period before returning to the field is spent in a flurry of last-minute equipment adjustments and trips to the head. It ends with the get-one-for-the-Gipper pregame speech. I spent the prespeech time getting the Redshirts ready to join the Varsity at the proper moment, then went back up front to catch Coach Anderson's remarks.

"Men," he began soberly, "I know you've all probably gotten pretty sick of me saying how important this game would be for us, but all you had to do was look up in those stands to see how right I was. You're going to be making sports history tonight because the game is an official sellout, and I hope you appreciate what that means . . . it's a once-in-a-lifetime opportunity for each of you to make your *mark*. I only hope you'll be willing to take advantage of it.

"Now, you're as thoroughly prepared as any team can possibly be for a game like this . . . you're ready to play. I've been in this business for a long time, and I *know* when a team is ready. You've had some hard knocks this week—as hard in one instance as I hope you ever have to endure—but you've come all the way back from that and you have the opportunity to turn it to your own benefit.

"We all know I'm talking about Don Slade, so let's bring it on out in the open. Don is what this whole game is about. Don Slade put those people in the stands and those reporters in the press box, but now the burden passes from him to you. Each and every one of you has an obligation to him to sacrifice yourselves the way he would have sacrificed if he were still with us today, and each of you will be ashamed the rest of your lives if you don't—just this once—give yourselves up totally to the greater cause . . . the dedicating of this game to his memory.

"Now get out there and give us some good, solid football and come in here at halftime with something Don would be proud of. What do you say, men? Will you get after 'em?"

Anderson, never a slouch, had done it just right. I'd never seen anything like it. After three or four seconds of stone silence, a roar seemed to erupt from every man in the room. Guys leaped to their feet and went crazy, pounding themselves, each other, the walls, anything in their way. I've never seen a team emotionally higher.

I'd had the foresight to take up a position near the door, so when the team finally gathered its senses enough to start heading for the field I was the first person to step outside. I hurried down to kick the weight room door so the Redshirts would know to come out and join their elite teammates. I hadn't mentioned the Redshirts to anyone since I last spoke to Coach Merritt, so I wasn't sure whether the coaches had assigned someone to go fetch them or not. I wasn't taking any chances.

Regardless of what was intended for them, the Redshirts blended smoothly into the stream of Varsity players that poured out of the dressing room. Even the ones wearing the old uniforms were in the chute and visible to the crowd by the time the coaches joined the team for that quick jog to the sideline. As far as I could tell, the coaches were too preoccupied to care *who* was with them now.

THE CEREMONY for Don was simple, moving. His older brother, Steven, represented the family and explained to the crowd that neither Don's parents nor his wife were recovered enough from the shock of his death to attend the game, but he thanked everyone for coming and promised to relay the warmth of the impressive turnout. After that our Athletic Director presented Steven with the number 42 jersey Don would have worn and the letterman sweater he would have won. At the same time he announced that for the rest of the season the team would wear a new game jersey with a black left sleeve bearing Don's number. A short prayer followed, then 83,000 people became totally silent for sixty seconds.

I have to admit the whole thing seemed tastefully enough done, but a jersey, a sweater, and a minute of silence aren't much of a tradeoff when you stop and think about it.

WE LOST the toss and elected to defend the north goal because a light breeze was blowing in from that direction. Conditions were ideal: the field was immaculate, the air cool and clean, the stadium a tense sellout. When the "Star Spangled Banner" was played, I felt chills. It may seem a boring ritual on television, but not from the floor of an arena seconds before combat begins.

Our kickoff unit took the field and lined up as the referee handed the ball to Helmet and Rabbit counted noses with a flourish. The absolutely least demanding position on our team was safetyman on the kickoff unit. For other teams it was a position of serious responsibility . . . kickoff safetymen trailed down the field behind their teammates and were the last line of defense when the other side broke the return. In our case, Helmet put ninety percent of his kickoffs in the opponent's end zone, so there would very likely be no returns for Rabbit to deal with this season. It was a situation designed by the hand of God to satisfy Rabbit's old man and keep the coaches riding in their new Pontiacs.

The whistle blew and Helmet approached the ball with his sidestepping soccer motion. There was a solid thunk as his foot made contact. The game was under way.

The Texas deep-backs had lined up on the goal line to receive the kick and so had no trouble drifting back under it as it came down in the end zone. The left side deep-back, number 37, caught it but elected not to run it out. Texas' ball, first and ten at their twenty.

Their first drive took four minutes and eighteen seconds to score. I was surprised it took that long. They executed their plays so well, it seemed as if we hardly got in their way. That smoothness and precision showed why they were number one, and it showed the kind of night we could expect against them.

While the Longhorn drive was in progress I wandered up and down the sideline, tense, excited. After the Texas score I went back to midfield and found myself next to Wheeler as the Longhorns lined up to kick their extra point.

"How about it, Jimbo? How're you feeling?"

"Only 4:18, man? Only 4:18? It seems like *forever*, doesn't it?"

"Yeah, right, but how do you feel?"

"Fine, fine, I'm all right! I feel strong and good, but everything is so fucking *slow!* I want to get *out* there!"

The ball went cleanly through the uprights and our kick-off return unit took the field.

"ALL RIGHT!" Wheeler suddenly screamed to the heavens. "LET'S GO BIG OFFENSE! LET'S TAKE IT TO 'EM!"

There was no doubt that he'd taken enough speed to get crazy. I only hoped he could handle it his first time out.

TRAVERS AND Colter were our deep-backs on kickoff returns, and Travers took that first one at the five with a full head of steam. He got right behind the wedge and they plowed out a path to the twenty-seven, where number 89 for Texas made the stop.

Meanwhile, Hackler had gathered the defensive line around the communications table, and I eased over there while the offensive unit took the field. The communications table was located at the fifty and stood five yards from the sideline. It was covered with microphone headsets so the coaches could maintain instant contact with observers in the press box. Hackler had a headset on and was shouting into its mouthpiece. "Goddammit, did they seal or pinch on the inside trap? That's all I want to know!"

There was a momentary delay, then Hackler glared at Craig Bonham, the left defensive tackle. "He says they pinched!"

Bonham steadfastly shook his head. "It was a seal, coach, I'm sure of it."

Hackler tore the headset off and flung it on the table. "Fuck it! Play to the inside if they give you air either way . . . they won't go outside till we stop 'em up the middle . . ."

I got back to the sideline just as the offense lined up over the ball. Our first play was always called in the dressing room before the game, so I knew this would be a slam-dive between left guard and center. Wheeler and the Bull were going to double-team Stoner while Lawrence followed their block with the hand-off. A lot always depended on who could establish initial dominance in the line, but an extra measure rode on dealing with a player of Stoner's caliber.

At the snap Wheeler fired out and drove his face mask square into Stoner's chest. Stoner met the charge with a forearm shiver that got under Wheeler's chest and seemed to hit his abdomen, while the Bull slammed into both of them to carry out his part of the block. Though not really moved out of position, Stoner was neutralized and Lawrence blew by him for a five-yard gain.

"All right! All right! All right! Way to hit in there, big offense! Way to stick!"

The sideline went wild at the success of our first offensive play. Then we saw Wheeler weaving back and forth on his knees and trying to struggle to his feet.

"Hancock!" Coach Marshall called out. "Hancock, get your ass out there!"

Sandy Hancock had been last year's starting center, but as is often the case, someone with equal talent and a little more enthusiasm had come along to roll him off first team. Though much depended on how badly Wheeler was hurt, Hancock was being given one of those rare chances to reestablish himself.

Wheeler was on his feet by the time Trainer Hanson waddled out to him. Hanson, with his special pride in being the picture of controlled efficiency, never made a hurried movement to help anyone. Which was why all our players wore mouthpieces and dreaded collisions violent enough to make them swallow their tongues. They knew they'd be turning blue by the time Trainer Hanson arrived.

Wheeler jogged off the field after a whiff of an ammonia cap broken under his nose and Marshall met him at the sideline.

"What happened, son?"

"Got the wind knocked out," Wheeler replied shakily.

"All right," Coach Marshall said as he patted Wheeler on the rump. "That was a good block, we got five off it. Shake off the injury and go back out for the next series."

Wheeler nodded and headed for the bench.

WHEELER'S INJURY seemed to set up our offense. That kind of thing can take all the air out of your sails if it's serious enough, but this one had a galvanizing effect. Wheeler had met Stoner head-on and left the field under his own steam, and that somehow rendered the Longhorns less invincible.

We scraped out a first down at the thirty-eight, then they measured for another at the forty-eight. We were grinding it out so slowly that the referee was reaching for a delay-of-game flag each time Hancock snapped back to Davis. Nevertheless we were getting just enough of our blocks and they were missing just enough of their tackles to let us pick up three or four yards a crack.

On first and ten after the measurement, Davis took the snap and moved left. Stoner took an immediate cross-step to his right because we'd been running straight hand-off dives up to that point. As soon as Davis pivoted back and handed to the Bull up the middle, Stoner must have known he'd been had. He made a lunging-backward move attempting to refill the hole he'd vacated, but Hancock was already there sealing to the inside. Hancock fired into Stoner's off-balance position and knocked the monster flat on his ass. The Bull bolted over center, cut left around a safetyman and picked up nine yards before a closing cornerback nailed him.

The beauty of the play got to us, as did seeing Stoner knocked down for the first time. Not only were we looking like a real football team, we had second and one at the Longhorn forty-three! Getting into their territory on our first drive was an achievement none of us had dared to hope for.

Coach Anderson grabbed Del Stevens, a second-team guard, and yelled above the noise, "Screen right! Screen right! Everybody *block!*"

Stevens sprinted out and relayed the call. The Bull faked a play similar to the one he'd just run, and Stoner held his ground up the middle. Lawrence, meanwhile, had swung right on a fake pitch, which left him alone in the right flat to receive the screen pass.

Davis got the ball out a little high and behind him, but Lawrence pulled it in and looked upfield. He had Stevens and Dan Watterman, the two guards, ahead of him, and Moe Polaski, the right tackle, on the way to help, but the Texas cornerback and safety were closing fast from upfield. Then Stevens took the cornerback outside and Watterman took the safety inside, and Lawrence was left with nowhere to go but between their blocks.

Stoner had gotten into the pursuit flow as soon as the Bull had come through the line empty-handed, and was bearing down now on Lawrence with all the speed his muscular bulk could generate. Polaski, our biggest and best offensive lineman, planted his near-equal bulk directly in Stoner's path to seal off an outside alley for Lawrence.

Stoner must have sensed the setup, because instead of evading Polaski's block in an attempt to make the tackle, he grabbed the initiative and became a blocker himself, blasting into Polaski's chest in a move that was totally unorthodox and unexpected—and completely successful.

Polaski had prepared himself to deliver a blow instead of receive one, so he flew backward into the air like a giant piece of kindling off an ax blade. An incredibly loud *"Uh!"* went up from the crowd as Polaski's flying body cut Lawrence down at shoulder height like a scythe cutting a shock of wheat.

Lawrence had already turned his attention away from

Polaski's assumed block, which left him unprepared for the blindside blow he received. The ball popped from Lawrence's stunned grip and bounded into the Texas secondary, where their offside safetyman had little trouble falling on it for a successful fumble recovery. As Lawrence and Polaski untangled themselves and shook away the cobwebs, their confused look symbolized for us all the certain knowledge that Stoner was indeed a breed apart.

The magnitude of that kind of disaster takes more than a moment to sink into the victim's consciousness. While the recovering team bounds around gleefully and quickly makes its way off the field, the offensive victims stagger off in shock. Levels of frustrated energy have to be dissipated on the sideline instead of in combat, and the defense is also thrown out of sync. They have to reenter the battle with little or no chance to gear up emotionally, and that inverted state often leads to disaster for them as well. If a 2:38 drive for a score can be seen as a disaster, then Lawrence's fumble led to one for us.

WE WERE down 14 0 and there were less than five minutes left in the first quarter when Wheeler went back out at center for our second offensive series. Even though Hancock had done an admirable job against Stoner on the first drive, Wheeler would be given the right to reassume his starting role.

Our first play of the second series was a trap over center. Davis faked a dive to the Bull over right guard to pull Stoner to his left, then whirled back and handed off to Lawrence up the middle. Wheeler and Watterman cross-blocked, with Wheeler knifing left to intercept Watterman's man while Watterman pulled right to execute the trap block on Stoner.

Stoner took the Bull's fake and stepped left, Watterman kept him from refilling the hole while Lawrence headed into what looked like a good opening. Unfortunately, Wheeler missed his block and number 74 for Texas nearly stole the hand-off. Lawrence was tackled for a two-yard loss and the coaches blew up.

"What the fuck happened?" Marshall screamed into a headset. "Was seventy-four offsides?" He waited for an answer from the spotters up in the press box, then looked over at Anderson. "Wheeler missed him clean, coach. Slow off the ball."

Coach Anderson kicked the ground but quickly composed himself.

"All right!" he shouted between handclaps, "this is the one! Let's get 'em this time!"

The next play was a fullback sweep right, the same play that had killed Don. The Longhorns were playing second and twelve a little loose, so the Bull got seven yards before being tripped up. Wheeler got a barely decent cut-off block on the tackle who'd beaten him on the previous play, but it seemed to appease the coaches for the moment.

On third and five we tried a play-action pass, but Texas blitzed Stoner. Wheeler completely missed Stoner's charge and let Davis get creamed for a four-yard loss that would have been worse if Stoner hadn't hit him so quickly.

As the punting team went on and the offense jogged off, Anderson and Marshall closed ranks to confront Wheeler.

"What the hell's the *matter* with you, Jimbo?" Marshall said. "Are you *scared* of those boys?"

Wheeler hung his head and seemed not to understand what was happening.

"Answer him, son," Coach Anderson said menacingly. "Are you afraid?"

"No, sir," Wheeler insisted, "I just can't seem to get off the ball properly. I can *see* what's happening and I *know* what I'm supposed to do but my body won't work right."

Anderson and Marshall exchanged arched eyebrows. Players never gave intelligent or truthful answers to explain their failures, normally answering accusatory questions with "Yes, sir" or "No, sir" and let the chips fall. Wheeler's straightforward answer was a tribute to his befuddlement.

"Sit it out till half time," Anderson said curtly.

EVEN THOUGH the score denied it and most observers would never realize it, we played some of the best football I'd ever seen us play through the next few series of downs. We were having the standard isolated breakdowns that most teams suffer on every play, but our patented wholesale fuck-ups were being kept to a minimum.

Texas also revealed something interesting throughout that period: they seemed determined to avoid looking like complete assholes by stomping us into the ground. Their coaches knew they were in the national spotlight right along with us, and it wasn't hard to figure how many ranking votes they'd lose by running the score up on us. After all, how impressive is it to kick a bereaved family when it's down?

At any rate, after notching touchdowns the first three times they had the ball Texas put their second team in the game and left them there. Ordinarily even their second team would be more than a match for our first units, but it was a decent contest as long as we played so far over our heads.

Late in the second quarter, though, with the score at 21–0, the Longhorn substitutes put on a drive that seemed sure to score again. I was standing near midfield as they crossed our thirty, and it was just after that when I noticed Coach Marshall grab Coach Anderson by the arm. Marshall motioned toward the communications table and indicated a headset, so I casually walked over and back to eavesdrop.

"I think we ought to put him in if they score this time," Marshall said. "The Texas kicking team is loafing down now and he can break one."

Coach Anderson didn't acknowledge verbally, apparently listening to the report from upstairs in the press box. Then I heard the headset go down on the table followed by Anderson's voice.

"Tell Wade to come here," he said flatly.

In a matter of seconds Marshall had brought Hackler to Anderson, and the three of them stood talking just a couple of yards behind my back.

"Wade," Anderson began, "I'm going to put him in on this return if they score. We'll be down 28–0 and it will only get worse if we don't do something to fire our people up."

"Dammit, T.K.," Hackler shot back, "playing a bad apple like him is a *mistake*. . . . It'll be just like that fucking Kraut. He'll undermine respect for us with the others, and we won't be able to touch him . . . no, it's not worth that sacrifice, I don't care *how* you rationalize it—"

"Look, Wade," Anderson went on, "I'm sorry you still feel so strong about it but Paul and I are outvoting you on this one. We played it your way as far as we could go, so now I expect you to play it our way. Do you understand me, Wade? We're in a unique situation here and—principles or not—we have no choice but to break precedent . . ."

I heard a grunt and a noise that sounded like someone kicking the bench or the table or something, then Coach Marshall's voice came rasping through the crowd noises.

"Goddammit, Wade, quit being such a fucking sorehead . . . listen to what they say upstairs—he can break one and get us back in this ballgame, and I'm not gonna risk my job because of your lousy grudge. . . ."

I heard nothing for several seconds, so I risked a glance sideways. Marshall and Anderson were several yards to my left, and Hackler was down the right sideline, yelling at his defense to keep Texas out of our end zone.

TEXAS WAS at our fifteen with a second and seven as I hurried into position alongside Tom. I jabbed him with an elbow and motioned for him to move back away from the sideline so we could talk in relative privacy.

"Can't it wait?" he asked. "I don't want to miss the score."

I looked at him as intensely as I could.

"It's a fucking bombshell!"

He gazed back at me for a moment and then shrugged in resignation, but his eyes stayed on the field as he stepped back with me.

"This better be good," he grumbled as we reached a relatively isolated spot near the bench.

"Prosser's going in for the kick-off return after this touchdown."

Tom's head snapped left to look at me, his face a picture of disbelief.

"*What?*" It was like hearing proof-positive that there *is* a Santa Claus.

"You heard me. I overheard Anderson, Marshall and Hackler just a minute ago. The gist of it was that the score is getting out of hand and they realize their jobs may be riding on the outcome. They hope Prosser breaks a return to give our guys a shot in the arm."

"Oh, Jesus, that's perfect!" Tom said as the logic of it began to sink in. "If they only use him as a specialist—like Helmet—it's less a concession to his attitude . . . why didn't I . . ."

His words were drowned out by the crowd's roar as Texas fumbled at our eight and we recovered.

"Oh, *shit!*" Tom and I blurted without thinking.

We were both upset because we knew Prosser might have lost his shot with that fumble, but several guys near the sideline in front of us turned around and gave us dirty looks. I could only think to smile weakly at them, but quick-witted Tom was on top of the situation.

"Sorry!" he called out. "From back here it looked like Texas recovered!"

As our offense sprinted out to take possession and the defense came off the field, Tom looked at me. "Do you think Anderson will go ahead and put him in when Texas scores again?"

I shrugged. "I guess we'll have to wait till the second half to find out."

THE OFFENSE had worked the ball out to our forty-five by the time the first-half clock ran out. The crowd gave both teams a polite round of applause as they jogged off the field, but a pall had been over the stadium since the middle of the second quarter. Even though, by our standards, we were playing inspired football, Texas was ahead of us by three touchdowns and no amount of crowd encouragement could change that fact.

Halftime procedure begins when the players file into the dressing room and find ice-cold cans of Coke on the floor in front of their cubicles, which they sit down to drink while waiting for the whole team to file in and get settled in a similar fashion. Talking is allowed—boisterous if we're winning, subdued if we're not—until the coaches make their appearance.

Surprisingly, by the time the team was assembled in the dressing room and waiting for the coaches, it was evident that most of them felt no sense of gloom. Except for Wheeler and a couple of other victims of extreme misfortune, they seemed pleased by their first-half performances. The 21–0 score was taking second place to the purity of their efforts, and I was glad to see that they hadn't completely lost the capacity for self-congratulation.

Meanwhile, the coaches were outside analyzing the team's first-half effort and collating opinions to help Anderson form a strategy for his halftime speech. Of course, coaches perceive a game from an entirely different reality standpoint than players, which means they're rarely able to give a head coach sound advice. So whether he tried to be abusive or encouraging or any combination in between, Coach Anderson almost never came into the dressing room on the correct wavelength. This time was no different.

He and the other coaches moved inside with frightful scowls of anger, apparently convinced that a tongue lashing was all the team needed to close the twenty-one point gap. I don't think the incongruity of their attitude was lost on any of the players, but all reacted correctly: smiling faces went blank, heads dropped in feigned shame.

Perhaps in an effort to leave no doubt about his own fabricated mood, Coach Anderson hit on a dramatic illustration. He spotted an unopened Coke can still standing on the floor and savagely kicked it toward the other end of the room some fifty feet away. Whatever his proposed halftime strategy had been, he ended all hope of achieving it when he kicked that can of Coke.

In the far right-side corner of the dressing room stood a large metal garbage container. Sure enough, whether directed by existential will or dumb coincidence, the can tumbled end over end all the way across the dressing room and landed squarely in the container, producing a metallic clang astonishingly loud in the otherwise silent room.

Nearly every eye had been on Anderson when he executed that kick, and every eye must have been on the Coke can when it disappeared into the garbage container. Of course, players in the target area had maintained the closest watch until they were sure it would land in an unoccupied zone, but by and large the takeoff, flight, and landing had held everyone in the room mesmerized; everyone, that is, except Helmet, who was sitting directly adjacent to the garbage container when the can rattled home. Without missing a beat, he leaned over and looked inside as if officially to verify the sanctity of what we'd all just witnessed. Then he calmly looked back out over the room and, with every eye on him, threw both arms upward in the classic referee's signal that a kick has been successful.

It brought down the house. One by one, the players began to choke and sputter, struggling to keep from laughing out loud, while the assistant coaches turned away to keep their reactions from being seen and interpreted as disrespect toward Coach Anderson. Their efforts proved unnecessary, because as soon as his initial astonishment faded, Coach Anderson burst out laughing, and that set us all off. The people standing outside the dressing room must have been amazed to hear a team down 21–0 laughing like that. When we began to regain some composure, Coach Anderson raised a hand for silence and quickly got it.

"Men," he began, "I'm glad we were all able to share that moment just now because it brings out something we, as coaches, often tend to forget. Football is supposed to be fun. It's good to remember that every now and then, because if you don't have fun at something you just can't do it very well. That doesn't take away from the importance of winning, but it gives our situation here tonight a different perspective than I'm accustomed to admitting. We're getting beat, men, the score tells us that. But we're not getting our asses whipped! We're playing the best goddamn football I think it's in our capacity to play, and I'm proud of you for that.

"Now, I had intended to come in here and tell you that since Texas scored twenty-one points and held you to none in one half, there was no reason why you couldn't go out there and do the same to them. Well, I'd still like to see that happen, but let me just ask you to go out there this half and play as hard and as tough as you played the first half. Do that and I'll be as proud of you as I am right now, and the score will take care of itself."

Randall was right when he said Coach Anderson was no slouch. The man sure knew how to adapt.

NEARLY ALL the rest of halftime was spent going over technical details with individual coaches, and relieving oneself between rounds of such talks. Since the Redshirts and I had little to do except stay crammed into the far alcove and keep out of everyone's way, Tom and I were two of the first people into the toilet area after Anderson's speech. Tom had already had to help me piss several other times, so we were long past feeling embarrassed about it.

As I stood at the urinal with Tom at my side, Wheeler came in and knelt down in front of a commode. He gagged once, then again, then stuck a finger down his throat and deftly emptied his stomach. Tom shook the dew off my lily and zipped me up, then we went over to Wheeler.

"You okay, Jimbo?" Tom asked.

Wheeler nodded, got to his feet and made it over to the sink to rinse his mouth, then took a deep breath before turning around to face us.

"That pill fucked me up," he finally said. "I had to get it out of my system if I could, that's all."

I felt genuinely sorry for him because he was too late on two counts: First, the drug had gotten into his bloodstream soon after he took it, and now the best he could hope for would be a rapid dissipation of its effects. Second, he'd already lost his first-team job and had next to no chance of getting it back unless Hancock was seriously injured.

No matter his excuse, Wheeler had folded when the chips were down and Hancock had come through. Now Wheeler's only hope was to stay second team until Hancock graduated at the end of the year. He'd have to be lucky, though, very lucky, to have any chance of working himself back up in the spring.

WHEN THE referee stuck his head in our dressing room door and said, "Five more minutes, coach," everyone stopped what they were doing and gave Anderson their attention. For the last time before rejoining the battle he went over the routine trivia of our game plan—a litany he'd recited hundreds, maybe thousands of times.

"All right, men," he began, "what are the things we want to always remember out there? We want to go all-out on every play and give it one hundred and ten percent effort at all times. We want to be first off the ball on both offense *and* defense . . . you can't be a winner sitting on your dobber. We want to drive through our blocks and lock our arms on every tackle. We want to punish the runner and not stop hitting till he's down or the whistle blows. We want to play the *ball* on pass defense— not the man. And, lastly, we want to concentrate on all phases of the kicking game because *it's there the breaks are made!*"

That last quote is a staple in football but not without basis, so Coach Anderson always gave it special emphasis. This time it led into the blockbuster announcement he'd planned earlier out on the field.

"Now, speaking of the kicking game, we're going to be receiving this half and we've made some changes in our return formation and personnel. Coach Marshall has the details. Coach."

Marshall, standing at the blackboard, quickly drew a diamond pattern of zeroes while the players exchanged furtive glances. Changing a formation like that was almost always the result of injury or back-to-back fuck-ups, and our kickoff-return unit had sustained neither. Consequently everyone except Tom and I had a perfect right to be confused by such a breach of procedure.

"All right," Marshall said as he turned from the blackboard to face the room, "we're changing from the standard two-three box we've been using to this one-deep-three-up configuration. We want a seven-man front line with Rodriguez added on in the middle. Duggan, Thompson and Johnson stay as the wedge. And Prosser goes back here in the key."

You could almost hear the silent reaction—Prosser! Is he serious? Holy shit! Football players are trained from day one to accept almost any dicta from coaches with no outward sign of reaction, so there was not even a blink as Coach Marshall went on:

"Do any of you have any questions about how to execute the one-three diamond return?"

No one had.

"All right then. Now, we're doing this because we think we have a solid chance to break one and get ourselves back in the ball game. The spotters upstairs tell us Texas is loafing down on their coverage, so let's go out there and cram it down their throats. What do you say, men?"

The team sent up a roaring "All right!" and then clambered out of the drooing room with what seemed like even more noise than before. They all knew that if an opportunity to break a kickoff return did indeed exist, no one had a better chance to pull it off than Prosser.

As I stood watching the team file out, fired up by its new enthusiasm, I wondered if Randall and Carla would appreciate Prosser's chance for vindication as much as we did. Because I was one of the last people out of the room, I know for a fact that Hackler did not.

My fondest football memory will be the look he gave me when I passed him on my way out and asked him, "Coach, do you think his sore back is going to slow him up?"

WHEN I got back out to the sideline I saw Wheeler sitting on the bench, his head in his hands. I knew he'd somehow gotten the word about being permanently demoted and I wished there was something I could do for him, knowing that at least for a while there really wasn't. Besides, the kickoff teams were lining up and I didn't want to miss the return.

We were defending the south end this quarter, so I looked to my right to watch Prosser and the others preparing to receive the kick. Prosser had gone through a rush warmup session along the sideline as soon as the team got back on the field, but now he seemed ready and was in position along with everybody else on the return team.

The Texas coverage unit was lined across the field along their forty-five as their kicker placed the ball in the tee at the forty. All kickoff units—Texas' included—cover kicks from the same basic ten-abreast-with-one-safetyman pattern. The field is divided into straight-ahead lanes, and each player is responsible for protecting his own lane until the ballcarrier commits himself to a specific direction, at which point they leave their lanes and converge for the tackle.

Opposing the coverage unit is the return unit's front line and its wedge. The front-line members try to disrupt the pursuit pattern by knocking holes in it, while the wedge is usually responsible for trying to clear one or more adjacent lanes in the middle of the field. Even when kicks are deliberately returned down the sideline, the wedge rarely leaves the middle.

Its members drift back under a kickoff and then come together several yards in front of the deep-back who receives it. From there they have the unenviable job of turning upfield to try to knock holes in the pursuit wall after it's passed through the front line's blocks. Those defenders are coming downfield under full throttle, and in turn are trying to flatten the onrushing wedge in order to stop the runner tucked in behind it. The situation creates the most consistently violent collisions in all of football, so it was no wonder that Quink, Duggan and Johnson were twitching and pacing nervously as the Texas kicker raised his right arm to signal that he was ready.

Prosser stood centered on the five yard line with his arms folded across his chest as the referee's whistle blew, and then he dropped into a slight crouch as the kicker started moving his way. With the wind at his back and a good foot into it, the kicker got the ball all the way down to our goal line. Prosser drifted back under it while Quink, Duggan and Johnson hurried back to form the wedge in front of him. They were all proficient blockers, so Prosser had a decent array of firepower leading him when he gathered it in and headed upfield.

As the wedge turned and began plowing straight down the middle of the field, Prosser hit the ten yard line and veered sharply to his right. It seemed a senseless move at first because there were no more than twenty yards separating him and the Texas defenders when he bent away from his escort, and, true to form, as soon as he made the move to his right, all the Longhorns began to sweep in that direction. The ones nearest him began to break stride and get themselves under control so he couldn't blow past them, while the ones on his left began to stretch out in an attempt to get to him. When it seemed certain he'd blundered into an inescapable trap, he knifed back to his left.

When Prosser had first cut to his right, the Texas defenders to his *left* naturally relaxed a bit, and that moment's relaxation created gaps in their assigned lanes as some rushed ahead of others and some bent too sharply toward the ball. As soon as he stepped back into the teeth of their sweep, the gaps were apparent to everyone. A gasp went up from the crowd as they recognized the moment of possibility. Prosser had picked his spot and shot through it before the gasps could turn to cheers.

While the wedge and everyone else were blocking their asses off up the middle, Prosser was streaking down the sideline in front of our bench with nothing but seventy yards and the Longhorn safetyman in front of him. We were all going absolutely crazy—even the coaches—jumping and screaming and marveling at the beauty of what we were watching.

I think the groan from the stands registered on us before what we saw did. We had all completely discounted the Texas safetyman because, even though he had an unbeatable angle on Prosser, we all knew Prosser couldn't be stopped one-on-one in the open field. That's why we were so shocked when he was. The safetyman had gone straight to the cut-off point somewhere near the Texas thirty, and Prosser met him there as cordially as could be imagined. No wrinkles, not one fake; just two people running to the same spot and then colliding.

Scattered booing and catcalls began as Prosser got up and

jogged back to the sideline. Coach Marshall met him in an absolute rage, demanding to know what the hell he was trying to prove. Prosser didn't say a word. He brushed his way past everyone, sat down on the bench next to Wheeler, and proceeded to concentrate on the ground beneath his feet.

THERE WASN'T much time to dwell on Prosser's actions. We had first and ten at the Longhorn twenty-eight, which was by far our deepest penetration of the night, and we seemed certain to get at least a field goal out of it.

To everyone's amazement, Texas stayed with its second-team defense while we went all the way for a score in seven plays. The Bull would not be denied and looked tremendous on the drive, slashing and hammering for those tough goal-line yards. We could hardly believe it when Helmet kicked the extra point and brought the score to 21–7.

Our satisfaction at having scored was characteristically brief. Texas put their studs back in on offense after the kickoff, and they lost no time starting to cram it down our throats again. I was wondering if we'd be able to hold them for even four or five minutes when I felt a tug at my elbow.

"What's with Prosser?" Tom asked.

"He tanked it."

"I *know* he tanked it. Do you think he's going to tank the next one, too?"

"Could you blame him?"

"You're damn right I could . . . let's go talk to him."

Prosser was still on the bench where he'd gone after his run, but Wheeler had moved away. He was staring out at the action on the field as Tom sat down to his left and I moved in on his right. No response to our presence, so Tom began speaking in the polite tone that somehow seemed appropriate when addressing Prosser.

"Pete," he said, "we'd like to talk to you a minute . . ."

Prosser continued staring at the action on the field.

"Listen," Tom charged ahead, "are you planning to tank every return like that last one?"

223

Prosser slowly turned to face him. "Redshirts are supposed to do it wrong the first time, *every* time. I'm doing what I've been taught."

He turned away then to look back out over the field.

"Hey," Tom said, "you've got every right in the world to pay them back for all they've done to you, but just remember one thing, Pete. You're reflecting on every Redshirt who wants to move up some day, and you're not giving any of us much to hope for."

"God knows you don't owe anybody anything, Pete," I added, "but the Redshirts are the closest things to friends that you've got out here. This is one time you can't screw the coaches without screwing them too."

His gaze stayed on the field. Tom was just opening his mouth to try another tack when Prosser suddenly spoke up.

"Save it," he said softly, "I heard you."

"Then you'll think about it?"

Silence made it obvious that Prosser had said all he was going to say. And a graceful exit was possible when Texas scored and we could turn our attention to the field in response to the crowd noise.

If Prosser did consider what we'd said, he didn't have much time to make up his mind. It took about a minute for Texas to kick their extra point, and seconds later he was jogging back out to receive his second kickoff of the night.

WHEN ANY coverage unit has a kickoff broken against it, it's extra-careful next time out. Heads roll after back-to-back long returns, so the Texas defenders were understandably determined to maintain proper lanes as they swept downfield toward Prosser.

The ball dropped in at the ten, five or so yards to his left. He gathered it in with a fair degree of forward momentum, then cut sharply right to get behind the center wedge. Instead of stopping when he got behind his escort, he continued driving to his right in an apparent repeat of his earlier effort. The

Longhorns on that side reacted as before, breaking stride and bringing themselves under control, but the offside defenders didn't repeat their mistake. Instead of lengthening their strides and moving toward Prosser, they maintained proper spacing and alignment. As a result, when he cut back left as he'd done before, he faced a solid wall of defenders ready to repay him for their earlier embarrassment.

He was also ready. He'd taken no more than three steps left before he again cut back right, and that movement brought him into perfect, centered alignment behind the heels of the wedge. A quick burst brought him directly behind his convoy as it blasted into the three Texas defenders who'd been left to guard the middle by their flank-conscious teammates.

Again crowd reaction was only moments behind the action on the field. A huge groan went up as the contact took place near our thirty, but the anguish just as quickly turned to joy. Duggan and Prosser had survived the collision and were still on their feet, with Duggan in the lead and Prosser clinging to the back of his jersey. You couldn't tell if Duggan was pulling or Prosser was pushing, but like tandem stampeding horses they were heading toward the fast-retreating Texas safetyman.

By the time he'd backpedaled to the fifty, the safetyman must have known there'd be no angles to play this time. Whichever way he committed himself, all Prosser had to do was cut the other way and be gone.

The safety had a hole-card, though, which he played at the forty-five. Instead of taking Duggan on an angle and hoping for the best, he faked left and then dove at Duggan's ankles. Prosser, unfortunately, had stayed glued to Duggan's back, and the safetyman's move caught them both by surprise. As Duggan tumbled over the prostrate safety, his feet slashed back and knifed Prosser's legs out from under him at the Texas forty-three.

The abrupt termination of that apparent touchdown run brought new groans of dismay from the stands—and the sidelines. Still, this time it was much less clearly Prosser's fault, and he'd given us good field position for the second time this half.

Everybody realized that it could have happened to anyone. Except most of us knew damn well that Prosser wasn't just anyone.

OUR DRIVE was stopped at the Longhorn twenty-seven, at which point Helmet came through with his first field goal of the season. Actually, I was relieved we only got three points because it meant Texas might still leave their studs on the bench with a 28–10 lead.

As we lined up to cover our own kickoff, Texas shifted its return to the one-back-three-up diamond we'd used against ~them the last two times. It looked like they intended to give us back our own, but they ran a secondary reverse instead and caught several of our guys out of position. In typical fashion, Rabbit failed to react normally to what they were doing, and so wound up in perfect position to make the tackle. The last thing I saw was Rabbit sailing waist-high into the Texas return-man near our sideline at their thirty-five.

Everyone near me was so blown-out by the crisp efficiency of Rabbit's tackle that we looked at each other in disbelief instead of down where Rabbit and the Texas man had tumbled out of bounds. By the time we refocused on the game, Texas was preparing to run its second play and someone was calling for "stretcher." As the one normally responsible for responding to such requests during a game, I was particularly attuned to that word. The stretcher was always folded and lashed under the communication table, where Stanton was already ripping it loose from its bindings as I came over. "What happened, Chris? Who needs the stretcher?"

He finally yanked it loose with the surge of panicky energy I'd felt so often. "Rabbit hit a down marker . . . broke his leg." And then he was gone.

I hurried over to see for myself. Sure enough, Rabbit was still on the ground with a blanket thrown over his legs and his left arm covering his eyes (trainers encourage that because, they claim, shock often isn't so severe if the victim can't actually see his injury).

Bud, the assistant trainer, told me what had happened. "The chain man didn't get out of the way in time. Somehow the down marker replanted when they hit and Hayden's ankle wrapped around it."

"It broke his ankle?" If so, it could be much more serious than a cleanly broken leg.

"Yeah, he tore it up pretty bad. It's dislocated and twisted backwards . . . my guess is he'll have to hang it up like you did."

I went back to midfield to tell Tom what had happened. He looked shocked for a moment, then shook his head. "Wouldn't you know it would happen the one time he finally does something right?"

"Yeah, and it wouldn't have happened if he'd been out of position like everyone else. Out of position for the *right* reason."

Tom nodded. "You figure this means the coaches lose their Pontiacs?"

I let it pass, Tom was entitled to a little bitterness. "Well," I said, motioning toward Heape, "as one career ends, at least so begins another." Heape had finally made his long-awaited Varsity status.

"True. Should we tell him now or let him find out on his own?"

We watched Heape edging toward where Rabbit was being strapped onto the stretcher. "I think he already knows," I said.

As I'd hoped, the Texas second team went back in on offense after Rabbit's score-saving tackle, but we were no longer able to hold out against them. We'd given it all we had for nearly three quarters, and had finally run out of gas. Their second team drove down the field as efficiently as their first, and they scored with the same apparent—and by now monotonous—ease. The only light at the end of that tunnel was the prospect of another kickoff return by Prosser.

"You think we should go have another chat with him?" I said to Tom. "I couldn't tell if he tanked that last one or not."

"What good would it do? He already knows how we feel.

Besides, they won't kick it anywhere near him."

Sure enough, the Texas coaching staff took no chances on another long return by Prosser. Their kicker laid the ball flat on the tee and kicked a squibber that barely reached our wedgebacks. Quink tried to scoop it up on a short hop, bobbled it, then fell on it at our thirty. Prosser didn't even get close enough to throw a block.

TEXAS STARTED substituting even more frequently when it became apparent we'd shot our wad; we played against their third string the entire fourth quarter. It wasn't a dull quarter, really. There were several good plays, some adequate drives and even a few stick-out individual efforts, but it looked like Texas was content to let the score stand at 35–10. To tell the truth, we were grateful for their charitable intentions and were happily preparing to celebrate a bona-fide "moral victory" when Lonnie Fulton, one of our second-team safetymen, shook everything loose with a jarring tackle.

There was 1:29 left on the clock and Texas was grinding out one last drive against us when it happened. They had third and five at our forty, which was the longest third down they'd faced in the series. Their quarterback decided on a quick slant to the flanker, who was split left; an easy, routine pass play. The flanker took two driving steps off the line to get Ferragino, the cornerback, moving backward, then cut sharply to his right and looked for the ball.

The pass was on target but high, so the flanker had to leave his feet and stretch out to get it. Lonnie arrived just as the flanker's feet touched back down, and he didn't flinch or even lower his head. He put his face mask right on the ball and smashed squarely into the flanker's chest. The pass was such a surprise and the lick so brutal, the impact noise went up into relative quiet. People had started filing out midway through the previous quarter, and I'd guess there were only fifty thousand left in the stadium when the two players collided.

A slow, rumbling roar began as the ball popped high into the air—perhaps as much as fifteen feet—but we had no one even close to it except Lonnie, who was lying stunned on the grass. The Texas tight-end was running a clearing pattern from right to left, and that put him in perfect position to continue his route and recover the airborne fumble. He caught the ball in full stride as if it had been intended for him all along, and then had nothing to do but set sail for a thirty-five yard cruise into our end zone.

I've forgotten his name—Marston, Hairston, something like that—but I remember his number, 84, running down the middle of the field like the hounds of hell were after him. And because he was just an adrenaline-soaked third-teamer playing in his first college game, he made a play I'll never forget.

As he caught the ball and took off, the crowd cut loose with a tremendous roar, the loudest since Prosser's last run. The noise seemed to startle number 84 into believing someone was on his tail, because he immediately lengthened his stride and— in defiance of one of football's cardinal rules—looked back over his left shoulder to try to spot his imagined pursuer. That combination of movements threw him slightly off balance, and he began a slow, agonizing forward lean.

The obvious remedy would have been to ease up, regain proper balance and then sweep on into the end zone, but the crowd noise deceived him again. As soon as his stumble became apparent, the crowd roared even louder at the mistake and, misinterpreting the noise as confirmation of imminent danger, he refused to waste even a moment to right himself. Instead, he continued his excruciatingly slow forward incline, and made it worse by trying to glance over his right shoulder to see his phantom pursuer.

When number 84 hit the fifteen, our closest defender was still ten yards behind him. Of course by then his running angle had tipped over to sixty or seventy degrees, and the only issue was whether he could make it into the end zone before falling flat on his nose. As it worked out, he couldn't. A small cloud of chalk dust went up as his left knee hit the ten yard stripe, and he ignominiously plowed to a halt with his head nearly touching the five. A final roar went up from the crowd as he came to rest, but it was a roar of derisive laughter, the kind you hear when someone makes a fool of himself in front of fifty thousand people.

There wasn't much compassion along the Cajun sideline. We'd taken it in the ear too often too long. Besides, number 84's choke was a real stunner, and we kept giggling like idiots while Texas drove in for the score. Afterward we noticed the crowd gradually quieting down, and felt a new tension take over the people as the kickoff return unit got back on the north end of the field, and Prosser moved up to the fifteen in anticipation of a flat-ball kickoff.

THE CLOCK read seventeen seconds. The score was 42–10. The Longhorn kicker signaled ready. The whistle blew and he kicked another squibber that went twisting and bounding toward our up-backs in the wedge. Again Quink was there to stop it, but this time he got a decent hop and was able to field it cleanly. Then, with no hesitation, looking just as if he'd been practicing it all his life, he turned and shoveled a crisp lateral to a surprised Prosser. No one, least of all Cajun State's sideline, had expected him to get another opportunity to run, but there he stood, stockstill at the twenty, the Texas defenders bearing down on him.

At first Prosser seemed unable to decide what to do . . . the return pattern was shredded, he had no organized help. He took a tentative step to his right, but the Longhorns on that side immediately broke down and got themselves under control. He stepped back left and that side broke down as quickly as the other had. He took one more stagger-step to his right, and must have realized he was trapped.

Prosser then headed straight upfield, obviously out to squeeze as much yardage as he could from a tight situation. Two big rangy defenders pinched in on him from either side. He didn't bother trying to take them, just ducked his head and drove forward as the two men crunched into him at the same instant.

Sometimes, more often than you might imagine, the physics of a collision allows a runner to undergo violent impact with

230

little damage. When the two Texas defenders slammed into Prosser from opposite sides, he had ducked into a crouching position directly between them. As their bodies crunched into his and their helmets met just above his back, the combined force they created was enormous. It criss-crossed through his body and knocked both of them off him as if they'd touched a twenty-thousand-volt cable. Each defender had hit with near-equal impact, so that Prosser's body became nothing more than a conductor of straight-line physical forces. Of course, if their heads had met *on* his body instead of over his back, he would have stood free for a moment and then slumped forward, probably with some broken bones. As it was, both players simply bounced off and left him stumbling forward through the first wave of defenders.

Still, there wasn't much to be said for Prosser's prospects after that first collision, even though he'd come out of it on his feet. Duggan had gone down on a block, Johnson was in the process of throwing one, Quink was out of the play after fielding the ball and the front-line men were scattered everywhere after throwing their first blocks. Nevertheless, he somehow found a gap to his right and started heading straight for our bench.

One of the interesting things about football is that sometimes nearly everyone sees and reacts to situations in the same way and at the same time. In this instance we all saw number 24 for Texas coming on from the left as Prosser drew a straight-ahead bead on the sideline trail-man, and we started shouting above the crowd noise, "Blind side left, blind side left!"

Prosser must have heard us because he immediately turned his attention from the trail-man in front to number 24 at his left. He had less than a second to react because number 24 had already lowered his head for contact, but his move astonished everyone. Somehow he managed to jump high enough into the air to let number 24 pass beneath his feet and at the same time spin 180 degrees to wind up facing the center of the field instead of our sideline.

The Texas defenders had begun sweeping toward our bench when Prosser committed himself to that direction, but his dramatic mid-air twist now left him facing directly against the grain of their flow. And that put them all in the same vulnerable positions he had exploited on the first return. Only the safety-man, who had already proved his abilities when he'd stopped Duggan and Prosser in the open field, maintained a perfect defensive position.

Prosser hit the ground and sped into the teeth of the coverage just as he'd done before, but this time there was no opening wide enough to slip through. Number 72 had him bottled up-field to his right and number 63 had the lane to his left, and neither seemed out of control in their pursuit. Prosser saw it and slowed abruptly. Understandably he seemed frozen, except for a lean upfield toward number 72's looming grasp.

About seven yards from number 72 Prosser suddenly grasped the ball with both hands and faked a basketball chest-pass di-rectly across number 72's path. It was a child's playground trick, the hokiest fake imaginable, which is probably why it worked. Number 72 instantly reacted by accelerating his speed and jerk-ing his hands out to intercept the bogus pitchout, and that automatic reflex created all the room Prosser needed.

The Longhorn went steaming by completely out of control and only inches from Prosser's right side. It reminded me of bullfights, and Prosser's skill and courage did indeed compare favorably to matadors toying with enraged bulls. Anyway, by leaning in so close to number 72, he'd also escaped the out-stretched arm of number 63 on his left, which put him free at our forty-five with only the Texas safetyman, number 10, be-tween himself and the goal line.

Prosser now bolted straight at number 10, who reacted by drifting into the controlled backpedal he'd used twice before. Obviously he wasn't the type to plant his feet and leave himself open to a hip-fake. Prosser sized him up for a few strides, then cut left. Number 10 immediately mirrored the move by cutting to his right. As soon as number 10 took his cross-over step, Prosser cut back right, and number 10 had no option but to mirror that move as well.

The gap between the two was rapidly closing, so that when Prosser cut *back* left he was no more than five yards away from

232

number 10. As number 10 turned back to his right to counter Prosser's move, Prosser darted forward and performed his most outrageous maneuver of the night. He grabbed the back of number 10's jersey the same way he'd grabbed Duggan's on the earlier run, and for a moment it looked as if number 10 was leading interference for his opponent.

The safetyman's surprise couldn't have been much greater than ours. We'd thought we knew what the man was capable of. We were wrong. We were watching a genius perform. From the stands it may have seemed more luck than talent, but every player on both sides of the field knew what they were seeing.

As soon as number 10 realized what had happened he whirled to his right, but Prosser shifted left behind his back. He twisted left, Prosser shifted right. And all the while they were moving toward the Texas goal line. Finally number 10 wrenched back to his right in an apparent repeat of his first futile effort, but halfway through the move he dug his heels into the ground and shoved backward into Prosser. He was standing on his own twenty-three and facing his own end zone when his brilliant counter-offensive caught Prosser unprepared. Prosser was in the middle of a corrective cross-over step when number 10 slammed backward into him, and it was impossible to avoid a collision. The only problem for number 10 was that he had no way of locking his arms around Prosser's legs to seal the tackle. He scrabbled desperately behind his back for something to hold onto as he fell, but Prosser's luck held. He was able to bounce back a step and keep his feet away from number 10's thrashing arms.

It seemed as if every person in the stadium was screaming his alarm as Prosser staggered to regain his balance. The defenders and several of our guys had maintained a steady pursuit of Prosser and number 10, whose collision had delayed Prosser long enough to give everyone at least a chance to catch him. Now it was a twenty-yard dash to the end zone, and it quickly became apparent that Prosser was running out of gas. The pursuit pack's lead-dog was number 47, and when Prosser hit the ten it seemed certain he'd be caught from behind. I started cursing bitterly as number 47 reached out his right arm and dove at Prosser's back, and there were thousands of groans as contact was made.

Maybe it was possible from the stands to see what was happening as Prosser bent away from our sideline toward the far corner of the field, but I know that from the bench there was no way to see what was developing in front of the screen of players strung out behind him. At any rate, whether he set it up or not, Prosser managed to lead number 47 directly into Quink's path.

Somehow Quink had crossed the field and then circled from the off-side in an attempt to intersect the pursuit angle, an effort that made it possible for him to pick number 47 out of midair just as the man's arm was about to circle around Prosser's neck. As the two bodies crashed to the ground behind him, Prosser had only five yards to go, which it seemed clear were just about all he could manage.

Our sideline went crazy when Prosser finally did cross into the end zone. Even after watching it we found it hard to believe that one of our own could have completed such a magnificent, improbable journey. I didn't see what happened right afterward on the field because I was swamped by leaping, screaming, pounding players who forced me to move back to protect my hands. Later I found out that Prosser had dropped to his knees in exhaustion, rolled the ball toward the trailing official, and then was smothered by teammates. I'm sorry I had to miss that part.

When the sideline had calmed down some and the field was being cleared for our extra-point attempt, I saw number 10 jog over to Prosser and offer his hand in congratulation. Prosser looked at his opponent in surprise before giving the hand a shake, and I suddenly realized that Prosser's ability was finally out of the closet. It was sweet satisfaction to hear the thunder from the stands as Prosser jogged toward our bench. I wonder if *he* heard it.

THE CLOCK had run out sometime during Prosser's run, so there was nothing left of the game except Helmet's extra-point attempt, which he laced through with no trouble. Final score: 42–17. As bad as we'd been beaten, it was a finish none of us had dared hope for.

I can't recall my exact thoughts as I jogged across the field, but several images will always be with me . . . people swarming all over the field, more than any I'd ever seen after any game I'd ever been part of . . . the scoreboard's light shining beacon-like through the stadium's upper-level haze of mist and smoke . . . Coach Anderson and the Texas head coach meeting at midfield, uncharacteristically friendly, obviously happy, as though they too realized something special had been shared this night. . . . But most of all I remember Prosser surrounded by dozens and dozens of kids wanting his autograph, begging for his chinstrap. And I remember Tom trying to fight his way through that crowd to reach Prosser after Prosser had called out to him and asked for help. *Prosser had asked for help.*

THE VARSITY dressing room was like no loser's dressing room I'd ever seen before. It was as if we'd just won the biggest victory of our lives, and no coach dared pretend it wasn't so. There were no big postgame speeches or prayers or anything. Only Coach Anderson made a brief statement:

"Men, you gave it all you had and I'm as proud of you as I can be. They're the best and they deserved to win, but you've got nothing to be ashamed of. Go out, have a good time tonight, no curfew. Practice at four o'clock tomorrow in sweats. Come out prepared to get ready for Mississippi State!"

Cheers rattled the windows as Anderson moved on into the training room to begin his postgame sparring with reporters. He was going to have a hell of a lot of explaining to do about Prosser—particularly to the out-of-town reporters, who hadn't known anything about him before tonight—and I suspect he knew it. I wondered how he planned to go about making it all sound plausible.

Two reporters Anderson didn't have to deal with, though,

were Glenn and Dave, the big-time sports columnists from New York. They seemed in no hurry to crowd into Trainer Hanson's back office with the local fry, preferring to drift around the locker room on the hunt for quotes.

"Hey, Larry," Dave called out when he saw me standing near the far alcove. "That's as much heart as I've seen in a long time . . . lotta guts in this room."

"You can say that again!"

"Hey! And that Prosser kid! I'd say your friend Randall had *him* pegged just right. Glenn called T.K.'s hand on what Randall told us about Prosser being a secret weapon and all, and T.K. verified it. He said they'd been wanting to Redshirt him to fatten him up a bit, but if they got very far behind . . . well, you saw it just like I did. Anyway, they weren't shitting us. That kid can be a *great* one before he graduates."

"For sure." Like always, T.K. had known how to adapt.

"Hey, and those smug cats in the pressbox, it would have done your heart good to have seen them after that last run! They were fucking pale, man."

He grinned happily. "And when that German kid kicked the extra point, they died. . . . It's great to see high-rollers lose their asses every once in a while, keeps them human . . . well, I gotta go give the Texas side a tumble. You be sure to catch our piece. We'll have some good things to say about you too."

"Will do, Dave, and thanks—"

"Sure thing, buddy. You got a real live one here. . . ."

As soon as Dave left I headed for Peso's cubicle. Peso greeted me with a huge grin. "We really fixed those motherfuckers, didn't we, Sage? We kicked their number-one asses!"

"What happened to the point spread?" I asked. I'd completely lost track of it after Peso said it would get down around twenty.

"It never got below twenty-six! I thought sure it would go lower but I guess the high-rollers overbet and the word didn't get out about Prosser."

"You're right, it didn't!" And now I understood what Dave had been telling me about the high-rollers losing their asses.

"So we beat the spread, man! We won!"

I shook my head in disbelief. The team had done all right after all. Prosser and Helmet, the two biggest jerk-offs on the team as far as the coaches were concerned, had saved their fucking jobs.

I turned and headed for the weight room, where the scene was nothing like the Varsity's brightly lit hubbub. The Redshirts were standing in the dim light and talking with subdued voices. There were no shower facilities so several of them were already dressed in their street clothes, waiting for the others to finish. Redshirt policy, as always, was to hang together. Better than separately.

Prosser and Tom, delayed by their late exit from the field, were still in their undershorts when I arrived. I went over to Prosser, offered congratulations which he politely accepted, then moved on across the room to where Tom was pulling on his socks.

It was all I could do to keep from shouting out loud. "Guess where the spread finished?"

"Peso said somewhere around twenty, didn't he?"

"Wrong! Try again!"

He broke into a grin. "You're kidding! What? Twenty-five?"

"Better!"

"Twenty-six? We beat the fucking spread?"

I nodded vigorously.

"Oh, Jesus!" he mumbled. And then he turned away for a moment, looking around the cramped, dimly lit room. When he turned back to me his eyes were brimming. He made no apology. "I wish Don were here," he said.

I nodded.

One of those uncomfortable silences came over us then, which I broke as Tom pulled on his shirt by glancing over at Prosser. "I've got some news on him too," I said, lowering my voice.

"What's that?"

"You know those two reporters Randall was blowing off to about Pete?"

He nodded.

"One of them told me the story the coaches are going to put

out to explain Prosser. . . . It's the old one about wanting to hold him out for a year so he could get bigger and stronger. . . ."

"Perfect!" Tom muttered angrily. "And they'll probably get away with it." He buckled his belt and looked out across the room. Prosser was just finishing up too, so Tom raised his voice loud enough for the whole room to hear.

"All right," he said, "it's over and done with. Let's give these monkey suits to Cap'n and split. Nobody told me, but you can bet we're not invited to the postgame buffet at The Sewer, so let's just keep away and not have another scene like this afternoon at the pregame meal. . . . Anyone object to that?"

Tom's question was aimed at Prosser, who had more than earned the right to attend, and Heape, who was now on the Varsity by default. Neither man spoke.

Just then the door swung open to reveal Teekay Junior framed in the outside light. He made his announcements with no preliminaries: "Prosser, be up front in five minutes for interviews. Larry, they want you in there too. Prosser and Heape are welcome at the buffet tonight, and both of you report for practice tomorrow afternoon. You're on the Varsity now."

After Teekay, Junior, left, there was nothing to say. Everyone quietly gathered up his uniform bundle and began moving out the door. Prosser hung back, trying, I figured, to avoid flaunting his new success in the faces of his teammates.

I stood with Tom at the end of the equipment check-in line as he waited to have Cap'n take up his uniform and roll.

"Jersey, pants, jock, shirt, socks, towel . . ." Cap'n checked each item off in a monotone.

Tom and I were now the only ones left in line. Suddenly there was a clatter of plastic behind us. We looked back to see Prosser depositing the entire mass of his gear on the equipment shed counter: shoulder pads, leg pads, helmet, shoes; the works. We looked at him in total disbelief, but Prosser's gaze didn't waver for an instant.

"I quit," was all he said before moving past us and walking out after the others out into the night.